SECRETS THE THAT SAVE US

LIZ HOBAN

This book is a work of fiction. Any references to real people, events, establishments, organizations, or locales are intended solely to provide a sense of authenticity and are used fictitiously. All other characters, incidents, and dialogue are drawn from the author's imagination and are not to be construed as real.

THE SECRETS THAT SAVE US

For my brother, Steven, a first-responder during 9/11 and my inspiration for this book.
I love you.

PROLOGUE

My story begins at the end. Truth is I have no regrets, not a solitary one. My life was spared all those years ago, and it is time to give back. It's that simple. There is so much that's out of control in this world, but as I amble up the steps of the local police precinct, empowerment is all mine.

Catching my reflection in the glass entrance, I turn away from my ghost-like image shimmering in the windowpane. Instead, I take in the city- the warm summer sky, the raucous and the sublime, the pervasive smell of subway steam roiling with the allure of salty street pretzels. In the incessant blaring of taxi horns, my whispered *good-bye* is lost.

Inside the precinct, the city noises disappear, replaced by conversations buzzing like an out-of-tune radio. My gaze drifts to the line of orange chairs riveted to the floor and the few strangers randomly occupying them. No longer on the thin precipice between before and after; this *is* the after and I've become one of *them*.

Shuffling in the direction of the main desk, I nod to the familiar officer standing behind the two dispatch sergeants. Lieutenant Jenkins recognizes me right off and makes his way around the security divider. With a toothy grin he embraces me and I'm aware of the creaking well-worn leather of his thick holster belt. My own weapon is concealed mere inches from his, still coated with fresh gunpowder residue and my fingerprints.

"Haven't seen you in like a decade." His Brooklyn accent is much heavier than I remember. "How've ya' been?"

When I don't answer, he narrows his eyes and gestures to a couple of empty seats. I oblige while he settles in next to me. He's gained weight, has the debut of grey at his receding hairline, but I pretend not to notice. Below generous lids, his brown eyes meet mine, his attention unwavering.

"So what brings you down here? No offense, but you don't look so great."

I figure I've nothing to lose so I begin at the end with these three words. "I killed someone."

PART ONE

Some anniversaries should always be remembered,
but never celebrated.
~ Ron Carnel ~

ISABEL

She wasn't dying after all. When the plus-sign on the test wand leached blue in less than a minute, Isabel Henry slumped against the cool porcelain vanity for support, certain her heart was about to box its way through her ribcage. She'd feared the disease that had claimed her mother's life was responsible for the stomach cramps and fatigue which had plagued Isabel the past few weeks. Instead, she was being taken down by something no bigger than a pin-head. She should've been relieved but panic seized her insides. Isabel jolted when knuckles chattered against the bathroom door.

"What are you shooting heroin in there?" her sister, Piper, barked. "You've been in there for a half-hour!"

Isabel was grateful Piper didn't wait for an answer.

"If you're still alive, do ya' mind hurrying? You've made me late twice this week and it's only Tuesday!" Piper's sarcasm seeped like smoke through the door cracks.

"Sorry, I'll be right out." Isabel's voice quavered.

Her sister stalked away and grumbled something but Isabel wasn't listening. Fingers fumbled as she wrapped the test stick in tissue and dropped the mummified evidence in the trash-bin. She washed her hands and splashed cold water on her face. Catching her gaze in the mirror, she knew she couldn't pass her sister's scrutiny at the moment. She waited until she heard the clacking of Piper's Prada heels descending the stairs, then slipped out the door and moved toward the bedroom at the end of the hall. A gentle tap and Isabel entered.

Her father appeared to be sleeping, and she eased down on the edge of his bed. She smoothed back his fine silver hair. His lips twitched with a barely suppressed grin: one eye closed, the other squinting up at her.

"Morning, Daddy." Isabel felt seven again, remembering when the school bus chugged its fumes up their street without her. "We missed the train."

"Get the next train. For heaven's sake, it's New York City, there's always a *next* train." His voice was gravelly and he was suddenly wide awake and rearranging himself. He gestured to the pillow at the foot of the bed. "Would you put that behind my head, Izzy?"

As the goose-down settled beneath him, she caught the muted trace of after-shave mixed with the sweet, rye scent when his insulin was kicking in. Eyeing the waste basket, she spied the used syringe and its packaging, crumpled together like origami. The dosage log on the side-table indicated Mary, his nursing assistant, had given the injection while Isabel was locked in the bathroom.

"Ah, much better." He was as comfortable as possible given the bullet list of infirmities he'd developed since his stroke. "What a gift you are," he sighed, patting down the end table for his glasses. She retrieved them and pressed them into his hand.

"Here, Daddy."

He propped the glasses low on his nose: a sharp nose like a pointed finger that seemed to grow more prominent while the rest of his features drew inward. She couldn't imagine a time when her father wasn't around and yet here he was, fading away right before her eyes. She leaned in and kissed his speckled forehead.

"So-long," Isabel whispered as Piper charged through the door.

"What? ... Am I missing something profound – my old man's last words? His final breath?"

Isabel had no clue why her sister was speaking in a Southern accent as though auditioning for *Gone with the Wind*. Piper smiled broadly in their father's direction then glared at her younger sister.

"From now on I'm having a driver take me to the train. I can't wait for you anymore." She paced court-room style and pointed a burgundy lacquered fingernail at Isabel. "I was the one who asked the firm to hire you, so how do you think this makes me look? We'll be lucky if we get to the office before noon! Do you realize I was never late, *ever,* until *you* started working with me?" She sighed like a disappointed parent, closed her eyes and shook her head. "*Isabel will be late for her own funeral.*" Piper parroted the assertion Isabel had heard all her life and she forged on.

"For the record, Izzy, you'll never be late for *your* funeral because *I'll* have made the arrangements. I, on the other hand, will end up wrapped in trash bags in your car's trunk until you bury me in some vacant lot." Piper turned on heels resembling knitting needles and strode back toward the door. Apparently, she'd rested her case.

"Bye, Dad," Piper chirped and waved over her shoulder ... for the *second* time this morning."

"Fifth ... But who's counting!" Their dad enjoyed the dramatic talents of his oldest daughter. Isabel would've been slightly amused as well if she wasn't going to be crammed in a train with Piper for an hour.

Piper snorted. "I'll be waiting in the car, emphasis on *waiting.*" She sang the last word and flounced out the door and down the stairs as though just crowned Miss Congeniality.

"Why would anyone want to be on time for their own funeral?"

Her father shook his head. "I'd want to be so late you'd have to reschedule it."

Isabel tucked the blankets under his feet the way he liked them and refilled his bedside water glass. "Need anything else before I go, Dad?" She cringed at the distant bleating of her car's horn.

Her dad touched her forearm. "Yes, Isabel, actually there is something. You can stop feeling so responsible for me. Don't get me wrong, sugar, I love having you by my side but Mary's here to help out. Stop worrying and go have some fun with people your own age. Meet a nice man and settle down … C'mon, Izzy, there must be *one* respectable guy out there worthy of caring for my beautiful girl. I'm not getting any younger, you know. I tell Piper the same thing. Both of you should be thinking about starting families of your own."

There had been someone. A charming businessman from a major law firm on the ninetieth floor in the North Tower had shown an interest in Isabel a few months back, said she was special. He was so sexy with dark eyes and sharp features and a body to die for: all topped with a tumble of dark, curly hair. He smelled of mint and apples fresh from an orchard, and it had lingered with her long afterward. Just when she was sure she was falling for him everything changed.

"You listen to me, kiddo, no more of this *late for your own funeral* nonsense; I don't want to hear that anymore." Her dad probably assumed Piper was the reason for her frown. "Who says we have to obey time? Where's the spontaneity, the romance?"

Isabel's brain calculated from July fourth to that morning was exactly nine weeks to the day: perfect timing for a healthy abortion. *There's an oxymoron if ever there was one.* She had spent two months pretending the relationship had never happened, only to be rudely awakened by its resurrection in the form of a tiny blue cross.

Her throat tightened and her eyes stung at the thought of an abortion. *What was that all about?* She made her way to the door to avoid her father reading her expression. Instead, he read her mind.

"Izzy-bella … honey, listen, it'll be okay. When it's your time, Mr. Right will come along. We'll talk some more but you'd better get going before Piper has a heart attack."

She turned and he blew her a kiss. As always, she pretended to catch it, then she slid out of the bedroom just as the car's horn blared again. On the brink of tears, Isabel had to giggle when she heard her dad's voice from the other side of the door.

"Jeez, Piper, relax! You'd be early for your own execution."

~~~~~~~~~~~

Riding the train to New York City that warm, sunny September morning, Isabel examined the thin space next to her seat in case she needed to vomit. Her nausea was unpredictable, and she was relieved that the only passenger within view was a portly, balding man in the opposite seat across the aisle. He was dirty and disheveled, his head tucked to his chest, solely responsible for the maleficent odor. The man was either sleeping or dead and no one dared to sit next to him. As usual, Piper was handling business on her cell phone and this annoyed Isabel. Granted it was 2001, the new millennium, post-Y-2K and all, but people disregarded the purpose of owning a cell phone: *only to be used in emergencies.* For all Piper knew she may unwittingly be responsible for derailing the train or skipping the conductor's pacemaker.

"Are you joking? How can I possibly defend that a kiddie-meal toy choked a grown man? I'd have to be Johnny Cochran." Piper winked at Isabel, then turned her focus back to the conversation. "Fast-food is right up there with hotdogs, baseball, apple pie, and sex." All her interactions were laced with brief periods of silence and occasional bursts of laughter, mostly at her own jokes.

"Listen, the drive-thru has perpetuated the human race. Over the years it's given mom a little extra energy for hubby at the end of a long day. Throw in the minivan and she can feed her little critters without ever setting foot in the kitchen, all the while sitting down. I'd rather have a colonoscopy than take this case to jury selection, but I'll do it for the sheer comic relief."

Isabel's stomach groaned at the reference to intestinal procedures. She tuned out the rest of Piper's banter and wondered how pregnancy, a blessed state which in most cases should be euphoric, could feel so horrible. Lately, she didn't just miss the train; she misplaced things including her train of thought. She figured when a woman was ready to have a baby, actually planned it, all the difficulties associated with the condition would be tolerable. Happiness would over-ride the negative symptoms which, in and of themselves, would be a constant reminder of the beautiful path the body was journeying down. She'd have to be a real cynic not to see the whole experience as miraculous. It just felt so wrong and of all people, she was sure Piper would understand this particular decision. If the Henry girls were anything at all, they were practical. *So, why the pervasive feeling of guilt?* She had to stop focusing on the wrong things. She'd let her sister afford her that humiliation.

"You do realize you look like you're in crack recovery. What the hell is the matter with you?"

Isabel's answer would only precipitate an avalanche of further grilling so she didn't respond.

"Here." Piper passed her a sports bottle that read: *Get a real Bush in the White House – elect Hillary.* "Drink some water. You've got bags under your eyes resembling avocados."

As they trundled through northern New Jersey, Piper peeled her banana while Isabel tried to block its pulpy smell with sips of water. Peering past the smudged window, she focused on the detritus littering the landscape: smashed cans, glittering shards of glass, a brown loafer on the lam, a twisted lawn chair. She followed the page of a newspaper blowing by, clinging to the rail-yard's chain-link fencing only a second later to be swept back out and gone like old news.

When the remnants of a discarded baby stroller passed her view, a lump rose like yeast in her throat. If she was going to get through this whole ordeal, the imaginings of a baby cooing inside her had to go, along with the pregnancy. She wanted a baby, just not this one.

PIPER

Here she was, a high-powered New York City corporate attorney, Princeton grad, funny and intelligent, the perfect personal ad – but Piper Henry still wanted to grow up to be her taciturn and adorable kid sister. Granted, her sister's personality adversely affected many things, not the least of which was getting to work on time, but she had always been the decent one of the two of them: the angel to Piper's devil.

Piper knew something was bothering Isabel; something she'd likely have missed if Piper hadn't moved back home a few days a week. After ten years of living in the city, Piper convinced herself the move was about her father's precarious medical condition. But that was only part of the truth. There were things she needed to come to terms with, secrets she had kept for too long that needed to be released, but she had yet to find the right time to share her true thoughts and feelings with anyone, even Isabel. The past couple of months Isabel had been preoccupied and moody. For starters, Piper couldn't recall the last time Isabel went out. Not just dates. Piper had been home quite a bit over the summer months and was hard-pressed to recall Isabel going to dinner even with a friend. She tried to keep herself in check when it came to Isabel's enmeshment with their dad. Isabel had cared for him for so long she became an abused cliché; *no one else could fill her shoes.* It was obvious nothing would change for Isabel until their father was gone. Five years ago the doctors had given him just a couple years to live and yet he was still treading water.

"Seriously, Izzy, what the hell is wrong with you? You've been acting really weird lately. Okay, so I yelled at you to hurry, but hello? I was supposed to be taking a deposition this morning at nine with a Wall Street, corporate --"

"Kiddie-meal? Is that it, Piper? Oh no! Planet Earth is in jeopardy!"

Mocking the law profession was below the belt but Piper decided to once again hold the harsh words poised on the tip of her tongue. "Hilarious," Piper said. "Well at least you still have some remote sense of humor left in that cute little head of yours but here's a news-flash, Sis-kabob, *I'm* not the enemy. Besides, *that* client is the same fast-food freak who's paying the firm's salaries next month. Honestly, I'm not missing a thing. As we speak, I'd be sitting across from a 300-hundred-pound horse's ass and I'd be asking the most tedious questions about food and toys, subjects about which I know nothing." She paused as it occurred to her that these were two of the many reasons she wasn't married. Piper hadn't played with toys since her sister was born, and she couldn't cook worth a damn. In fact, she needed to be reminded to eat and, ideally, men wanted homemade food, if possible, served between a woman's legs on the fifty-yard line.

"Trust me, Izzy, nothing is more irritating than listening to a 50 -year-old man who claims he choked on a plastic cartoon figurine." Piper rolled her eyes and her head simultaneously. "You know Jen Wilkes, that cute intern going Associate next month who's always working the perky? She's covering for me." She smirked at Isabel. "Thanks to your reliable unreliability I have been spared the first deposition of the morning, but that's not the point. What's going on with you? I don't care about the client; I just don't want you to lose another job. I realize I can be a bitch sometimes … okay … often, but something else is bugging you. It's me, Iz." Piper pointed to herself with both index fingers. "*Talk* to me."

Isabel tried to brush her off with a wave of her hand but then sighed. "Nothing, Piper, really, I'm just exhausted worrying about Daddy and all, really, that's it. Honestly it's all good. I'm fine. Promise. I swear."

"Me thinks she doth protest too much." Piper saw right through her lies. "And good god, Izzy! *'Daddy'*? Really? You sound like you're seven." Whatever her issues, she'd get it out of her eventually so Piper lightened up. "Okay, so you don't want to talk about why you're so Betty-bipolar lately. Fine, but if you decide to spill, I'm right beside you practically all the time now." Piper winked at her sister and Isabel winced.

"I *know*. Don't remind me."

"Hey, where's Mom's charm bracelet? You never take it off." Piper was sure her sister was feigning nonchalance. Piper didn't often pay attention to details outside the courtroom – but since she'd been spending more time back home, her mom came to mind regularly. She'd even dreamt of her. Their mother had died from a very rare genetic form of lymphoma at the age of thirty-five. Piper was just seven and Isabel a toddler. The sound of her mom's voice, the smell of turpentine and oil paints, her smile; Piper feared her memories were fading, dulling. Seeing that bracelet had always brought her back.

"I need to get the latch fixed."

Piper prayed Isabel hadn't lost it; it'd be one more arrow in her bleeding heart. She'd been a little jealous of her sister for the first time when, after their mom died, Isabel got the charm bracelet. Instead, Piper had inherited her mom's wedding ring along with her request to take care of Isabel. The ring was in a memory box in her childhood bedroom closet, but as far as looking out for Isabel; that began long before their mom was even diagnosed and would continue until Piper's final day.

She'd wanted her baby sister from the moment she set eyes on her swaddled in her mother's arms. It was as if Isabel was a rare and precious gift given to Piper by their parents. When their mother was sick and Piper was just a little girl herself, Isabel would climb in bed with her after a bad late-night dream. Sometimes she was scared of the simplest things like Santa, the refrigerator, or the wind. When life overwhelmed her on such occasions, as it often did, Piper would tell her everything was going to be okay, always. Isabel wasn't a kid anymore though and sometimes life needed to be handled head-on and not masked with useless mollycoddling. Piper glanced over at Isabel. Her sister's hands were cupped on the side of her head and tears dropped to her lap.

"Wednesday, Thursday, Friday?" Piper's genteel way of saying; *what the fuck*? She grabbed Isabel, mucous and all, and drew her into her Chanel blazer. If that wasn't unconditional love, she wasn't sure what was. "What is going on with you? Wow, c'mon, what's going on?" Piper knew she sounded chirpy and blamed the three cups of coffee she had while waiting for Isabel to get out of the bathroom earlier that morning. Shoulders relaxed, Piper let go of her sister and took a deep breath.

"Who is there to take care of you when you need it? Huh?" Piper hoped she had her sister's attention. "Remember when you had the flu last year? I came home, made soup for the first time, okay not from scratch but still. I even cancelled a court appearance. Who bought you this amazing Coach bag?" Piper pointed to her side where the smart, classy purse sat between them like a well-behaved pet. "And who got you the job when the library laid you off? Who gave you the down payment for the Honda because you have bad credit?"

"Oh well, now I feel so much better about myself." Isabel rolled her eyes and laughed through a sob.

Piper wrapped her sister in her arms again. What else could she do? Maybe Isabel was getting her period.

"I didn't mean it like that, silly. I'd give you the world and you know that. I'm here for you. Why would I drop the ball now? I promise to be by your side through the entire ordeal with Dad 'til the end." It felt awkward consoling her over a death that had yet to occur, but Piper held her fragile sister together just the same.

Isabel pushed her away and leaned back against her seat. She took a deep breath as though Piper had been suffocating her. "Piper, you don't get it. Of course you'll be with me. He's your father too. Just drop it, okay?" Isabel's face was flushed. "I'm running out of time. I need to make something of my life! I'm going to feel worthless when Dad dies because I haven't made him proud. He tells me he worries about me. Not you, Piper, he doesn't lose sleep over you." She paused and Piper gave her a tissue and a bemused look she hoped implied: *Please wipe your nose and go on.*

"You've made something of yourself. What have *I* done? I have difficulty paying my library fines – even when I worked at the library. Dad doesn't want to die until I meet someone who'll take care of me. Do you know how that feels when he says stuff like that?" She blew her nose.

"Hello? Bitter? Party of one?" Piper attempted levity but failed, not even a lip twitch from Isabel. "Listen, Izzy, he says the same shit to me, really, stop feeling sorry for yourself. You're an awesome human being. And, while we're on the subject of Dad, let's be real here. You look and act just like Mom, the only woman he's really ever loved besides us. Let's face it, you're her."

Isabel wasn't stopping Piper's diatribe, so she kept at it.

"And whom do I bear resemblance? Creepy Uncle Earl, the family drunk with the bulbous, veiny nose who always loosened his pants and sniffed our heads whenever he hugged us. This is my legacy."

Isabel chortled despite herself. Piper had her, so she pressed on.

"Dad loves both of us equally, but I'll tell you one solid truth— he feels way closer to you." She gave Isabel one last shoulder squeeze and hoped they could finally relax. "We good?"

"We're good." Through a sheepish grin Isabel half-heartedly laughed. At least she wasn't crying.

Gazing at her sister, Piper took in the thin tracks where dried tears had stained her cheeks and Piper's breath caught in her chest. With her smooth skin and button nose, those full lips, soulful brown eyes, that thicket of wavy blond hair – Isabel hadn't clue-one of the beauty she exuded. Quiet and sweet, yet dark and contemplative, she was almost tragic. Piper wanted to believe she'd always been Isabel's pillar of strength but as irony would have it, over the years, her kid sister had taught her about real love. Piper patted Isabel's knee.

"Everything will be okay, Izzy."

The need to reach for her took over and Piper gave Isabel an awkward sideways embrace and then they both rested back against their seats for the last ten minutes of the commute. Piper glanced up just in time to notice the old disheveled man seated across the aisle from them; he was no longer snoozing but was wide awake, nodding and giving the *thumbs-up* sign while smiling a toothless grin of sentimentality in their direction. Nothing entertained better than New York City public transportation.

ISABEL

Tears seemed to flow without much provocation, so it was a relief when Piper finally backed down. Isabel was surprised when her sister inquired about the charm bracelet. Since being named a partner in the firm, Piper had been so preoccupied with her profession she wouldn't have noticed if Isabel's wrists had been slit. If Piper knew that the bracelet was gone along with Isabel's menstrual cycle for the past two months, she'd throttle her for answers.

Since Piper despised taking the subway, they'd have to take a cab from Penn Station to lower Manhattan. It would cost a kidney and Piper would have to cover it. When they were on schedule they bought coffee at some expensive kiosk and walked part of the way, then they'd grab a bus, but they obviously couldn't do that this time. Isabel wouldn't miss the coffee; the thought produced an image of more coming back up than going down.

Isabel couldn't wait to get off the train and get distracted by her lengthy to-do list and away from Piper. She longed to submerge herself in work and stay lost in the hive of cubicles without anyone noticing her or the trash bin parked between her legs. She really didn't want Piper to cover for her and take the blame again for their lateness. Piper would understand Isabel's strange behavior soon enough, but for the time being Isabel needed to adjust to the idea herself.

"Nan Goldberg's got it in for me, Piper." Of all things, Isabel wondered why on earth she'd said that? Of course her boss would have an issue with tardiness. That was one of the main reasons to have a boss, so employees actually showed up for work.

"Well, I could say I told you so, but I won't. Besides, Izzy, I don't believe you even like what you do every day."

"I don't know what you mean." Isabel did know. If Piper only knew how scared Isabel was that she wasn't even good enough to be herself.

"Yes you do." There was irony in Piper's laugh, a private joke only she herself understood. "I mean seriously, Izzy: an *archeology* degree – you're afraid of insects *and* air travel. Piper sighed. "Oh well, you still have a whole life ahead to pursue whatever the heck you want." She stretched her neck. "Hey, you've always been a natural born writer; you live for books. Go back to school for a fine -arts degree and notch up your resume."

Isabel couldn't believe what she was hearing, and Piper wasn't done yet.

"And don't worry about Dad either." Piper leaned in and nestled her head on Isabel's shoulder. "If you really want to go back to school, I'll be there for him whenever you need me. I'll even pay for it." She squeezed Isabel's hand. "Anyway, back to reality. Brown-nose Goldberg— the stiff with her eyeglasses on one of those beaded chains around her neck? Tissues up her sleeves? Couldn't get laid on a conjugal prison visit?" Piper pinched her face like a closed string bag. "*That* Nan? I'll have a little chat with her."

Isabel laughed. "That would be the one, and no, please, Piper, it's fine. Promise me you won't say anything. You've already covered for me way too much."

Isabel recalled with fondness her first day of work at the firm when the cab dropped the two sisters off at the base of the World Trade Center. Isabel had stood, mouth agape, dizzy and staring up at the two infamous skyscrapers. She felt paralyzed at the thought of being swallowed up whole in those enormous behemoths. Piper, always so in-tune to her sister's feelings, sensed her unease that first morning.

"Quit gawking like you're a fucking tourist from Mars." She pointed up at the towering buildings and grabbed Isabel's hand in hers. "See those two pillars? That's you and me, kid, standing tall, side by side, invincible."

From then on, whenever Isabel felt overwhelmed by lower Manhattan with its inexorable hustle and bustle and its claustrophobia-inducing skyline, she garnered strength from the image of the two of them, together forever. Isabel was jerked back to the train and reality.

"Christ almighty!" Piper shut her cell phone's cover. Glancing around, she opened it again in a fit of compulsion, like the smoker fumbling for a cigarette she couldn't spark-up. She glared at the screen and sighed. "Check your cell, Izzy." Piper scowled and thumped the buttons with her restless fingers. "I can't get any reception."

"Uh … I left my phone at home." Isabel cringed knowing her sister would shake her head and roll her eyes. As usual, Piper didn't disappoint.

"Did you at least bring your head?" Piper went back to fiddling with her phone but the satellite gods weren't responding. "This cell service sucks!" She shook the device and blew into her palm as if it were on fire.

The technology of a cell phone, something a few years ago would've meant a corded telephone located in a jail, was incredible and complaining about its abilities was unacceptable as far as Isabel was concerned.

"We can take pictures of Saturn but we can't improve cell reception." Piper spoke as if she had a side-job with NASA. "It's not the battery because I charged the phone all night. What if this were a *real* 9-1-1 situation?"

Isabel snapped a snap she didn't know she had in her – a snap that may have been building since the 80s. "Christ, Piper, can you just shut the fuck up for one minute, please! Just shut-up about the damn phone. We're in a city with more phones than the seventeen million people who live there and you'll have all the damn service you need. Oh, I forgot! A pay phone is probably beneath you. Just buy a new cell phone, or better yet, buy your own fucking satellite." Isabel sat back down, shrinking into the seat as if slowly deflating. It felt good for a nanosecond.

Her sister stared down at her, brows so narrowed they nearly connected. Piper was speechless for maybe the first time in her ... well, *ever*. Isabel was relieved until Piper mimicked in a childish, sing song voice, "Ooooh ... you said the F word ... twice. I'm telling Daddy."

~~~~~~~~~~~~

A little after half-past eight in the morning, the train screeched to a halt on time as opposed to Isabel and her sister. They'd be close to an hour late for work. While Piper strode from the platform and up the escalator a few paces ahead with professional city chic, Isabel followed her, skipping and stumbling like a misfit. She worked in a city that didn't care much for her, a place that had already devoured her and was just waiting to spit her out.

The queue outside Penn Station was short and it was less than ten minutes before they pulled themselves into the taxi cab. The driver, with way too many consonants in his name, turned to Piper in the back seat and studied her face suspiciously, only breaking away his stare when a loud static screech came from his radio accompanied by the rumble of what sounded and felt like thunder, but in a cloudless sky. Loud noises in New York City were a regular occurrence, but one normally didn't *feel* them.

"What was that?" Isabel glanced sideways at her sister. The cabbie shushed them before Piper could answer. He pushed buttons on his handset as another squeal shrieked from the receiver and forced the sisters' hands to their ears.

"What the fuck?" Piper drew her face back in indignation. She turned to Isabel. "Are my ears bleeding?"

The driver shot Piper another disgusted look, eyes birdlike in intensity and mumbled something about *salty talk* and *typical American irreverence*. He turned back to the windshield and slowly eased his livelihood into bumper-to-bumper traffic.

While Piper scrutinized her cell phone, Isabel's thoughts were on the excuse she'd give her boss. *A dental emergency?* She had used that pathetic excuse a few weeks ago, but perhaps it was chronic gum disease. *At twenty nine?* She could say her dog was sick. Unfortunately, she didn't own a dog and didn't want to get caught up in some pedigree discussion with colleagues wanting to see pictures of her adorable, but invisible, pup named Sunday.

It was after nine in the morning, rush-hour was nearly over, but traffic was still gridlocked. People along the street were moving faster than the cars. Isabel stared ahead and absentmindedly watched as the driver tried to connect with his dispatcher but to no avail. The crackling static and frequency squelches of the car's two-way radio bounced between Isabel and Piper, disallowing conversation. After several blocks, the radio was awakened again in the form of a shrill voice from the receiver that cut through the static.

"K4, K4, ya' dare, guy, hey, Mon," came through clear, as well as the next grammatically incorrect exchange. "Holy sheet, dude, Twin Tower been crashed into. Fooking crazy sheet. Da tower wit' plane steeking out da windows! Ya' dare, K4?"

K4, as he was obviously known in the garage, shook the handset and mumbled something, but the connection broke and the harsh static resumed. Isabel would never know if K4 was offended by his own colleague's salty talk because at the next light, Piper threw a 50-dollar-bill on the seat next to him, reached across Isabel, opened the cab door and nudged her to get out. They walked, pressed in the crowd, not really sure of where they were headed. Visible a good fifty blocks away they saw the black billowing smoke.

"Oh god, Izzy! We need to get to a landline that works and call the office to find out what exactly is going on down there. Keep your eyes peeled for a cop. They'll know what's happening." As a prestigious lawyer in Manhattan, Piper seemed to know everyone in law enforcement.

A noise Isabel could only liken to a sonic boom echoed in the air. "What was that?"

"I don't know, Izzy."

"Shit, Piper, I'm scared."

"Something bad happened but bad things happen all the time in New York. Calm down and let's just find a television."

People were running and yelling, but then folks these days were always noisy and impatient. This was New York City and of course there was an elevated level of frenetic energy. But there was something more visceral. Horns were blaring in useless discord as traffic in all directions solidified from sludge to concrete. Cars were stopped in fire-zones and double parked, intersection lights ignored. A few vehicles appeared abandoned, driver and passenger doors left wide open. To the south, a cloud of gunmetal gray churned and widened while the crisp clear blue sky just above them seemed to mock the chaos.

A bearded and dreadlocked, frail looking man, dressed in a soiled raincoat with Army patches on the lapels and a purple do-rag lopsided across his temples, stood on the opposite side of the street and shouted in a heavy Jamaican accent. "*… At that time the Son of Man will appear in the sky and all the nations of the earth will mourn …*" Cold fingers wrapped themselves around Isabel's heart just as Piper grabbed her arm.

"Izzy, don't listen to that shit! He's there on that corner everyday spewing the same crap." Piper was lying and she knew Isabel knew it. Without apology, her sister veered her in the opposite direction of the street prophet but which avenue they took, Isabel couldn't be certain.

"Maybe it isn't as bad as it looks." Isabel wanted Piper to slow down but Piper spun on her. She took hold of Isabel's shoulders as if she were about to shake her.

"Hello? You see the black smoke don't you? Something horrible happened."

Isabel was officially frightened. In the middle of another intersection, Piper tried to get a police officer's attention. Piper reached out and touched his arm.

"What's going on down …?"

"Two commercial jets, one hit the North Tower and the other, the South Tower." He brushed her aside and kept moving in the opposite direction.

Piper turned, face blanched and befuddled. "Oh dear god, Izzy, we gotta find a TV."

Around the next corner, Piper swerved them into a bodega. A thrumming crowd gathered around a television mounted high on the far wall. The scents of humanity sardined in this small establishment caused Isabel's stomach to lurch and her head swam. The news reporter spoke in Spanish, but language didn't matter. Everyone watched the screen in fascinated horror as the surreal scene unfolded like a nightmare from which they could not awaken. The images told the story just as the cop had said; both towers had been hit by hijacked commercial airliners and both buildings were ablaze. The realization that this was obviously not an accident, but well-calculated and synchronized attacks, paralyzed Isabel with terror.

"This is way worse than what happened in '93 and that was tragic. There are no words for this." Piper's tone intended to sound in control, but fell short and landed on fear. Her firm had been uptown in the nineties and Isabel remembered it had given Piper pause over employment in such a vulnerable city or as the investigators called it, a *soft* target.

"We'll stay in here for a bit, get our bearings." Piper always had a plan. In spite of this awful situation she was still all business. Or so Isabel thought.

Over and over the news replayed the shocking footage of the planes flying into the towers. No one could look away – until the television showed people jumping from windows of the burning towers. There were audible gasps around them as some watched in resigned disbelief while others covered their faces. Isabel wondered why they would televise such raw and hopeless human desperation. The fact that the plane struck the North Tower a few floors below their law firm did not escape Isabel's notice, only her comment.

When a booth opened up, the sisters grabbed it. Piper ordered coffee, Isabel ordered nothing. Instead Isabel just looked across the table and watched as her sister's face became more and more pinched, lips thin as a strand of yarn. Tears leaked from the corners of Piper's eyes, but she brushed them off before they got past her cheekbone.

"I feel like I am going to have a full-on anxiety attack. My heart is beating so fast –can you hear it?" Piper began to weep openly. "I know you don't want to hear it but I can't even call anyone because my phone still doesn't work."

"No, not true, Piper, this is certainly a time when a cell phone should be used. I get it and I'm sorry I didn't bring mine."

"There's no reception anyway. The satellite towers on the top of the building are probably knocked out. It's possible no one in the lower half of Manhattan has cell phone service." Piper put her head in her hands. "I wasn't there but I should've been. We *both* should have been in that building." She sobbed into a napkin and Isabel moved to her side of the table.

"It'll be okay, I promise." Isabel had no clue what she meant by promising but she patted Piper's back just the same. "We're safe for now. We are so lucky, Piper." Isabel needed to stop talking – how could anyone possibly know what to say? Piper was right; there were no words. Isabel sat with her and let her cry as Piper twisted and pilled napkin after napkin.

Then, the unthinkable happened. The crowd groaned in unison as though they were all simultaneously punched in the gut. The sisters sank back against their seats, slack-jawed and at a loss for words. Before their very eyes the South Tower collapsed. They were frozen in place knowing the North Tower was not far behind.

PIPER

An eerie gloom settled in like an estranged enemy announcing it had come back to exact revenge. Store owners took protective stances in front of their modest shops, faces petrified in consternation. Grated metal curtains were pulled and dead-bolted as was typically done at the end of a long day, only it wasn't even noon. Piper had never felt so disoriented, trapped and helpless in the overwhelming face of what was happening.

Clare had moved into Piper's city apartment as a house sitter. She was a stunner; Brazilian descent, mocha skin, tall and slender with a heart-shaped face and shiny wavy layers of chestnut hair. She was a bartender at Windows on the World, referred to by the regulars as WOW. The five-star restaurant was located on the 106th and 107th floor of the North Tower of the World Trade Center. Piper and Isabel met up there occasionally after work and before heading back to New Jersey. For Piper, WOW was ordinary and it always tickled her to see Isabel's expression of awe each time those elevator doors opened to those panoramic views.

"My place is as safe a place as any. I'm sure Clare kept the fridge full. She's good like that. Oh, god, I know I'm an atheist but please let Clare be okay. Please, please, please." Piper prayed to whomever would listen. "We can unwind there and use the landline to call Dad."

32

"If Dad saw the news, Piper, he's probably worried sick."

"He doesn't know. The man equates television with laziness, hasn't watched television since the days when you had to get up to change the channel." She gave a weak laugh. "Thank goodness for small favors."

"Daddy is going to freak, he's not going to want us to leave the house after this. You do realize that?" Isabel was pale and stone-faced.

"You'll have to call him. I don't think I can manage it, besides you're better with breaking bad news." Piper knew Isabel would do it.

"I will, I'll call him."

Piper caught a glimpse of her own reflection in a storefront window. She resembled a member of some eighties metal band. Large, blackened mascara smudges highlighted her wide, unfocused blue eyes; her straight, blond hair fell from the loose chignon at the nape of her slim neck and formed parentheses around her face. Her right earring was missing and her attaché case was gone but she didn't care. Her usual fastidiousness was not a concern, and she used the building she was standing next to for support. Then she just slid to the concrete walkway, her backside on a *graffitied*-wall, her legs splayed out on the filthy pavement in front of her, torn nylons, high-heels sticking out from the maw of her purse, her blazer tied around her waist. *Silks and sartorial suits be damned,* she thought. Isabel settled in next to her and rested her head on Piper's shoulder like a puppy who wasn't going anywhere without her lead.

They weren't sitting long before the dazzling sun became a mere yolk of its earlier self. Sepia crept over the massive, industrious island. And yet how incongruous was the preamble to every news program from the moment the story broke the news.

"What began as a beautiful Tuesday in the Northeast ..." Piper was certain beautiful Tuesdays in September would forever remind her of this tragic day and she knew for years to come, if they lived that long, the very question that would dominate many a conversation: *Where were* you *that Tuesday morning?*

She realized at a certain point she was viewing herself in a movie: present but not really there. Sooner or later she'd have to face the fact that on top of everything else, her career lay beneath the rubble of the Twin Towers. What storyline she'd follow next eluded her. Eventually they stood and together hobbled the rest of the way to Piper's apartment. She was never so relieved as when she turned the apartment key in the door and then closed it with a thud behind them, locking them safely inside.

Without stopping to even put her purse down, Piper ran to the bedroom and leaned back on the door frame in relief when she saw Clare was sound asleep in the bed. She'd get Isabel settled in and then wake her with the bad news. She gently shut the door and then rummaged in a hallway closet.

"Here." Piper threw a wad of cottony clothes at Isabel. "Happy pants just for you, Izzy. Might as well be comfortable in all this misery."

As soon they were changed, Piper woke Clare. When Piper broke the news to her, she screamed something in Portuguese and then crumbled to the floor. As a bartender for many years in Windows on the World, Clare knew more about the people in those buildings than any other employee. The three of them had survived and shared in the suffering of millions.

"I know Clare," Piper hugged her and patted her back. "It feels like pure evil. The god-damned devil himself came to the Big Apple this morning and took a fucking bite."

ISABEL

Isabel put on the tea kettle in the kitchen, while Piper helped Clare to the sofa. They cried and hugged and Isabel was relieved to have the task of boiling water. She knew the two of them had an immeasurable amount of grieving to do, and they'd have each other for support. Of course they'd have her too, but when they learned of Isabel's situation, they certainly wouldn't perceive her as a pillar of emotional strength. Isabel gathered strength to call her dad.

Sooner or later she'd have to face the fact that on top of everything else, her job lay beneath the rubble of the Twin Towers. What storyline Isabel followed next eluded her. Potential employers would wonder why she hadn't been in work that day; *no one takes a Tuesday off.* Hanging onto her sister's coattails in the job-hunting market made Isabel cringe, but she wouldn't let pride stand in the way of earning a living. Being single and unemployed at her age was bad enough, but an abortion on top of all that was the epitome of baggage. Not to mention the painful circumstances surrounding the pregnancy.

Isabel had cheated her co-workers when, of all of them, the tardy ones were the ones who deserved punishment. She certainly warranted firing and as horrid as it was, it had literally happened the other way around. Isabel didn't deserve to be alive as opposed to many of those successful, responsible people who never left the building. *Shift*, Isabel thought, she needed to switch her focus, which was easier said than done. She had a loathing for herself and needed to put it into perspective. How many life-altering situations would she be subjected to in one day?

After a deep breath, Isabel picked up Piper's kitchen phone and dialed. Her father had no idea what had occurred, but as soon as he heard she knew he would turn on the television against his better judgment, and the only consolation was he knew she and Piper were safe for the time being.

"Hey Dad." Isabel's voice came out stiff and overformal, and she tried to loosen up a bit. "It's me, Izzy."

"What's wrong? Everything okay? Piper okay?"

"Yes. Yes, Dad. Everything's okay with Piper and me." Isabel switched the phone to her other ear. "Listen, there's been a very bad accident … incident that happened this morning to the World Trade Center, our building and the South Tower, Dad."

"What happened? Is it on the news?" His voice was rising. "I should put on the television?"

"Dad, the buildings are gone. They collapsed after commercial airliners crashed into them." Isabel stopped at that. He needed to absorb what she'd just said.

"Izzy, what is going on over there?" He coughed and cleared his throat. "You better be safe. Are you safe right now?"

"Dad, calm down, listen to me. We were so late for work today that luckily we weren't even close to the buildings when all this happened. We'd just gotten off the train and into a cab. Anyway, we're at Piper's apartment uptown so we're fine …"

"Don't tell me you're fine, I've got the television on right now. It looks like goddamn Armageddon. I need the two of you to get back home here to New Jersey as soon as possible. It's not secure there, Isabel Rose Henry!" He'd rarely used her full name, and it caused Isabel's jaw to clench.

"Dad, we'll be home tomorrow. They aren't letting any public transportation in or out of the city, and it would cost us a whole lot of money for a private car."

"I'll pay it!"

Isabel hadn't heard that much adamancy from her father since before his stroke.

"It's that simple. I'm calling a car service."

"No, Dad." It was odd standing up to him. "We're staying here tonight. It's a war zone out there — no kidding — and we're here with Clare, and she knows how to make cocktails so …"

"Don't even joke, Isabel, this looks like nothing I've ever seen before in all my seventy years." He let out his frustration in a moan, and then was silent for several seconds.

"Daddy, you still there?"

"Jesus Christ, I hate to give in here, but I guess you're right. You and your sister should stay put. But be sure and call me when you get your bearings about what time you want to leave the city tomorrow. I'm sending a private car, you just say when and I'm not taking 'no' for an answer."

"Hopefully the trains will be running again, at least out of the city, but a car would be awesome. We really have no idea what tomorrow will look like. I'll call you, probably not until tomorrow afternoon. After things calm down. It's a madhouse in the city. But we're safe here." Isabel had no idea where her assured confidence was coming from. "I love you, er … we love you."

"Love you too, and tell Piper she'd better take care of my little girl."

"See you tomorrow." Isabel hung up and smiled. She was his little girl and Piper was the big sister looking out for her. Her father still saw her as a child, the world was still burning and Isabel was still pregnant, but she was a very fortunate human being.

PIPER

Fists clenched with wadded tissues, tea cups untouched, the women huddled together on the sofa in front of the television. Piper couldn't help thinking about the people in those upper floor offices, just moments beforehand, diligently working or goofing off in the copy room, spilling the morning's first cup of coffee on their desk, or grabbing the last glazed donut.

Of course she mourned her colleagues, the partners and associates she saw every day. But it was also the nameless acquaintances, elevator buddies, those rushing in the lobby's revolving doors with the obligatory courtesy *You first, ... no, you* and *have a great day ... Right back at ya'*. Colonies of cubicles always buzzing like a hive by nine every morning, dozens of people in their mini "offices" with their half walls tacked with family photos and abstract kids' art; their desk accoutrements, anything from a Rubik's cube to Simpson's figurines. So many desks, each one told a different personal story that was gone forever.

Her brain was like a rolodex flipping through all the colleagues she'd never see again. The plane hit the North Tower just below their firm's floor, so there was no way out. Co-workers in the office with no escape other than up to the roof, or dare she imagine jumping. On the trek to her apartment, Piper found herself sinking deeper and deeper into oblivion. And her mental rolodex kept spinning.

Each of them made a list of all the people they knew from the two towers. Isabel's list was just first names. Under other circumstances, Piper would have found that pathetic but in this case she was relieved for her sister –less mourning for her to endure. Both Piper and Clare were on the reverse side of their papers and still writing down names.

They spent a painful hour calling every phone number Piper and Clare had in their address books, but to no avail. Not one person answered. Clare was able to reach a few of her coworkers. Since WOW didn't open until ten in the morning most of them were still at home when the planes hit. It was the long list of beloved regulars that Clare was trying to come to terms with.

It was quite possible Piper and Isabel were the only employees left from the firm. Everyone else was dead unless they were running late, but Piper knew better. Her firm was one of the most cut-throat in the business, dealing in international corporate litigation. Most of the partners were in their offices at dawn, already on their third cup of coffee by the time Piper arrived at eight each morning.

Piper could describe each and every one of her colleagues, the photos of loved ones on their desks, where they ordered their lunch and their choice of sandwich down to the condiments, if they took cream in their coffee or lemon in their tea. It was endless, her connection to so many dead in the blink of an eye. She had lost more than ten years of relationships, just like that. Why was she one of the lucky ones? Piper was more than acquainted with survivor's guilt having watched her father go through it after they lost Piper's mother.

Shock had obviously rendered her incapable of controlling the direction of her thoughts. One pressing thought was she prayed they died quickly, painlessly. It amazed her the ways people consoled themselves at unfathomable depths and with ridiculously sad prayers; *they didn't suffer, they called a loved one for closure, they died from a heart attack before hitting the ground.* One didn't need to be a grief counselor to know that the worst part for Piper was just beginning. She hated funerals and imagined that over the next several weeks, she'd become a professional mourner. There wasn't enough little black dresses or Xanax on the planet for her near future. Piper was going to need Isabel and her friends, whoever was left anyway and of course, Clare.

Finding something positive about that morning was like looking for a needle in a stack of pins. There was, of course, the miracle that they were still alive. But there was a cleaving that morning, a clear and definite before and after. The severing of past and future was swift and final. What began as a beautiful Tuesday in September ended in a dramatically changed world.

ISABEL

The three of them comforted each other. Their choreography was gentle and polite as each of them yielded to whomever was triggered by a thought; an unnecessary and exploitive image on the news or a memory of yet another coworker or friend they'd forgotten to remember. They were puffy-eyed and weary, but tried to be constructive with their thoughts. *How could they help?* Piper had suggested they could give blood but what else? Isabel tried calling the hotline number just to ask if they could be of any assistance; it wasn't in service yet. They felt useless and hopeless all at once. Occasionally they managed a laugh, but those moments were few and far between and always smothered by the heavy truth of the day.

The sky outside Piper's elongated windows was dirty despite the perfect, cloudless day. As the news reports played out they learned that many people who did not work in those buildings were also killed, including many firefighters and cops. Isabel thought of Rosie's Pizza where they'd met for lunch once a week to jazz and razz around with the cities' finest who hung out there. Rosie had been fortunate to have both the fire department and the 6th Police Precinct right around the corner, so she showed her appreciation by making the best pizza this side of Ohio. Rosie would laugh and admit her secret ingredient was simply water.

"We use spring water while the rest of the schmucks use city water," Rosie would say. "It doesn't take a genius." She was legendary from Harlem to Brooklyn. Rosie's Pizza was in ruins, smoking rubble where a thriving business once resided. It was right there, or rather wasn't there, on the evening news. Hundreds of people were fleeing lower Manhattan, and then there were the few hundred that were headed toward the catastrophe, to try and find their loved ones. After three hours of watching news programs, Piper announced that they had witnessed the towers collapsing at least a hundred times, and it was best to shut off the television for a while.

There were long stretches of silence, punctuated by the occasional sob. Isabel knew Clare and Piper's heads were swimming with images far worse than her own. She took a chance at changing the tone. After all, it was Isabel's turn to put Piper back together each time she broke down in whatever way Isabel could.

"Let's talk about something else." Isabel gave it the old college try. "So, Clare, do you like house sitting? Your place is in Soho, right?"

"Oh, sure," Clare glanced over at Piper. "Okay, yes, yes I do, Isabel, I love it here."

Piper turned to Clare and then faced Isabel, but before she could say anything, her sister sat forward on the couch. "We need to chat, Iz." Piper looked somewhat flustered and for a second, Isabel wondered if she was pregnant too and waiting to spill her story.

"How bout I make us some real drinks first?" Clare stood and made her way to the kitchen. "It's afternoon, right? Somewhere? Isn't that what you say?"

Isabel heard ice being ground from the freezer and clinking glasses and the distraction was enough to fill the silent void, so she didn't feel the need to speak. Her head felt swimmy.

"Our own personal bartender." Piper attempted small talk, but it was apparent she was deep in another place.

Clare returned with a tray replete with cheese on crackers, a secret concoction of pink liquid, and three bottles of water.

"This cocktail will put some hair on your dog." Clare curled up next to Piper.

"You either mean *hair of the dog* or *puts hair on your chest*." Piper laughed a bit and nudged Clare who then rested her head on Piper's shoulder.

Levity was welcome albeit brief. While the two friends sipped from Y-shaped glasses, Isabel chose water to no comment from either of them. Even if she wasn't keeping this baby, Isabel was not going to be so callous as to subject an unborn child to alcohol. Then again, was there anything more callous than abortion? The thought was disconcerting, and Isabel needed to get out of her own head.

"What is it you need to chat about – sounds serious? Er … well I mean besides today kind of serious. I'm all ears."

Piper was probably going to tell Isabel she'd be moving home permanently after all this and Isabel welcomed that news at this juncture. She wanted nothing more than to be closer to Piper. Sure her sister was a bit over the top, a force to be reckoned with and all, but when their father was gone she'd be all Isabel had. Truth was Isabel loved her sister's outrageous company.

"So I need to tell you something and here goes, little sister." Piper took a deep breath, and Isabel couldn't for the life of her imagine what she had to say. When Piper spoke, Isabel felt a rush of sound in her ears, and her skin prickled and flushed with heat. As quick as it came on, it just as swiftly disappeared taking Isabel along with it.

She woke with a start, a cold compress on her forehead and

Piper and Clare looming over her. Isabel's head was cradled in her sister's lap.

"What happened?" Her brain had a dull ache. The two friends were laughing. After all they'd been through that day, Isabel couldn't imagine how any of this was funny?

"Well, I'm sure someday you'll laugh at this, too." Piper cleared her throat. "I told you I'm gay, and you passed out."

PIPER

"That went well." Piper was taken aback by Isabel's reaction. She hadn't expected her sister to react with such drama. For all Piper knew, Isabel had figured it out a long time ago. Piper hadn't been in a sincere relationship with a man since her senior prom. Sure, in her line of work she was surrounded by men, and it behooved her to flaunt her femininity. She knew she couldn't beat a man at his own game so she never tried. Instead she lured men into wanting to play her game, a bit histrionic but it worked.

Isabel had always been a very open-minded person. She was the last person Piper expected to be shocked over sexual preferences. Piper didn't get far enough in the discussion to tell her the best part of the news— that Clare and she were lovers. She was pretty sure Isabel knew Clare was gay but maybe not since her sister had apparently checked out of life months ago.

Isabel sat up on the couch. "You're gay?" She shook her head like a cartoon character trying to jiggle sense back into its brain. "Ouch, did I hit my head?" Isabel tried to stand up, but Piper wouldn't have it.

"Simmer down, you only tapped it on the side arm of the sofa. You fainted though."

"Are you sure, Piper? Does Dad know?"

She could picture the questions flooding into Isabel's throat.

"Yes, Izzy, you fainted, and how could Dad know? It just happened ten seconds ago."

"I don't mean …"

"I know what you mean." Piper smiled down at her. "Yes, I'm sure I'm gay and no, Dad has no clue." Piper winked at Clare, their practiced signal for Clare to cut in.

"She's a lipstick lesbian. Not to be confused with a diesel dyke." Clare sat down opposite Isabel on the loveseat and bore a smile that reached her eyes for the first time all day. When she spoke again, her voice conveyed a soft accent. "As tough as this is for you to comprehend, imagine how we felt when we had to accept this fact within ourselves, like we were born freaks of nature or something. We've faked through a decade of relationships and orgasms only to come out on the other end completely confused and unfulfilled."

"You're gay, too?" Isabel's eyes widened, and she drew back her face. "Holy shit, am I stupid to have not known? I feel so … I don't know …"

"Straight?" Piper knew acceptance would take some time. "Listen, Izzy, I didn't even know for sure myself until maybe ten years ago."

"Ten years?"

"Yes. I just thought I had put men second because of my career. Clare and I," Piper moved to where Clare sat and plopped down next to her and slung her arm around her shoulders, "have decided to try and make a go of it, we sort of came out together, it's so cliché it's trendy." They laughed, but Isabel did not.

Isabel's brow was furrowed. "You two are lovers? Seriously?" She pointed her index finger lackadaisically between Clare and Piper.

"Yep." Piper knew she sounded confident. The beverage Clare

had whipped up gave her a slight buzz and a false sense of bravado. Funny part was Piper had zero courage when it came to telling her father. If it was challenging getting her bleeding-heart sister to understand then her father may have to go to his grave without the knowledge that his overachieving daughter was a lesbian. She'd banked on Isabel knowing the exact move as far as their dad was concerned.

"I didn't faint because you're gay. I don't know why I passed out, probably all the stress. Does anyone at work know?" Isabel pressed her face in her open hands, and Piper knew she was crying again. "What am I saying, there's no one left besides us, is there? I don't deserve to be sad, Piper, I'm still here, still alive. Now I feel like I really am late for my own funeral."

The three were hugged-out, only reserving them for very large moments, but Piper couldn't help herself, and she stood and went to Isabel and leaned down and embraced her.

"We need to lighten up here, Izzy, realize how fortunate we are." Piper wanted this optimistic buzz to last, but she knew that was impossible. "If we don't appreciate every breath then we're disrespecting all those people who lost their lives that day." Piper looked at her sister. Isabel shook her head.

"It's fine, all good. I'm happy for you two, seriously. When I somehow reconcile this day, I'll be okay. You're both going to really need each other in the coming weeks, and me too, so for what it's worth, I'll be here for both of you."

Isabel was right. There would be a tremendous amount of emotional work ahead to resolve the mix of emotions: *can't feel happy or I'd be selfish, can't feel sad or I'd be ungrateful.* It was simple, yet lent itself to such complicated resolutions. Piper experienced a sense of relief. There was no more faking her way through life. Her greatest fear had been having the partners, a term used ironically more these days for homosexual couples than staunch Republican esquires, to discover her secret. None of that mattered anymore. She would be starting a whole new life with Clare, and she needed to embrace her great fortune of being alive. If it weren't for Isabel's lateness, they'd be dead, she knew this with certainty. She vowed to live every moment to its fullest, grateful for life only after she fell apart. The latter was inevitable.

"So, Izzy, I shared my dilemma with you, now it's your turn. Go ahead — change the subject and it better be good."

ISABEL

Piper waited for an answer, but Isabel was at a loss for words. "I'm all talked out. I think I just need to rest."

Consumed by the events of the day and the continuing tragic broadcasts, the last thing Isabel wanted to talk about was this pregnancy. She wasn't about to contribute to the insanity of the day. She'd have to wait a few days before scheduling the abortion, so she didn't need to tell anyone just yet. Didn't have to take that personal day off after-all, Isabel was permanently off.

It amazed her how Piper managed, once again, to steal the limelight. Not that it was a bad thing – for Piper, one-upmanship came as natural as breathing. It's just that Isabel assumed her news would be major, but it paled in comparison to Piper being a lesbian. Isabel was sure her fainting had nothing to do with Piper's news because she'd been feeling strange since they'd shut the door of the apartment hours before. The only issue Isabel had was how blind she'd been to her sister's life. She never once considered that Piper wasn't having relations with men all over the world. Whenever Isabel had inquired about her sister's love life, come to think of it, Piper was always in-between relationships. It never occurred to Isabel to ask the gender with whom she was sharing her time.

At some point in the following few days, after they all had

some decent sleep and nourishment, Isabel would tell Piper about the pregnancy. Meanwhile, she needed to lie down although sleep would be difficult. Finding relaxation was like trying to outmaneuver an enemy that was both outside and within her. The news footage of events was seared in her brain. She knew the attacks demanded that the media gave such hype to these sorts of events, but it added to the victory for evil. All the publicity these terrorists received was probably giving them everything they ultimately sought, notoriety and power.

Isabel lay on the couch and Piper tucked her in with a pillow and cashmere blanket. Piper and Clare sat on stools in the galley kitchen and whispered and cried. Isabel shut her eyes, but shutting down her thoughts proved impossible. Her mind drifted back to that afternoon in May when she rode the elevator to another floor in the tower and a man got on with her; had said her dress was beautiful. Isabel's arms had hugged her torso as if she could hide herself. She flushed with embarrassment, not used to a man in an expensive suit paying attention to her.

"You're blushing." He'd said and then winked at her. "Don't be shy. What's your name?"

"Sorry … er … I mean thank you. Isabel, my name is Isabel." She was never so grateful when the elevator doors parted. She wasn't even aware of the floor she'd gotten off on, just relieved to be free of that confined space.

"Hope to see you again," he said as the doors shut.

She wanted to see him again too.

Her eyes stung with tears at that memory, their first encounter. She forced her thoughts back to the present.

What would she and Piper do the next day? Would they even wake up the next day? If they did, would they venture out? Isabel honestly didn't know. She was sure of only one thing: that for the moment, she was safe under a blanket on her sister's plush suede couch. She needed sleep. After an hour of begging her brain to turn-off, she must have fallen asleep because when she awoke the apartment was dark. Clare and Piper were no longer in the kitchen, but probably asleep in the bedroom. Good for them. They had each other.

Isabel got up to relieve her pressing bladder and then squelched her sour, ravenous stomach by rummaging through Piper's kitchen cabinets. The warmth of the couch beckoned her and she once again ensconced herself back under the blanket. She didn't dare turn on the television or look out the windows. Somehow she fell back asleep until the sun came up.

Isabel awoke to a peanut butter cracker stuck to her cheek, and Clare announcing she was going out to grab the newspaper and bagels. Isabel showered and dressed in a tailored warm-up she found in Piper's hall closet. Piper emerged when she smelled the coffee Clare had put on before she left the apartment. The two sisters shuffled around the narrow kitchen, dull-eyed and featureless. Conversations were monosyllabic, interspersed with the occasional sniffling or throat clearing.

"Are we going back to Jersey today?" Isabel felt compelled to poke the elephant in the room because at this point, it was her responsibility to keep them on track, a reversal of roles again indeed. Isabel prayed it was only temporary because sooner or later she'd need Piper strong and by her side, back in Isabel's comfort zone. "Whatever you want to do is fine with me, but we *are* going to need to go home at some point."

"I know, I know, Izzy." Piper's eyes were so red they looked as though they'd been bleeding. Her face was mottled and puffy. "We should try and get home this afternoon sometime." She stared down at the floor. "Listen, Izzy, I know this is going to sound crazy, but just hear me out, please." She took in a long pull of air through her nose, exhaled through her mouth and looked straight at Isabel.

"I need some sort of closure before all the staged memorial services. I know I sound like a Sylvia Plath poem, but it's like someone has removed all my insides and replaced them with glass, if I move too quickly I may break open. Scraped raw on the inside sums it up for me at the moment. I need to go to Ground Zero, breathe it in one last time before I say my staged good-byes at funerals."

"I … erm … I don't even know how to respond to you, Piper, but okay. I think? It's a crime scene, so I'm not sure how close you'll get." Isabel looked around the room and toward the front door, desperate for it to open and for Clare to come back and tell her girlfriend she was crazy. The last place Isabel wanted to be was Ground Zero, but she didn't know what was logical at that point. "What does Clare think?"

"I haven't mentioned it to her. She has to go see her parents in White Plains today. They went out of their minds when they heard the news." Piper twisted her hair into a knot at the nape of her neck and then walked to the sink to dump her coffee. She rinsed her mug with her back to Isabel. "They can't shut down the entire Financial District, no way. I'm sure I can get close enough to feel some small bit of what happened. I was supposed to be there, Izzy. I've lost everybody."

You didn't lose me, thought Isabel, but she kept that to herself. "Okay. I really don't need any more images of what I saw all day yesterday, but you shouldn't do this alone even if there's nothing left to see." Isabel wanted to pull back her words when Piper winced. "I mean, I'm sorry … you know what I'm saying. I was only with the firm a few months, and you, well, over a decade. I'm just saying I get it, I think. I'll go with you."

Piper hugged Isabel and when they released, Isabel looked down at the Mickey Mouse pajama bottoms Piper was wearing.

"Relax, Izzy, I'm not going out like this. In fact, I'm going to take a quick shower."

As soon as Piper closed the bathroom door, Clare walked in *a day late and a dollar short* for the conversation. She began spreading cream-cheese on a sliced bagel and pushed the *NY Times* across the kitchen counter toward Isabel without a word.

Isabel knew what would be on the front page. Those same photos would be on the front page of every paper around the world. Isabel had promised herself she wasn't going to watch television, so when Clare flipped on the news, Isabel stayed in the kitchen. It was impossible to block out the incessant reporters' dramatic voices. When she had had enough, Isabel told Clare she was taking Piper's apartment key and going out for some air. Clare just nodded, her large, watery green eyes never wavering from the reporters on the screen.

The air outside smelled charred, and the sun was visible through a thin layer of smog. The day before seemed eons ago, the pregnancy test, bickering with her sister over minutia like her cell phone; such trivial nonsense in the scope of things. Isabel sat down on Piper's front stoop and watched people traversing the sidewalk, no one looking at anyone else, but all wearing the same resigned expression and trying to be small, unseen as if carrying on with their lives was wrong.

Isabel couldn't fight her thoughts from going back to June. She had seen the man a few more times since he had complimented her, and they had introduced themselves. One evening on her way out of the building she found herself in a crowded elevator and when the doors opened she looked up and saw him. They'd shared coy smiles, but neither of them spoke because there were several other employees coming and going. Something had passed between them on that occasion, the sexual tension was palpable. Another week had passed and just when she figured she'd never see him again, there he was casually leaning against the side wall elevator. He straightened when she stepped into the car. His delicious smile ran ear to ear.

"What floor?" He had asked, finger at the ready to push the button of her choice.

"Eighty-two please." Isabel couldn't meet his eyes for fear she'd implode. Instead, she glanced at the panel of lit up buttons.

"I'm up at Charles & Dean Finance, ninetieth floor." He moved a little closer to her. "What do you do?"

"I, umm, I work for my sister's law firm, just a secretary."

"No, not *just* a secretary, a one-of-a-kind secretary. I can tell, you're special." He looked at her in a way no one had ever looked at her.

"No, I only started working there a month ago." She was just filling the silent void. "What do you do?"

"It's not what you do that's important, it's what you want to do, what you're meant to do." He leaned over to the panel and tapped the emergency "stop" button mid-floor and leaned in for a gentle kiss. At the time she'd thought *who had the nerve to do that in the World Trade Center?* She was all at once surprised, impressed and flattered. In the weeks following the elevator kiss, she slowly let her guard down. They had coffee a few times during her lunch hour and got to know a little about each other. When he invited her to a Fourth of July picnic in Battery Park, she realized they were moving from casual to the next level and it felt so right. She had trusted him. How could Isabel not have seen the huge mistake she was making?

Two months later she was still trying to put all the pieces together. There had to have been clues, but she was apparently too naive to recognize them. There on Piper's steps in the aftermath of

9/11, Isabel felt a sense of being torn between grief and relief. She looked down and took in her body language: arms wrapped around her knees and crouched inward. Isabel shuddered, stood and turned to go back inside. This was going to be a long journey, the path to trusting the world again seemed endless. She had no clue what her future held. One thing was certain: for the first time in their lives, Piper had it worse.

PIPER

When Piper emerged from her morning rituals, Clare was on the couch watching the gruesome, repetitive news, and Isabel was nowhere to be seen. In a one bedroom set-up, there weren't too many places to hide. If Isabel changed her mind about coming with her to Ground Zero, Piper would understand.

"Where's Izzy?" Piper said.

Clare looked up at Piper through tears. "She went to get some fresh air. This is horrible, just so horrible. I want to do something, but I don't know what to do."

"I'll tell you what to do; turn the damn TV off!" Piper acquiesced with an apologetic smile when Clare snapped her head toward her. "Don't go to White Plains. Come with Isabel and me to Ground Zero."

"Did you eat a bowl of crazies this morning? Ground Zero? Are you fucking nuts? I may never venture south of Canal Street again." A heavy, nervous accent punctuated her words.

Piper sat down next to her on the couch and kissed her cool cheek. She wrenched around on the couch to look out the window next to them. "Where is Izzy getting this fresh air you refer to because it ain't out there?" Piper shot her thumb out gesturing to the window, but Clare wasn't looking.

"She just said she was going out." Clare shook her head. "I'm sorry but I don't want to go with you. I have to go see my parents before they have nervous breakdowns. I know how superstitious they are, and if they don't see me in the flesh and blood they won't believe I'm okay. I have to go home, no choice."

Piper smarted a bit at Clare's *home* comment. Sad part was her lover had never even lived in White Plains. She'd wanted Clare to feel that the apartment was her home. Piper stood just as the apartment door swung open and Isabel walked in.

"Ready?" Isabel clicked her fingernails on the entry table and glanced at the vintage Route 66 wall-clock in the kitchen. Piper knew Isabel didn't really want to go to lower Manhattan and Piper appreciated her sister's willingness to accompany her despite the obvious misgivings. The truth was Piper couldn't wait to plant her feet in New Jersey, but New York had spared her and she was compelled to pay homage. It would be the beginning of a long road of grieving.

"You both are insane. Go." She gave a dramatic wave-off. "You will be sorry though. Now go, we'll talk later."

"Okay. Give my love to your *Ps*. Oh and honey, can you lock up?" Piper didn't wait for her to answer—Clare obsessed over safety and security. Clare had an innate distrust of people in general. Piper assumed it was rooted in something tragic from her childhood in Brazil. Something Clare tried her best to leave behind, but it manifested in paranoia. Piper shut the apartment door behind them, knowing Clare was cussing her. They opted for the stairs instead of the elevator.

Once outside, fear began seeping into Piper's system like poison. Guilt and confusion were just the tip of the iceberg. Her world had been turned upside down like a filthy garbage can, and it would be a long time before she was ready to accept that she'd lived to talk about it. If she was going to get through the next several hours, she'd have to keep all those negative demons at bay.

"We'll grab a cab," Piper said. "I don't care how much the fare is, we'll have him take us as far southwest as possible, at least below Canal Street."

"I don't mind going with you, but I won't cross police lines and get shot like a criminal, Piper. How pitiful would that be after surviving the worst disaster ever?"

"Calm down and let's just see. Okay?"

Miraculously, they weren't on the street more than five minutes before a cab pulled up in front of the apartment, and they squeezed in the back seat together.

"Canal Street." Piper stated matter-of-factly, but crossed her fingers.

"Oh, no, no, no. Can't go there. No way." The cabbie stopped the car and turned in his seat. "Four dolla' and please to get out of my cab."

"Four bucks? The car hasn't moved." Piper was in no mood. "Wait, if I can't go there, where can I go? Take us as far southwest as possible."

"Okay lady, but it got to cost you."

She was mildly comforted by the familiarity of the old New York hospitality of cab service. "I wouldn't have it any other way." Piper winked at Isabel, who looked disappointed they weren't thrown to the curb.

The sisters got as far as Soho when the driver stopped and dropped them off on Bleecker. They'd hoof it the rest of the way. It was a long trek, cutting over to the Westside Highway and then a few miles to Ground Zero. This was the day after one of the worst moments in history. They could walk.

Twenty blocks later, Isabel started lagging behind. She had

been quiet and there was a pinched look on her face. Before Piper could ask if she wanted to go back Isabel said, "I don't feel so good, Piper." Isabel quickly turned to a narrow alley, the gap only large enough to fit her head, and vomited.

"My god, are you sick?" Piper snickered nervously. "How stupid of me, of course you're sick, you just puked." Piper took a tissue from her handbag, a bag that one could survive out of for weeks. "Here."

Isabel took it and wiped her mouth. "Wow, I had no idea that was coming, must be the coffee on an empty stomach. I should've had a bagel." She leaned against the wall, her face pale and covered in a sheen of sweat.

It made Piper uneasy seeing her sister like that. She didn't want to think of Isabel having some severe illness like their mother. Piper resisted the urge to tell Isabel that it was not her gourmet coffee or lack of breakfast, but rather the stress of their existence at the moment. They lived in a surreal sort of apocalypse, headed toward the eye of the storm. Piper was nervous and nauseous just like Isabel was, but her role had always been to keep it together even if she didn't have a hint of how to do that.

"Let's get you something to eat."

"No, really, I can't eat anything until my stomach settles. I'm feeling a bit better Piper, so let's just keep moving."

They got just north of Manhattan College, still several blocks away from Ground Zero, when they came to the first barricade, manned by armed guards. Piper took in the chain-link fencing along the riverbank of the Hudson. Singed papers clung to the gaps, blown into the thousands of linkages. Ash polluted the air and every so often they had to brush dust off themselves. The ashy remnants reminded Piper of the pictorials she'd seen in history books of the aftermath of Pompeii. The trees were whitened, littered with detritus and even though there was a moderate breeze, the branches were unmoving as if laden with heavy snow. Cars were blanketed with an inch or more of debris beyond the barricade. They were standing on the border of New York City and ancient ruins.

"State your business."

Piper's disorientation was interrupted at the barricade by the square-jawed Marine. She and Isabel pulled out their work IDs which displayed the WTC logo and their names. They were allowed to pass, but barely. Before the next barricade, the air thickened with smoke and who knew what else. The murky smog could not be good for their lungs. Piper grabbed Isabel and shoved her toward a small grocery store to get some fresh indoor air.

"We need something to cover our mouths and nose, and some bottled water," Piper told Isabel.

Once inside the small establishment, Piper noticed shards of glass and wood splinters jutting from where the store front window had once been. The floor was sprayed with specks of glass. A dark-skinned man was holding a broom and dustpan and was having a heated conversation with an apparently on-duty New York City fireman. The grocer was ranting about some hoodlums that had threatened his business that morning.

"I am Egyptian, not from Pakistan like they accused. I am a legal citizen and have lived in New York for twenty-five years and now they throw bricks through my window! What is next? A hole in my head?"

The fireman calmly handed the store owner what appeared to be his receipt after scribbling something on the back. "Here's my cell phone number, Manny. Anyone bothers you or threatens you again in the slightest, call me and I will personally take care of them." He turned.

Piper wasn't surprised to see a handsome, dark-haired man. If she were straight she'd have been all over him. He seemed good-natured to boot, a rarity in this city. When Piper nudged Isabel into paying attention to the hunky fireman leaving the store, Isabel collapsed at her feet like a ragdoll.

ISABEL

Isabel woke up to the smell of smoke and after-shave. She blinked several times and when her vision cleared, she found her face mere inches from a stranger smiling down at her, so close she could see the pores from where whiskers sprouted.

"You okay, Miss?" He was cradling Isabel in a semi-sitting embrace.

Way too close. She pulled away from him and crab-walked to the corner of the store.

"Isabel, honey, calm down." Piper's voice echoed in Isabel's ears as if she were underwater. "You passed out and this nice fireman is only trying to help." Piper appeared in her line of vision and squatted in front of her. Through gritted teeth, she whispered, "Don't blow this one, Izzy. He's not wearing a ring." Then Piper winked at her and Isabel would have laughed had she not been trying to comprehend what just happened.

From behind Piper, the man who smelled of smoke approached and extended a strong, calloused hand in a gesture to pull her to her feet. Isabel accepted the help while Piper supported her around the waist.

"Name's McAfee, Thomas McAfee, but my friends call me Mac. Glad to meet ya'." He firmly shook the hand he was already holding, eased her onto a chair and then gently released her. "I'm no doctor, but you should get checked out at the hospital. People don't faint for no good reason."

"I'm fine, just bad coffee." Isabel knew she sounded like an ass. Even if his grammar was atrocious, he was sweet as well as right. There was a reason she fainted, the very same cause of her puking twenty minutes earlier. "You're really kind but I'm fine – just tired."

Maybe it was his proximity, the overwhelming smell of smoke on the man, but Isabel leaned over and threw-up right there on the floor at his feet.

"Oh shit! I am so sorry, I am …" Isabel felt a warm flush cross her cheeks.

"And here I thought you liked me, said I was sweet." He patted her shoulder. "You pregnant?"

The gulp of water Isabel had swigged to get the acid breath to settle down came out every possible opening in her head except her ears. Her ears had their own brand of humiliation by turning red with heat. Mortified, she jumped from the chair but he gently pressed her back down.

"I'm so sorry. I'll buy you new boots. But really, I'll be okay." Isabel knew she wasn't convincing anyone.

"You stay right here until help arrives. And don't worry your pretty head about my boots, they've seen worse, trust me on that." He turned from her and still holding her shoulders, shouted, "Manny, get me a mop, I'm calling an ambulance."

"Yes, sir, right away, friend." Manny snapped to attention.

Isabel tried to protest, but Piper waved her off saying she had ample insurance, which she never used and Piper was in full agreement – Isabel should be seen by a doctor.

"You've puked and passed out twice in less than twelve hours and you know I've been telling you that you look like crap lately." Piper glanced up at the fireman then back at her sister. "I mean that in the most caring and concerned way, mind you."

A pang of guilt hit Isabel. Rescue workers had to be exhausted and limited and she was not about to drag them out here for an ailment that wasn't an emergency at all. It was time for her to come clean to Piper. Isabel looked into the fireman's steel blue eyes and without wavering stated the obvious.

"Please don't call an ambulance, Mr. Mac, I'm fine. I'm pregnant." Her eyes darted to Piper. "There, I said it and now you know." Isabel sighed with relief. "Nine weeks yesterday to be exact."

"I knew it, can always tell when a woman is expecting. Expectant mothers have a certain beauty, like the *shining.*" The fireman puffed his chest out and grinned wide at his apparent gift.

"Are you fucking kidding me?" Piper pressed her lips into a thin line. Her eyes darkened and brightened all at once. "What are you telling me, Isabel? Telling us?" She swept an arm across the grocery store as if the canned goods were all witnesses to Isabel's disgrace. Piper tilted her head and gazed at Isabel, waiting for a response.

"I just found out yesterday, honest, it's why I was in the bathroom so long and why we missed our train. I was going to tell you, but then everything happened. Then you had your *coming out* debut so I decided to hold off on more stressful news *until* … well, until now." Her adamancy was weak, at best.

"I didn't think you were even sexually active."

Isabel shot Piper a glance that said *too much information in front of fireman Mac and Manny,* but Piper didn't seem to care.

"Well strike me with lightening! Here I was beginning to worry that you inherited Mom's disease! Thank god it's not that." She planted a kiss on Isabel's cheek. "Okay, so I gotta hear this one. You haven't had a date in, well in I don't know, did you at least get dinner out of the deal?"

"Well, congratulations is all I can say, Miss or Ms. What's your name, little mama?" Fireman Mac was grinning as if this were a baby shower he'd stumbled into by mistake. "This feels so intimate and wonderful in light of yesterday's horror."

"Who are you? Jiminy Cricket in a fireman suit?" Piper dismissed him with a wave of her hand, forgetting that only five minutes earlier she had been trying to secure Isabel a marriage to this guy. "Hit the road, Mac."

Isabel ignored her rude sister and extended a shaky hand. "My name's Isabel, Isabel Henry and this is my sister, Piper. We both work on the 82nd floor of the North Tower, well, worked that is until yesterday." Isabel took a sip of the bottled water, and it eased the burning in her throat. "We missed our train yesterday because I was in the bathroom watching my life circle the drain."

"Well now that's some kind of miracle." Mac grinned and leaned on the counter.

"Who the hell is the father?" Piper was pacing.

Isabel had gotten this much of the story out, so what did she have to lose by telling the rest of the sordid mess? For some reason, she found that talking to a stranger made it a little easier.

"Hold off on the congratulations and cigars, Mac. I don't know who the father is because … well, because I was raped." Isabel knew a secret shared was no longer a secret, but she didn't care. She suddenly felt lighter.

"You what?" Piper didn't wait for an answer. "Holy fuck, Izzy, you poor baby, when … who, why didn't you say something?"

"I really don't want to get into any details here, Piper." Isabel wasn't about to tell anyone, not even Piper the particulars of what happened that July Fourth night. "Suffice it say, I was raped. Just wrong place at the wrong time." Isabel saw tears well in her sister's eyes and Piper leaned down and grabbed Isabel into her arms and held her for what seemed an eternity.

"Sure, sure, no details. I just can't believe you never said anything to me."

Isabel wanted to point out that Piper hadn't shared the lesbian thing with her for ten years, but she kept it to herself.

"I'm an attorney, remember? I could've helped!"

Mac let out a long sigh. "I should've guessed by your polite demeanor —another damn attorney."

Piper turned and her face said it all. If she wasn't a lawyer she'd have been a mob boss. "Shut up, Mick, or Matt or whatever your name is. Don't you have some fires to put out somewhere?"

He laughed. "I do, I'm on Ground Zero search and rescue. Lost half my buddies including my best friend, so I'm kind of feeling a little sorry for myself right now, too. I was in here to get away from the mound. Needed a break, ya' know."

Everyone was silent for a moment and then Piper cut in. "Sorry for your loss, but no one here is offering a sympathy blow job so why stick around?"

The handsome fireman chortled, but his cheeks flushed as though he'd been slapped.

"Oh my god, Piper! I know you're upset, so is he but you don't need to be nasty."

Piper didn't seem to hear Isabel. She straightened her shoulders as if squaring off with the man. "Listen, dude, I've got this under control."

"Of course you do – lawyers and money are the two things that never sleep, isn't that what they say?"

Piper glared at the man. "No, moron, it's *sharks* and money!"

"Exactly!" Mac smiled at his clever joke.

Any other time Isabel may have agreed and laughed along with him. Instead, she gave him a half-hearted, apologetic look just as Piper snapped her fingers toward the store's entrance in an effort to dismiss him and came to Isabel's side and put her arm around Isabel's shoulder.

"Izzy, I am at a loss for words." Piper didn't seem at a loss for words. "What did the police say when you reported it? Are they investigating or have they found the pervert?"

Isabel winced knowing what was coming. "I didn't report it."

"What? Why the hell didn't you report it? We need to report this! I do realize it makes the case so much more difficult without a rape kit but ..." Piper cocked her head at her sister waiting for a response. When Isabel stared ahead and didn't answer, her sister continued her interrogation. "Who was this jerk – do you know him? Where does he live because I will be sure justice gets served one way or another."

"Piper, I have no idea who the man was or where he lives, I thought I knew him, he said he worked in the North Tower, but it was all lies, his name, his supposed apartment, I was duped. He made it so there was no way it could be reported and please don't ask me why. I don't want to talk about this here, now." Isabel tried her best pleading look.

"So, okay, Izzy, you're not going to explain to me why you let a pig get away with rape, fine. We can discuss that mess later as well as what action I will take to be sure this man pays. For now, we need to get you to a doctor. You do see the value in getting this checked out by someone, don't you? You've been puking and passing out. We need to be sure both you and the baby are healthy." Piper stopped pacing and squatted down in front of Isabel and pressed her ear to Isabel's abdomen.

"What are you doing?" Isabel pushed her sister's head away and Piper fell on her backside, but she was beaming back at her. "I'm not having this baby, Piper! Are you serious? It's a rapist's baby."

"Oh, you'll have this baby, Izzy! It's part of you!" Piper got to a standing position as if to dominate over Isabel's decision but then took on a pleading tone, her hands in front of her in praying position. "This kid is a small part of me too, and I want to be an aunt! If you don't want the baby, I'll take it. It'd be a small joy amidst this world of shit we're in, don't you agree?"

Tears glistened on Piper's lower lashes and Isabel could taste salt on her own upper lip. Piper wasn't talking about trading a pair of Manolo heels, she was talking about a baby, and Isabel had never seen her so serious. In all of her meandering thoughts over the past twenty-four hours, it never occurred to Isabel that her sister would try and talk her into *having* this baby.

"Piper, I am not going to use a baby as an antidepressant." Isabel's voice didn't have as much conviction as she'd hoped. "Besides, it's my decision. As far as me not reporting the rape, I don't want to go down that road or even discuss the matter. Bottom line is I'm not having this baby. I just can't, the timing sucks! Besides, look at me, I'm sick as a dog. There's probably something wrong with the kid."

"If I may interject, it's the little lady's decision." Mac addressed Piper, and Isabel was grateful. "You should know that. After all, you're an attorney; the choice is hers."

Piper wheeled around and faced him. "Why are you still here?"

"Free country last I checked."

Piper gave a quick disgusted snort in his direction, but he didn't give her a chance to speak and instead directed his words to Isabel.

"But personally," he continued, "I'd give the kid a chance. Not his fault his old man's a loser. Lots of great people have shit for fathers. No such thing as a bad kid, just bad parents. The child is innocent."

"See!" Piper gestured in the fireman's direction as though she were a diplomat. "Even NYFD agrees – have this baby!" Piper was acting and sounding like a crazy woman.

"And there's nothing wrong with the kid, they say the sicker a woman gets in the beginning— the more solid the pregnancy." Mac raked his fingers through his thick, dark hair. "Hey, all I'm sayin' is at least have the kid and put it up for adoption, but don't kill it because of something someone else did. Give it to your sister if you don't want it although the kid may turn into the antichrist if you do that."

"Yes, yes, yes! Give it to me!" My sister jabbed a finger at her own chest. "I'm dead serious, Izzy, I'll raise the kid." She glared at Mac. "And the child will be a saint, dude."

"I ain't got kids, so I can't say for certain, but lots of single women have kids and the kids turn out fine." Mac reached out his hand. "Let's get you to a hospital, what-do-ya-say?"

Isabel took it. He pulled her up gently to a standing position. "I don't want to interfere with emergency medical efforts for possible survivors, but I promise ..." She hugged Mac in a thank-you gesture. "I will make a doctor's appointment first thing tomorrow to discuss options."

Piper laughed through tears, apparently ignoring Isabel's intentions. "We're having a baby!"

PIPER

Piper didn't have any answers, but she knew one thing for sure: Isabel's news made her smile inside for the first time in two days. The man Piper silently dubbed *handsome* fireman, Mac for short, helped Isabel to the curb and Piper stuffed her into a taxi with strict orders to return to the apartment. Piper knew Isabel needed to rest and digest the idea of her bared secret. This situation was so far out of Piper's control that she felt bludgeoned and heavenly all at once. Even so, Isabel was not going to complicate her emotional instability any further by having an abortion if Piper had anything to say about it. In the back of the cab through the open car door, Isabel tried to object going back to the apartment, insisting she needed to be with Piper for support.

"No one is going anywhere near Ground Zero. This is about the closest you'll get, well the next checkpoint that is." Mac stood on the sidewalk, arms folded across his chest.

"Bullshit, my entire office is in that rubble, and I have just as much right as anyone else to be there!" Piper wasn't sure why she was so angry with this stranger. "Just ignore me, us – better to just walk away, Fireman Mac."

"Whoa, whoa, cool out, darlin'. Maybe I can help you."

Piper wouldn't trust any man at this point, least of all someone they just met in a deli. She was determined to get as close as possible to her place of business and police be damned. This guy had no jurisdiction over her, he was just a frigging fireman, and she told him as much. It worked because Mac backed away. Before Piper could shut the cab door with Isabel safely inside, Isabel gave a parting shot.

"Piper! You are a real bitch, you know that? I feel like I don't even know you. How dare you say that to a brave New York City fireman, especially one who's lost all his friends and is risking his life trying to save your friends."

Piper put her hand to her forehead and stepped back, stumbling a bit on the sidewalk.

"Wow, okay. You're right, Izzy. I'm a mess. I need to get a grip." Piper feared she'd have a stroke right there outside Manny's deli. She spun and called after Mac who had crossed the street. "Hey! Mac! I am so sorry, I had no right speaking to you like that. C'mon back."

To Piper's surprise he turned and jogged back across the street.

"I'm just pissed at the world right now, not at you. Just the world. God, the terrorists, my sister's rapist, myself, I'm a fucking wreck." She held up a hand in surrender and he hesitated for just a second and then gave her an awkward and unexpected high-five. They were silent for a bit.

"It sucks. I get that." Mac was reassuring. "But if you don't get your anger in check you're going to do something you regret. I know this from personal experience, been a fireman for ten years and the job breeds rage." He took off his sunglasses. "It's not healthy to let it fester, but it's also not healthy to let it all out at once."

"I know, I know. I'm just so unsure of my next move. It's like I have no clue how to move forward so I'm moving backward, back to the rubble of my life before this all happened. Please accept my apology for being an asshole." Piper gave him her best smile and leaned into the cab to find Isabel smiling through tears. "See, Izzy, I'm being nice."

"Meters ticking even if we ain't moving," the cabbie announced.

"Hold your fucking pants on, dude!" Piper took a deep breath; *I will not freak out, I will not freak out.*

Isabel groaned in frustration from the back of the cab.

"Don't worry, Izzy. I won't punch anyone, and I won't get arrested. As soon as I get back to the apartment we're going home to New Jersey."

Isabel lolled her head in Piper's direction and mouthed a *thank-you* of relief. Piper reached in her purse and flashed a hundred dollar bill in front of the driver before handing it to Isabel. "Get my sister home safe and sound, please." Piper slammed the cab door after gently buckling in her sister and pecking her cheek. Isabel lackadaisically waved then pressed her palm to the window as the car left the curb. Piper turned to the fireman.

"So how close do you think we can get? It's important to me, Mac."

He looked down at her, forehead furrowed and eyes narrowed. "If I really want to go to Ground Zero, I can get you down there but you'll have to listen to everything I say. Have you ever done that before, actually listened to a man? I could get suspended for this, but I understand. You need to see it for yourself. You got some decent IDs?" He gave her a chance to nod. "Your colleagues are there – mine too if that means anything and it feels right to be present, but it don't feel good. We'll walk the rest on foot and at the NYFD trailer I'll grab us some gear and an all-terrain vehicle and I'll give you the grand tour. Be forewarned, it will take your breath away and not in a good way."

Piper couldn't fathom what he meant by gear and it gave her the chills even though it was at least seventy-five degrees in lower Manhattan. Regardless of what she was going to be exposed to, she had to do this for her own sanity.

"I owe you big time, Fireman Mac."

"You seem like a tough broad, a feminist sort of chick so your heartfelt apology before was a huge gesture." He had a cool confidence about him as he pointed in the direction they'd travel. "This way. And if you really believe you owe me one then how about giving me your sister's phone number?"

Piper stopped and he turned and walked backward to see her reaction.

"She's pregnant by a rapist! Most guys wouldn't go near her. You're either really awesome or really horny."

"No nothing like that. I just think she's special." Mac grinned at her and resumed walking forward. "Okay, I'll admit, I guess I'm pretty awesome."

"Really, dude, why do you think Izzy's special?" Piper already knew her sister was amazing, but how did he know it after only knowing her for less than an hour. Piper had to hear this one.

"I can tell. I may not be all *edumacated* like you, but I'm quite a good judge of character and besides that, she's gorgeous."

"She threw up on you then sprayed after-puke water in your face." Piper kept walking but turned to look up at him with a sideways glance. He was serious; he looked dreamy.

"I know, it's weird. It's just a feeling I got when I saw her, like I had to get to know her. Then I find out she was raped and just suffered through yesterday– that she's still here and to top it off, she lived all her life with a smart ass, self-righteous sister. That she hasn't given up? Well, that says a whole lot about the strength of her character. Besides, she has a nice ass."

She couldn't help but laugh because not only did he have Isabel pegged, he had Piper nearly figured out as well. She still wasn't going to give Isabel away so easily. "Cops beat, firemen cheat."

"Not this guy. Besides, after yesterday, I don't think I'll be sticking around here for too long. I got a best buddy who died yesterday in the collapse –knew him since kindergarten. He was a high profile banker — we bought some property in Pennsylvania with a plan to build a horse ranch where we could eventually raise our families. The property is beautiful, has a natural waterfall, views of the Pocono Mountains and at least twenty horse trails. Now, I'm stuck with it and on my salary, it'll take years to manage the funding on my own. The plan was he'd lay out the bucks for the property which was a steal. Then I would build us what we needed – I did construction work before I went to the fire academy. Don't care if it takes me the rest of my life though, I'm going to make something of that investment even if it breaks my bank account and kills me in the process."

They paused at the corner and then crossed the street. It's sort of like how Piper felt about coming to Ground Zero. Some things one just had to see for themselves in order to move forward and feel whole again. Piper wondered how Clare, Isabel, Mac and her had survived.

"How come you're still alive?" Piper knew on some level it was crass to ask, but she was curious how he'd survived when his job was to be there in the throes of action. "Were you there when it happened? You know my deal, what's yours?" He didn't answer and she felt the need to fill the silent void. "I mean, I get the distinct impression you're the *run into a burning building to save lives* kind of guy."

Mac cleared his throat. "I worked the weekend through Monday evening, so yesterday and today are my regular days off."

They stopped at an intersection and Piper noticed the traffic lights were out. When she glanced at Mac, she saw his cheek was damp with tears.

"I'm such a jerk," Piper said. "I'm a mean girl. I didn't mean to pry —I didn't think. I am so sorry."

"It's not you. It's personal for me too. I'm just as messed up as you are. I can't even imagine there'll come a day when I'll be able to move on from this catastrophe. This can never be in the past. How can it?"

Piper needed to keep the mean girl in check. They were both alive and everyone else was dead and she was pissed but directing it in all the wrong places. "I truly am sorry for all you've lost, Mac."

Mac didn't seem to hear her apology. "Monday I'd done a double, worked twenty-four straight, so at seven yesterday morning I went home, shut off my beeper and crashed. Didn't find out what happened until yesterday afternoon. I feel like garbage that I wasn't there for my firehouse. I let my brothers down."

Piper stopped short. What had she done to this poor man, thrown salt into a festering wound, cut him down to the bone? She tried to remedy the situation. "Now you're being an ass. You worked two twelve hour shifts – you're not a superhero ya' know."

He turned to her. "I went to the firehouse as soon as I heard about the attack, but it was way too late to do any good. Even stayed there all last night. This morning only four out of sixteen from the day crew showed up for work. Some can't handle it, others are still missing. I was at Ground Zero all morning. I can't be in the apartment – Sergeant told me to go home but I can't – I want to help but then it gets to me and I need a break. It's why I ended up in the deli." He rubbed tears from his eyes with both fists. "Okay, enough of this sissy shit, I've got to be strong."

Piper pulled him to her and wrapped her arms around him.

They stood hugging each other like that for several minutes, rocking from side to side and crying. He smelled of musky burnt wood and testosterone, and she could feel his heart pounding in his chest even through his thick jacket. There was nothing sexual at all about the embrace, but it was the most intimate moment she'd ever had with a man. When they let go of each other, they didn't feel the need to discuss what just occurred or the fact that they were complete strangers a little more than an hour before.

ISABEL

Isabel was never happier to be sitting in a smelly, New York City cab. She felt humiliated on so many levels; Piper had needed her support more than ever and here she was bagging out on her, unable to handle the pressure. To make matters worse, she'd thrown -up on a handsome stranger's shoes, and then admitted in public that she'd been raped.

She stared out the car window and watched a city altered by tragedy pass her by. As the cab crept further from the crime scene, every street corner had clusters of people standing and holding signs saying *thank you* to the stream of honking emergency vehicles that passed. New Yorkers were experiencing true gratitude for maybe the first time.

The traffic let up once they escaped the clutches of lower Manhattan. They left behind the police barricades and emergency vehicles and entered the illusion that was midtown, where New York pretended to be unfazed. Isabel knew better. The world was reeling and would be for a long while to come. They were all changed, even if they weren't sure yet in what way. Isabel's hand drifted to her abdomen. *Change piled on change,* she thought and grimaced.

Piper meant well in reference to the baby and Isabel loved her for it. At some point though, she knew Piper would see things Isabel's way. The very reason they were both alive was, ironically, a perfect example of Isabel being unable to look out for herself. What chance did she have of caring for a baby? Between her father's medical problems and her sister's impending grief, Isabel would have her hands full. Just the thought of explaining the pregnancy to her father made her feel ill. There was no way she could garner enough courage. Better to live with the guilt of having an abortion than to tell her father his little girl had been raped. It would break his heart.

The cab finally made its way into Greenwich Village. Isabel tapped on the smudged Plexiglas divider and asked the driver to pull over. Piper had given her enough money to warrant a trip to Boston, but Isabel wanted to walk. She needed to get some air and was in no rush to get back to Piper's empty apartment. She felt anonymous walking amongst strangers, yet oddly comforted.

Guilt-ridden and relieved Piper was being given a tour of the ruins by someone else, Isabel headed in the reverse direction. Mac seemed harmless enough, and Piper trusted him. The two of them had more in common with this tragedy than Isabel did with anyone – both having lost most of their long time coworkers. All in all, there had to be a sense of hope that they had survived. Unfortunately, their personal great fortune was trumped by the worst tragedy the world had ever seen.

PIPER

Mac and Piper engaged in small talk as they made their way to Ground Zero. It felt good to have a normal conversation and Piper tried to steer clear of sensitive subjects. This wasn't some pompous lawyer or arrogant bondsman. This guy was the real deal, and she'd already decided that Isabel would at least go on a date with him.

Other than the heavy presence of uniformed and armed guards at every barricade and the sounds of distant sirens, the streets were eerily vacant of moving vehicles. Piper's heart rattled every time a camouflaged officer carefully scrutinized her attorney ID and then her face. Mac lied to these armed men saying she was with the prosecutor's office, and he was assigned to bring her down to Ground Zero. She was amazed at his smooth manner. This guy could coax skin off a snake when he set his mind to it. He'd have made a decent lawyer, but she kept that thought to herself. At some point he turned to her and spoke calmly.

"Listen. You're entering a crime scene. *Illegally* entering a crime scene." His stern voice slipped into condescension. "So what are you going to do again?"

"Keep quiet and do what you tell me," she replied. That seemed to satisfy him and Piper intended to do just that. Any words of protest she may have had or the enormity of what lay before her settled into her gut leaving no room for her usual glib demeanor. She was truly frightened for one of the first times in her life.

The structures where Piper's career had flourished were no longer visible from blocks away. Was she still a partner in the firm? She wasn't sure. She wasn't sure if there *was* a firm. All she knew for certain was her sister and Clare were safe – and she was soon to be an aunt. That alone would be an incentive to keep going and not look back. First though, Piper had to come to terms with all she had lost – all that had been taken from her in one fell swoop.

A few blocks away from Ground Zero the air had grown thick with soot and smoke making talking impossible. Piper's eyes stung and she donned a pair of sunglasses, which was as effective as sunglasses at night. She covered her mouth and nose with a rag Mac handed her that smelled of aftershave and soot. The deeper they went into this strange dystopia, the more ominous and solid the gray curtain that was her air had become. Buildings and cars had windows blown out. Everything was covered in a thick pad of ash, including their feet and Piper was glad she had worn her old sneakers. She felt like she was walking on the moon.

A series of trailers appeared out of nowhere and Mac stopped in front of the one that read NYFD along its body. Inside, fans attempted to circulate the air and Piper was able to catch her breath without the cloth covering. The air was still flavored with dust, but not as cloying as outside. The trailer was empty except for two men who were talking on cell phones. Both sported dark circles under dulled eyes and wore slack expressions. They were brothers in arms, and she knew that they viewed showing any emotion as disrespectful to the fallen men.

A table in the corner held everything from boots to what looked like space suits and gas masks. "Drink this and suit up." Mac handed her a full get-up replete with a respirator mask and a bottle of spring water. She dressed without saying a word as per his instructions refraining from making a stupid joke about Star Wars or some such nonsense. This was not the time.

Mac dressed and spoke quietly with the men. One of them explained how they had found a cat in the rubble earlier that morning. "A little beat-up but alive," he said. "Can you imagine? Poor thing must have used up eight of its nine lives."

The other man slammed his fist on the table. "We saved a fucking cat!" He stood, shook a cigarette from its pack, lit it, then turned and exited the trailer.

Mac held the door open for the two of them to leave as well. Despite being in full gear from head to toe, Piper felt naked and vulnerable, not knowing what would come next. They stopped at ATVs parked on the far side of the trailer.

"All the equipment was donated," Mac said. "A deluge of donations of all kinds from all over the world, even though there's not really anyone to save. There's still hope. It's human nature for folks to want to do something – anything – in times like this. I love that."

Piper climbed into a little green all-terrain vehicle with gooseflesh-prickled skin under the layers of protection. She was about to see something that was unimaginable. Already the reign of destruction defied the senses, and they were still blocks away from the massive open graves where the buildings had stood, gleaming under the morning sun the day before.

Those two towers represent our strength as sisters, Isabel. Side by side forever.

Piper's eyes burned with fresh tears. She refused to fall apart after coming this far. Mac helped her with the mask.

"Can you still breathe?" Mac peeked in through the eye glasses.

"A little." It was uncomfortable and her voice sounded strange and muffled. Mac pulled the straps on the mask tighter. "Ouch! I can't breathe at all now!" She started to panic when Mac opened something on the side of the mask and she was able to pull in filtered air from the outside. There was a metallic taste to the air quality, but it beat the taste of smoke and dust.

"Let's go." And they did.

It was still early afternoon, but here, in the new land called "South of Canal Street," it was midnight. They were two blocks from Ground Zero. It would be several days before cars or even trucks would be able to get within blocks of here. Even with the ATV, progress was slow going. Trees and chain-link fences were yanked from the asphalt like molars with braces. Buckled pavement revealed rebar unable to keep the road intact under the tremendous upheaval and everywhere, there were thousands of unidentifiable things hidden in ash and dirt and darkness: perhaps a car door, maybe the side of a copier machine, maybe a shoe. Piper's eyes flitted from object to object, rather than lingering at the risk of discovering something too disturbing to comprehend.

Her first live glimpse of Ground Zero was from between two high rise buildings. She saw a massive mound in the din and tiny silhouettes moving along the stretch at the top. At that distance Piper could only liken it to an active ant hill. As they got closer, she could make out the rescue workers. They carried buckets and shovels and pickaxes -- the worker ants on top of their colony, sifting and searching. Words the media wasted on sports stars and fictional movie heroes; words like strong, courageous and brave were too shallow for these volunteers and the valiant job they were performing. Piper's chest ached and she had to look away.

The vehicle was brought to a halt at a police barricade blocking the outlet of the avenue they were headed down. The guard explained to Mac that a piano was precariously perched on the edge of a window ready to drop. People had not just existed in those apartments, they had lived and laughed and cried and shouted and made love. Some had played the piano. She wondered what had become of all those residents. If they survived, where would they live? Would they ever want to move back to the eye of the storm?

Mac saluted the guard who then lifted the 2x4 plank and allowed them to pass in the other direction without interrogation. The idea that Piper was now official terrified her.

"I'm gonna take you down each possible avenue they'll allow so you can get the full effect. I know it doesn't look too familiar to you, but you'll start to get your bearings." He was yelling but between the growing noise of the activity and the gas masks his voice was barely audible. "There are only two streets open to the actual mote."

"Mote?" Piper shouted but he had already turned back to the road without answering. Mac pulled away from the barricade, his attention was focused on navigating around chunks of upended asphalt and overturned vehicles. There were occasional signs that read "debriefing area." On one side street, Piper saw stations of showers and eye washes.

"We'll have to *debrief* before heading back to the trailer," Mac explained. "That means remove all the gear because even the dust is considered evidence now, and we can't carry it outside the perimeter of the crime scene." Mac was pointing things out to her and Piper strained to hear. His voice sounded boggy and her fresh sprung tears didn't help her vision or comprehension.

Piper had prided herself on never crying. In fact, she figured something was wrong with her years back when she didn't cry during *Schindler's List*. She even saw a therapist about it. Every tear she'd refused to shed had come home to roost, and she wasn't sure if they'd ever stop. Tears that never came after her mom died, tears from denying who she really was all her adult life, tears for Liam Neeson, and tears for all her coworkers: her friends who'd died. Piper's mask fogged over from the moisture. She felt like a coward and Ground Zero still was a ways before them in the distance.

They passed the remains of the shops and bistros that once lined the streets, blown out shells of their former high-end architecture and designs. There were massive cranes occupying the longer avenues, and Piper didn't understand why they were there or, better yet, how on Earth something the length of two city blocks had managed to wedge itself between the remaining buildings.

Nothing looked even vaguely familiar and Piper had completely lost her bearings. Then Mac pointed to the side of a building where someone had spray painted "Vesey Street." Inside her mask, Piper's mouth went slack with shock. Vesey Street was one of her favorites for its eclectic mix of unique shops and upscale residences. She'd travelled this part of it a hundred times. Now it was gone, replaced by something unrecognizable. More tears. So many she feared she may drown if she didn't take the mask off. Piper forced herself to stop and tough it out. Mac stopped the ATV and gently turned her mask toward his.

"This is a throughway to the mound, hang on to your hat!" His voice, muffled and thick, made the word *hat* sound like *heart*.

The ATV turned down a patch of road once known as Fulton Street and nearly tipped because the asphalt was so humped and buckled. Piper found herself facing head-on what used to be her tower. Turning that corner changed her life forever.

Three thick, twisted steel girders were the only sign that towers had ever been there at all. The mound was smoldering and she realized why Mac called this place the mote. There was a thirty foot gap between them and the mound, a circular trench down at least forty feet below what had been the Financial District's subway line. The mote ringed the massive pile of smoking rubble: footprints of the two massive imploded buildings.

There were rescue workers everywhere, searching for people, dead or alive. They were dressed like Mac and her, but with lights on their headgear. Dozens of fire hoses were strewn across the ground, spraying gigantic arcs of water from every angle. Mac stopped the vehicle and they sat there, watching in silence. It was too much to take in all at once. The photos on the front page of the Times that morning didn't come close to depicting the image before her.

After a while, Mac tried to explain the futile activity they were witnessing. At one point Piper was watching a team of spelunkers from New Mexico who had flown in to assist with the rescue efforts. But it was evident now that no one had survived the destruction of this magnitude. Not a chance.

Still, Piper found herself, the self-proclaimed atheist, praying: *Please God, let at least one person come out of that rubble. Don't let anything happen to the men and women rescuers risking their lives to search.* But any slim hope she had for any sign of life was crushed by the overwhelming reality of what she was witnessing. All this supposedly had everything to do with religious fanatics and yet this scene seemed abandoned by God. Nothing made sense. All Piper knew was she needed to be there at that very moment in time. For all those who would never know the devastation, she would forever be their witness, defend how hard they tried to save them.

They moved throughout the desolate landscape that afternoon, taking in the scene from different angles. Once an air-horn blew and Piper watched workers frantically run to a mound not far from where they were parked.

"They found a hot-spot," Mac explained. "There are a lot of fires still burning underneath all this shit.

"We used more than two million gallons of water yesterday to deal with the surface fires. We were hoping for rain today. Another prayer unanswered, I guess."

The rescuers doused the area with swollen fire hoses, but the mound was enormous and the workers looked like they were using garden hoses and their streams like those of a kid's soaker toy.

"This place will be burning for days, no matter how much water we dump on it. It's a massive fire pit, filled with furniture, toner cartridges, computers, office equipment. The EPA says anything burning that's ink-related is deadly if you breathe in the fumes." Left unsaid were the thousands of bodies that were adding fuel to the underground fires.

How many bottles of white-out did they have in the law firm alone? She had at least three bottles in her desk drawer. For the first time, she thought of what she may have left behind in her office, but then quickly realized she didn't care. It was all gone, but Isabel and Piper were both breathing. Piper wasn't about to worry about her signed Chris Evert tennis racket, or the crystal desk clock that belonged to her grandmother. None of it mattered.

Eventually they left the central mound with its klieg lights and dozens of workers, the noise of cranes transferring equipment across the mote. There had to be journalists amongst the throngs of workers, but Piper hadn't seen one person taking a photograph or interviewing anyone. Mac said photos were prohibited, but when did that ever stop the press?

It was impossible to circle the area with the ATV so Mac and Piper got out and walked, picking their way over the peeled-away asphalt of a four-lane highway pushed all the way out to the buildings on the far side of the street leaving gravel and slabs of concrete in its wake. What lay at Piper's feet and all around for as far as the eye could see were the cremated casualties. Mac had said the dust was evidence. Piper realized part of the debriefing would be leaving behind potentially identifiable remains. She carried the victims' DNA on her suit.

Piper looked up at the front of a tall building directly across from where the South Tower had stood. All the windows were blown-out. A couch hung halfway out of a gaping hole on one of the upper floors. On her right was a large emblazoned sign that read King's College. It was partially torn from its brackets and bent at a forty-five degree angle. Underneath it, another spray-painted message with an arrow pointing away from Ground Zero: "MORGUE."

Piper's breath caught inside the respirator and the mask started to steam again. This time she couldn't see where she was walking. When she stumbled, nearly going down on her knees, Mac grabbed her to break the fall. He released her mask and gently lifted it from her head. Piper was wrung out, her emotional batteries were drained.

"We done?" Mac cocked his head in her direction, his hands resting on her shoulders.

"I'm done." Piper tried to look at him but couldn't. He lifted her chin all man-like and she let him. She liked it in an avuncular sort of way. Truth be told, there and then, at Ground Zero that day, Piper was at Mac's mercy.

"Listen, kid, you had to do this and you did it, no regrets. The worst is over as far as wantin' to know." He slung an arm over her shoulder and they walked. The gas mask hung from Piper's fingers in resignation. "I just gotta make one more stop to grab some chow, then we'll get the hell out of here."

"Grab some chow? What are you a dog?" A weak attempt at humor. "How can you even think about food?"

"Guys gotta eat." He smiled down at her, and kissed the top of her head. She felt her neck stiffen and relax. No one had been this comforting since she held her dad's hand to cross the street. Piper looked back up at him, met his eyes and forced a smile.

"Thanks," was all she could say.

"I'm glad I was the one to escort you, my lady. Now gimme your sister's phone number, and I'll carry your skinny ass the rest of the way." He pulled her further in as together they stumbled over lumpy ground.

Along the square surrounding and facing the two towers there had resided swanky eateries and chic boutiques: all were gone. A few expensive restaurants opposite the south end were fortunate enough to have their kitchens still intact and makeshift food dispensaries were set up. Entire façades were missing. Shards of glass crunched under their feet, much of it melted into the ground and glistening under the harsh lighting. Piper felt so disoriented, lost in a place she'd spent every day for the past decade. Then she saw what was left of Rosie's Pizza.

Somehow a portion of the kitchen had been saved and served as what could only be described as a mess tent. The grills and countertops buzzed with activity, and if one stood in the right spot the aroma of garlic and onion rivaled the smoke. Inside the ruined establishment were weather-beaten, haphazardly positioned wooden benches. It was disconcerting to see picnic benches in the Financial District, but there they were. Rescue workers from all walks of life rested on the benches, many with hands over their faces, either crying or sleeping. More stood, heads hung over paper plates scarfing down food. As soon as their plates were emptied, they were tossed like Frisbees into trash receptacles as the workers returned to their assignments on the mound. Piper had never seen such morose expressions, no laughter to be heard. She wondered when they'd be able to laugh freely again without a lump nestled in their collective throats. They had all seen too much, lost too much.

Piper recognized some famous faces working the kitchen: a news anchor, a movie star, and of course politicians. Being in the midst of what they called the "A-listers" and having them cook and serve probably motivated the rescue workers. Truth be told, it was the rescue workers who were the real *A-listers*. No one asked the celebrities for autographs. Though the event was so wrong, the theme was so right – these anonymous blue-collar workers were the real heroes in this tragedy, not the entertainers turned mess workers, who typically garnered more attention for a simple indiscretion than fireman, police and healthcare workers ever received for saving lives every day. They were finally getting the attention they deserved, if only for this brief time. Piper was viewing a temporary humbling of New York City elite, her Upper West Side-self included.

"Want a plate of something?" Mac asked. Piper shook her head. He deserved to eat. Piper didn't. That food was not for her. Suddenly she felt too small for her own skin.

"I'm going to wait outside."

Mac was already attacking his food. "Put your mask back on."

Piper ignored him. Out in the dank and dusky afternoon air, she made her way over clay-colored puddles and chunks of pavement. She needed to get as close to the caution tape surrounding the mote as she could. Less than a few feet from the mote, Piper let go of the mask, removed her gloves and dropped to her knees. She scooped up a handful of sludge and held it up to the sky, rubbing it into her palms, the cool muddy substance dripped back down to the ground. The souls of her firm were gone to another realm and what remained had been returned to the earthen soil where they once walked with pride and purpose. Piper believed she may be losing it.

A hand appeared over her shoulder and she looked up to see Mac reaching for her. She must have looked so pathetic, kneeling in the sludge, face smeared with tears and dirt, hands held up to him like a character from *Les Miserable*. "My hands are dirty" was all she could manage but he continued to hold his hand in a gesture of support. She put her hand in his as he pulled her with ease to her feet. They got back in the vehicle but not before she had a chance to rinse off at an open hydrant. The water felt cool and clean and she was desperate for a shower. Piper was ready to get out of there, get Isabel and head back home to New Jersey.

They drove back in silence to the trailer where Mac dropped off the keys to the all-terrain vehicle. They walked to another trailer and following crime scene protocol, parted with the gear one article at a time. Mac walked her through the first three barricades until some of the roads had car service and she was able to get a cab. At each barricade, Mac gave away meals he had packed for some of the guys on post along with bottles of water. Piper hadn't even noticed he was carrying anything. She loved this guy, for Isabel; Mac was a major *I do* dude.

Before climbing in the cab he'd hailed for her by standing in the middle of the road, she gave him a long hug. When they separated from the embrace Piper held out a card between her index and middle finger.

"Still want my sister's number?" She waved the card.

"You bet I do. She's an Aquarius, isn't she?" He grinned wide and took the card from her fingers, tucked it in his left fire coat pocket and patted it.

"My number's on the front. If she doesn't answer let me know." Piper winked at him. "How'd you know Izzy's birth sign? January 28th." She slid into the cab.

"Well I'll be damned, that's my birthday, too."

"Are you serious?" Piper stared at him and he nodded.

"No kidding." He slammed the cab door and patted the roof as the driver pulled away from the curb.

~~~~~~~~~~

Piper left lower Manhattan and wasn't sure when she'd be south of Canal Street again. Thirty hours earlier she was bitching because she couldn't get decent cell phone reception, and she hadn't checked her cell phone in hours. Her priorities had dramatically changed. The baby, for starters, something she believed she was allergic to before 9/11, would give them both something positive to focus on. She was pretty sure Isabel would come around to her way of thinking, but what if she didn't listen? It was her job to point out such things as regret, loneliness, guilt, blah, blah, blah but in the end, as Mac pointed out, it was Isabel's choice.

When the cab pulled up to the curb, Piper saw Isabel sitting on the steps. She paid the driver and jumped out.

"Oh shit! I am so, so sorry. I forgot you don't have a key. How long have you been sitting here?" Piper sat down on the stoop next to her.

"Not long, I got out of the cab in the Village and walked a ways to a diner then took another cab the rest of the way. A lot of time to think. It felt good, Piper. To be lost amongst strangers, ya' know."

"Oh, for Christ's sake, don't be so fucking maudlin." Piper leaned back to stretch.

"Was it horrible? Ground Zero?" Isabel didn't look at her sister.

"All I can say is I'm grateful you didn't come, even if you were stuck outside without the key. I almost wish I could un-see it."

"Will we recover, I mean *we* as in the city itself?" Isabel's voice was flat.

"We may recover, but we will never forget. I can't imagine a day will go by in which I won't think about what happened yesterday or what I saw today." Tears pricked in the back of Piper's eyes, but she kept them at bay. "It wouldn't matter if the moon itself descended upon that part of New York to sit in place of the Twin Towers, nothing and no one in the city will ever be the same."

They were quiet for a minute or so. Piper slung her arm around Isabel's shoulders and made an effort to lift the mood. "At least we have a baby to look forward to, Izzy. In spite of all the death, you're bringing life into the world."

"Piper, I … um … I can't do this." Isabel continued her impassive stare and Piper's gut clenched when she realized she was losing this argument. "How can I bring a child into this messed up world where we don't know our enemy? It could be a classmate with a rifle, a dog with a bomb rigged in its collar, or a pilot on a domestic flight." Isabel looked at Piper. "Besides all that, and that's a bushel, how will I ever explain all this to Dad? Then, there's you. What about you getting through all this? For once in my damn life, I want to be there for you, Piper. Please give me that." Isabel put her hands in her lap and bowed her head again. "Besides, how would I ever explain this to the kid? Talk about dysfunctional." She started to laugh and beneath the layer of cynicism Piper thought she heard that familiar tinkle in her voice. Isabel eventually turned to look at her sister. "I'm in a fine pickle indeed, aren't I?"

They fell silent again. Piper reached over and gently laid her palm on her sister's abdomen.

"Maybe, little curly girl, but all of that pales in comparison to the real truth of the matter here." Piper waited for her to look up before she spoke. Slowly their eyes met.

"This *little pickle* growing in here saved our lives."

THE SECRETS THAT SAVE US

PART TWO

Above all, be the heroine of your life, not the victim.
~ Nora Ephron ~

ISABEL

"Hey Mommy? How come Grandpa gets to sleep in church?"

Isabel didn't think it was possible to whisper and scream at the same time, but her son managed to do just that at his grandfather's funeral service. She recognized that it had to be confusing to a four-year-old with his grandfather's open casket next to them in the aisle.

"Shh, love. It's almost over then we can go home." Isabel gently patted the child's knee. He smiled up at her, his green eyes almost phosphorescent in the chapel's dim light, and cupped his hands like parenthesis to his little mouth. Before Isabel could stop him, he hissed out another loud whisper.

"Hey, Grandpa, wake up! It's almost over!" His voice cut through the vaulted room and settled back between Isabel and Piper. Murmurs of disapproval and nervous tittering broke out.

Piper snatched the boy's hand and giggled her way out of the pew and down the side aisle with him in tow all the while asking in his most boisterous voice, "What's so funny, Aunt Piper, what's so funny?"

Their father had lived much longer than any of his doctors predicted and outlived many of his friends. Isabel was convinced the moment their dad found out she was pregnant with his grandchild, he got a second-wind. She had suffered a few indignities in her explanation to her father of how she found herself with a child. She'd long since decided she'd never burden him with the truth. Isabel knew he didn't judge her, but she made sure he didn't pity her.

In Dad's last few months with his daughters, they took turns staying in his room at night. In the end, they were lucky if he was awake and lucid for five minutes out of each day. The evening Dad passed was imbedded in a record cold winter, and he went quietly in his sleep under his favorite blanket at the age of seventy-eight. The service was simple, nothing lavish. Dad had talked briefly several months back about the service he wanted and just like their late mother's, it was carried out to the letter. Later that same week he would be cremated and joined together with her ashes which had waited so patiently all these years in a box in the back of the coat closet. In the late spring the sisters planned a sprinkling ceremony, their remains spread around the gardens in the yard of their homestead in Morristown where Isabel still lived. Isabel had spent all her life in that leafy suburb and she'd cherish the rich memories of her father that would be a part of the estate forever. She was by his side when he took his last breath, but not before he told her how proud he was of her and what a wonderful mother she'd become. In the end, that was all she ever wanted to hear. He never needed to know the truth.

Born on April 1, 2002 and perfect in every way, Isabel's son was officially christened Peter Michael Henry after her father. However, since the day after 9/11, when the sisters had sat together on Piper's front steps after she returned from visiting Ground Zero, Piper had nicknamed Isabel's unborn baby, *Pickle*, and it stuck.

Piper had been amazing through the entire pregnancy process, even participating in childbirth classes. If anyone ever questioned who the father was, she always responded with a wink and a whisper; *Mick Jagger*. Piper's pain had been palpable for a long while after 9/11, but when it came to baby plans she was all onboard. It was as if Pickle had saved their lives twice that year.

Pickle rarely cried and was a delicious baby and had blossomed into a sweet little boy. While most first-time moms had delusions of Harvard-attending sons, Isabel prayed, but less often lately, that Pickle would turn out to be a decent human being. He would start kindergarten in the fall and Isabel knew the day would come when he would ask about his father and she had no idea what she'd say. Like most mothers, she wanted him to be well-grounded, so explaining that his father was a rapist was not going to work. She'd figure it out when the time came, for the time being she'd shelter him and protect him from her dirty little secret.

When Isabel's father's service ended, she stood in the church lobby and greeted the mediocre crowd who'd come to pay their respects on such a bitter, cold day. When the attendees were gone she found herself on the church's broad front steps enamored with what she saw in the church courtyard. Piper and Clare were sitting on a bench with Pickle sandwiched between them, condensation rising in ghost-like images from their open mouths. It was a beautiful site, the three of them. She could only assume Piper was explaining to her nephew in her logical way about his grandpa's death. Isabel glanced around and spotted Mac patiently waiting at the base of the chapel steps for her. When their eyes met, he smiled and came up and took her hand.

"You okay, kiddo?" He pulled her in to him when she shivered.

Mac had gone to only one funeral after 9/11 and that was the one for his best friend, Sean. He made a decision that very day to never attend another funeral service. He deemed the entire process barbaric and was of the mind-set: *remember them when they were alive.* So when Mac told Isabel he'd be there for her but outside the chapel, Isabel was fine with that arrangement. Who was she to judge anyone on how they should grieve? She barely knew how *she* felt about all the death and dying rituals.

"I'm good now, just a little melancholy. Thanks for being here." Isabel leaned into his warm tweed coat. "Dad loved you, ya' know that, right?"

"Except when I beat him at backgammon." Mac took her hand and they walked toward where her family was sitting.

It had been easy over time for Isabel to fall in love with Mac. He had pursued her after that unfortunate day when they'd met in the grocery store, but she had refused to get involved with him until after the baby was born. He'd kept his distance for a while but Isabel had come to discover he had stayed in contact with Piper throughout Isabel's pregnancy. One day in early June on a mild, cloudless afternoon, Mac drove by her house in Morristown while Pickle and Isabel were outside enjoying the warm sun on the hammock. When he got out of his car, he acted like he was just *in the neighborhood,* but he brought a bouquet of flowers for Isabel and a football for the three-month-old infant. She found this so endearing. After they casually chatted about this and that and Isabel's face hurt from smiling, he asked her on an official date. They took it slowly because of the baby and because she was so reluctant to intimately trust any man after the rape. The longer Isabel had gone without sex since the rape, the harder it was for her to face the idea of being with a man. Thing was, Mac knew her history and listened when she expressed her fears about the attack rushing back in once she reopened that door. Mac read her perfectly and planned his moves accordingly. At first they were intimate friends, holding hands, the occasional kiss and loads of innocent flirting. Isabel was sure it had to mean several cold showers for

Mac, but he never once complained. Eventually, her guard came down and she was his for the taking.

The first time Mac and Isabel made love was wonderful, as though she'd already spent a thousand nights with this man. It wasn't about sex, it was about love and tenderness. Mac was slow and methodical, an amazing lover. It didn't take long for her to feel completely safe and secure in his arms. By the time they consummated their relationship, Isabel was already in love with him, pure and simple. It was so comfortable to be around him, they could do anything together and have fun, but what Isabel loved most was they could do absolutely nothing at all and as long as they were together, they were perfectly content. Isabel could cry with this man and laugh with him, snuggle with him, go all out sexy, and yet garner her own space when she needed time for herself. Following her father's service, Isabel knew Mac would be there for her when she needed him, but he also knew when she needed space.

"Mommy, can I go to Aunt Piper's house, pleeease?" Pickle ran to Isabel when Mac and she approached them in the churchyard.

Piper was living the vicarious life of a mother without having had to give birth and Isabel was so appreciative of the time Aunt Piper spent with her nephew. Pickle adored his aunt, and she was just irreverent enough to be a good influence on the kid. After 9/11, she'd shed her tough city exterior as though it were an ill fitted overcoat and a softer Piper emerged. She was the easy-going one, the one who sat in Pickle's room reading to him until he fell sound asleep when she babysat. She taught him silly songs and made him peanut-butter sandwiches sans crust and sporting smiley faces of jelly on the top. She taught him how to swim and when she and Clare took local jaunts she always invited him along. Isabel wasn't sure if Pickle would have a sibling so she wanted him to be exposed to as many people who would love him unconditionally, as she did. Turned out, Pickle was so easy to love.

"Okay, but you be good for Aunt Piper, I'll pick you up later." It was easy to indulge her son in this pleasure because Isabel wanted nothing more than to relax. She was grateful not to have to fake through the next few hours with an inquisitive preschooler who just discovered death. If there was anyone who could compartmentalize death in an orderly fashion, it was Piper.

It had taken nearly three years for Piper to snap out of her state of mourning. Isabel had just come back from grocery shopping one afternoon and there she was, propped up on their father's porch with a cigarette in one hand and a pen in the other writing down things off her laptop computer. When Piper saw Pickle running toward her, she stubbed out the cigarette and waved the air.

"Sorry, I really do hate cigarettes — just a little self-destructive behavior for one last time, promise." When she smiled at Isabel, smoky eyes and all, at that very moment, Isabel knew her sister was on her way back. Maybe not the same, but changed in a very profound and better way. They all were.

Another two years passed since that afternoon and they had healed enough to handle their father's passing without too much gloom.

"Don't be silly," Clare said, "Pickle will stay with us tonight. You two go and have a peaceful time of it." Clare smiled down at Pickle. "Besides, he is trying to beat me at Parcheesi, but can't seem to do it."

"Auntie Clare!" Pickle stretched her name into four long syllables and giggled.

"You're coming with us little man!" Piper scooped him up and they headed for their car.

"Kiss, kiss for mommy?" Isabel sounded pathetic but didn't

care. Piper let him down and he ran back over to his mom and hugged her around her hips. Isabel leaned forward and pressed her lips to the tufts of soft hair on his head. "Love you my Pickle-puss. See you for breakfast. Auntie Clare makes the best French toast," Isabel winked at her sister's partner.

"Darn," said Piper, "now we'll have to stop for powdered sugar. Queen Isabel, Prince Pickle and King Mac will be joining us for breakfast."

Isabel knew they would prepare an awesome breakfast in the morning and although they'd just lost their father, Isabel never felt as full of love as in that moment standing outside the chapel.

Mac and Isabel drove home in silence. She was aware he was respecting her emotional space and composure. The truth was Isabel was ready to move on. She had given up a chunk of her life to take care of her father and although Isabel had no regrets, she was ready to be free. She could travel and not worry about something happening to force a hasty return home. She was taking the whole "moving on" thing literally. She was going to sell her father's house and maybe get a condo. A place where there were kids Pickle's age for him to play with, maybe even a nearby playground.

Eventually, Mac reached for her hand and gently held it. "Whatcha thinking?"

"I don't know. Dad was a constant in my life all my life and yet I'm not devastated." Isabel turned to Mac. "Why is that?"

"Because you covered all the bases. No stone unturned. All there was to be said was said."

"I'm choking on clichés here!" Isabel laughed. "You're probably right though."

"Course I am. Some people have a tremendous amount of guilt when a parent dies because maybe they didn't get along or they had

had an argument or they hadn't seen each other in years and they have to come home for the first time to go to their funeral." He shook his head. "That's bad news. You did right by your dad, both you and Piper sacrificed a bunch to make sure he was able to spend his last years in comfort and his last days at home."

A small curl of dark hair just behind Mac's right ear made Isabel lean over and kiss his neck. His warm skin smelled of wood and aftershave. It was so vulnerable and familiar, she closed her eyes and leaned against the headrest and contemplated her good fortune.

"What's with that grin?" He rested his hand on her knee.

"Actually, I was recalling the day I found out we shared the same birthday, when you sent me birthday flowers a week after I threw-up on you. You knew it wasn't my birthday, but you also knew I would call you to say thank-you. So sneaky. Truth was, Mac, I held you in the back of my thoughts for a long time after that, knowing I would have to give you at least a chance after Pickle was born. You gave me something romantic to look forward to, and I love you for that. I'm finally ready to live the rest of my life and you've been so patient with me. Thank-you for everything." It had been over three years since they'd begun dating and at this juncture in her life, Isabel wanted to believe he'd be around for the long haul.

"I love you, Isabel Henry." He sounded so solid, so sure. "I have loved you before I even knew we had the same birthday. I fell hard the moment you puked on my boots, and I'm still in love. I lost my best friend on 9/11 and met the love of my life the next day. Sean had something to do with us meeting each other, I know it in my soul." He glanced at me in the passenger seat and smiled and then his eyes went back to the windshield. "Listen, love, if you need any space over the next few weeks just say the word, I'll take

Pickle and keep him busy." He squeezed her knee a few times ever so gently and Isabel placed her hand over his. Isabel was grateful for his generosity and kindness, but she was even more besotted with the way he was with Pickle. She prayed these feelings would never dissipate.

When they arrived at Isabel's home, they shared a bottle of wine out on the back deck of the house, wrapped in fleece blankets with a gorgeous, blazing fire in the outdoor pit. That night, despite her dad's funeral, was relaxing. Mac and Isabel snuggled together on a cushy lounger built for two. The few sips of wine made her head a little swimmy and her face felt flush. Isabel leaned over and kissed Mac on his lips, and he responded with a pleasant groan. His breath was warm and minty and she felt the debut of stubble on his chin. Isabel wished on the stars above to grant her a lifetime with this man.

When their lips parted Mac took her face in his hands. "You know how much I adore Pickle, like he is my own flesh and blood. I never told you this, but I was there when he was born. I was in the hospital that day. When I saw him in the nursery window, it was the most amazing thing I'd ever seen."

Isabel was so touched but feigned skepticism. "You were there? Like a stork stalker? A storker?" She couldn't help but giggle.

Mac ignored her. "He was so tiny and perfect, and I knew right then that I wanted a baby with you. If you could make that kid outa that pile of rubble back then, then what would you create with someone who loves you?" He lowered his hands from her face to her hands. "Let's get married. We can start there, what do you say?"

"Okay." There was no hesitation in Isabel's voice. It just surprised her that he'd ask her in such a nonchalant manner. It seemed out of character for him. "Really? Just like that? Of course my answer's yes but ..."

Mac put a finger to her lips in an effort to shush her and it worked. They rose simultaneously and he took her in his arms and hugged her close. They stayed like that for a long while just hugging. Then, he kissed her firm on her lips and slowly his tongue found hers. When he pulled back and looked into her eyes, Isabel found herself staring up at his perfectly straight, white teeth, and between them was a gleaming diamond.

"Mac! It's a ring?" Tears sprung and rolled down her cheeks. "How did you know, I mean when did you …? I'm speechless."

Mac removed the ring from his clenched teeth, buffed it on his shirt-tail and got down on bended knees. He took Isabel's left hand in his and stared up at her with warm, watery eyes. "Isabel Henry, will you marry me?"

"Oh my god!" Isabel knew what other women meant when they referred to amazing moments that left them breathless. "Yes, yes, yes! I'll marry you right now, right here!"

He slid the ring on her engagement finger and stood. "You just gave me the very best moment of my life so far, well, that is except the Christmas I got my first video game when I was ten." Mac knew to back away in the event he may be injured by Isabel's exuberant reaction.

She swatted his arm playfully then danced around the deck like she was still a kid. She couldn't recall the last time she was this full of joy. She'd spent over a decade worrying about her father and that was all gone, replaced by a new life. If Sean was responsible for Mac and Isabel meeting each other all those years ago then her father was up there at this very moment bestowing on them his blessing. Every time Isabel looked down at her hands for so many years all she ever saw was the empty wrist, the missing charm bracelet from her mother. This ring changed all that in an instant. It gave her a beautiful focus.

"I've never seen anything quite so beautiful as this ring, Mac." Isabel stretched her left arm out in front of her admiring its sparkle in the silver moonlight. She wasn't really a jewelry person, but this was exquisite and looked perfectly at home on her hand. It occurred to her that there was only one person with whom she really wanted to share her enchanted news.

"I have to call Piper!" Isabel looked at Mac and when he didn't say anything she figured out why. "You told her didn't you? That's why she took Pickle home. You are so sneaky!" Isabel shook her index finger in his direction.

"Not sneaky, I think it's called romantic."

"Does Pickle know?" Isabel was being a bit controlling, but wanted to be the one to tell her son since Piper already knew.

"Of course Pickle doesn't know, that kid couldn't keep a secret if I stuffed a sock in his mouth and duct taped over it."

"I am so in love with you, Mac. My life feels so right for the first time in years." Isabel flung her arms around his strong neck and they lay back down on the lounger. With the exception of Pickle, this was the best thing to ever happen to her.

PIPER

Time fell away like dominoes and Piper found herself somewhat healed from the trauma of 9/11 and the losses she had suffered along with that gruesome battle known as survivor's guilt. The gutting nightmares and cold sweats were all but gone. Isabel had been a godsend in that first year. They had attended thirty memorial services, sometimes up to three a day before Piper finally had to call it quits. Isabel stood by her side at every single service. That was just like her kid sister with her natural and thankless commitment to their family.

The best thing to come out of that whole tragic moment in history was Pickle. At first Piper understood Isabel's reluctance about having a child from such negative origins. Piper was determined to not have her make a mistake she'd regret forever. She'd succeeded in convincing Isabel; a victory that was more relevant than any court trial Piper had ever won. After he was born, Isabel held Pickle in her arms one afternoon when he was barely a week old, and stared down at him, brow furrowed.

"What if he turns out to be a serial killer?"

"Stop looking at him like that, Izzy, as though waiting for horns to sprout. Rape is a learned behavior and this baby is absolutely perfect, a clean slate, so don't fuck him up with your ridiculous paranoia."

Over time Isabel realized he was just a beautiful baby, nothing evil or untoward and he quickly became the blessing Isabel needed to get on with her life. Piper was fortunate to be able to share him and it didn't take long for him to become his aunt's partner in crime. Pickle had the ability to make his aunt laugh and it became his mission. Mac and Clare completed the whole picture and what an original family portrait it was.

Mac's plan to ask Isabel to marry him was perfect timing. He had taken Piper's advice and waited until their father passed to ask her. Piper got to take Pickle home with her where he would distract her thoughts from the dozens of memorial services she'd endured in the past years; the latest being for her father, the only man Piper had ever truly loved.

Pickle was a ball of energy, and he wasn't completely processing the fact that his grandpa had died and he'd never see him again. There would be lots of questions and Piper felt a little sorry for Isabel. If Piper was feeling blue, Isabel had to be feeling black and Pickle's persistent queries would've only made things worse. Piper counted on Mac to turn a bad day into a positive one. When her cell phone vibrated at ten that evening Piper knew exactly who was calling. Isabel was engaged. Piper feigned ignorance when she answered.

"Hello?"

"I know you already know so don't pretend. Oh my god, Piper, can you believe it! He even asked Dad for permission last week."

"Who is this?"

"Piper! Stop joking!"

"Okay, okay, of course I knew. Dad was so thrilled, by the way, and was busting at the seams to say something – he knew how happy you'd be. We both did."

"What a day." Isabel sounded wonderful and it was music to

Piper's ears. Life was good. "Oh and don't say anything to Pickle. I want to tell him."

"Of course you do, and of course I won't. I know he is going to be overjoyed – he loves Mac like a father already."

"I feel a little bad about being so excited on the day of Dad's funeral but I can't help it."

"Listen Izzy, Dad died of old age and had lived much longer than his actuary table predicted. More importantly, he died surrounded by all of us and at peace for the life he lived. He so wanted this for you, to be happily married, you know what a sap he was. Trust me. Now go back to your fireman and have a great night. We'll see you for that celebratory French toast breakfast at nine."

Pickle had fallen asleep in front of the television and Piper cringed at the idea that Isabel didn't allow television. She leaned down and scooped him up in her arms, kissing the top of his head. He was growing like a weed, but he still fit so nicely in her arms. She realized she was being silly, he wasn't her kid and all, but he really was. Piper couldn't imagine loving her own child more than she loved this sweet kid. If she were honest with herself, he was her only real shot at motherhood. She laid him down on the double bed she'd bought for him. Clare and she were so excited to find dinosaur sheets a couple of years ago, but he soon outgrew dinosaur obsessions and moved on to aliens and outer space fascinations. Dad explained to his oldest daughter at the time about childhood phases, how one always led in to the next. He was right as usual.

As Piper tucked him in, he woke up and in a voice riddled with sleepiness, he asked, "Where were they taking grandpa in that box? Is that his space ship to heaven?"

His query took her off-guard because since their chat in the churchyard he hadn't brought his grandpa up again.

"Yes, Grandpa is up there flying with the aliens having a good old time." This seemed to satisfy him and he drifted back to sleep like a leaf floating down to the soft ground.

Her nephew didn't understand death but really, who did? It was the one thing they hadn't figured out yet. They understood birth and the human body and the Big Bang and how they got here to this age of technology and yet no one could tell them, not even the greatest scientist, what really happens after death.

ISABEL

There was a wedding to plan and Isabel needed her sister's help. Piper dreamed of stuff like this, but it just wasn't Isabel's thing. She'd be happy to elope, but Mac's family was local and Irish. He'd have to wear a kilt which Isabel found hilarious. She'd met his family shortly after they'd started dating, and she saw a whole different side to family life. Mac came from a huge family and at thirty-five, he was the *baby*. Isabel loved his family immediately when she saw how much they adored their youngest and then took to Pickle like bread to butter.

It was a while before she could get Mac to open up about Sean, his over-achieving sidekick, but eventually he spilled out his childhood memories morsel after morsel and Isabel saw a bit of Piper and herself in his anecdotes. Mac shared that he'd discovered a year after 9/11 that Sean had left him a modest fortune. Mac was financially set for life. The pain of his best friend not being there to stand up as his best man was only nullified by the idea that Pickle would be his best-boy.

Mac and Isabel ended up laughing their way through the entire wedding ceremony which was only attended by immediate family and close friends out of respect for *her* absentee father and *his* best friend. A week after the pronouncement of vows, they planned a reception at the remote farm Mac and Sean had purchased in Pennsylvania. Mac had not made much progress on the land because there had been some surveying issues, but he showed Isabel the exact spot where ground would be broken in the coming months. Like an upside down mistletoe, they kissed on that spot throughout the day. Cut-offs and cowboy boots, horses, and a pig roast were all Piper's idea and of course, she had buy-in from Mac with that theme. Regardless of the grassy setting, Piper sported six inch heels and a red-hot dress. Every man she passed throughout the day just shook his head as if to say, *what a waste of a woman.* Mac hired a renowned photographer who shot beautiful images of all of them individually and together. The day couldn't have been better.

At the end of the reception, Pickle received his own colt as a gift from Mac, his new father. Isabel couldn't say she'd ever seen her son so excited. When Pickle recognized that the colt's patchy coloring looked like a jigsaw puzzle, that became the name Pickle chose for him: Jigsaw. *"Pickle was tickled ..."* was repeated well into the evening.

In the end, Mac and Isabel rode off on their own horses into a setting sun to a quaint yet luxurious barn tucked a few miles from the property in a hilly mountainside. This was where they'd spend the next few days relaxing and making love. Isabel fell instantly in-love with the place. It had lofty wainscoted ceilings, thick reclaimed wood beams and rustic ceiling fans with massive rattan blades. The floors were all knotty pine and the fireplace at the center of the barn was open on three sides to the kitchen, the great room and their favorite place of all: the bedroom. All the accoutrements had a country appeal, warm colors of greens and burgundies, throw pillows and cushions everywhere. It was the most comfortable little space she'd ever been and it seemed to be built just for them that weekend. The fridge was stocked with fresh lobster salad, exotic cheeses and gourmet desserts, not to mention several expensive bottles of champagne with cut fresh fruit and caviar.

This was the ideal honeymoon for the two and Isabel wanted Mac to know how much she appreciated having these many hours to bask in their love for each other. She was enamored at how well he'd planned everything from the stacks of seasoned firewood, the homemade honeycombs dripping over pancakes, the cashmere throws and woven baskets of gossip magazines and trashy novels, the homespun bed quilts and goose feather pillows. It felt like a dream come true.

They spent endless hours on their second day languishing in the cool sheets, sharing stories from their childhoods and laughing so often Isabel's ribcage hurt. Or maybe that was from all the intense lovemaking. She devoured his stories about growing up in a large family, and she was inwardly pleased when he repeated a few of the crazy times he had with Sean over the years.

Isabel shared what little she'd remembered of her mother and what it was like being raised by a single father. When she reminisced about going to Sea World with her dad and sister when she was in high school, how she swam with the dolphins and Piper petted a seven-foot shark, Isabel was brought back once again to the missing charm bracelet. That curved silver dolphin charm her father surprised her with when they got home was forever gone.

There was a lull in the conversation and when Mac asked her what was wrong, she explained the loss of her charm bracelet at the rapist's apartment. He listened while she told a brief, but sentimental vignette about each charm on the chain starting with the five that were on there from her mother: a silver paint brush, a heart from her father, initials for her sister, and an apple for my mom's love of New York City. Isabel told him how much the ring filled the emptiness she'd felt every time she looked beyond her wrist to her bejeweled hand. Eventually, all tuckered out from talking they managed just enough enthusiasm for making love again and fell asleep in each other's arms until morning.

On the last morning of their country honeymoon before returning to New Jersey, Mac and Isabel enjoyed the last few hours sipping coffee on the barn's plantation style porch. Isabel took in the golden sunrise gently pushing away the silver crescent moon and its attempt to hold back the day. There was a crisp feel to the air and they both hunkered down in their chairs in thick sweatshirts. It was tough to look past Mac's strong tanned neck, his cleft chin and sharp cheekbones, the way the yellowy shards of rising sunlight seemed to single him out. Isabel felt as though she'd been given a gift, a beautiful man in an amazing place. She could have stayed right there forever, but all good things must come to an end. As long as she had Mac, she'd be content to come up here once in a while and rent the property from the caretaker.

"I hate to say good-bye to this amazing place." Isabel gestured with a sweeping motion at the scenery, the purple mountains in the distance. "We need to come back here again sometime soon. I could live in a place like this. Pickle would love it here, too. Maybe over his spring break next year we could rent it out again. What do you think?"

"I agree. Pickle *would* love it here. Now that Pickle has a colt I'm sure he'd love a wide open place like this to exercise him. Mac turned to look at her and as usual Isabel couldn't help but smile. "The farm that supplied our horses the other day said they'd keep Jigsaw until we can find a better set-up closer to home. When I finish building the farmhouse, we can build a small stable."

"I know, at point you are going to need to carry on with the property you and Sean owned. I know it's very personal but since you saved me from myself, I need to help you heal. You've made me feel human again and I just want you to know how grateful I am for having you in my life." Isabel didn't know how to say this without hurting Mac, but she felt it was critical to start their marriage with honesty. "I was surprised at how little you'd completed on the farm in the past year. You've spent a lot of time up here and I can only assume you've hit an emotional wall. I want to join you in building some sort of memorial to Sean and then help you build our home, please let me. I owe you." Isabel meant it. She wanted to help him in whatever way she could. She owed him that much.

Isabel thought she saw Mac brush a tear from his cheek, but she couldn't be sure. "I love you Mac and feel like I have been negligent in being there for you all this time. You come across as so confident and strong – I know it's not an excuse for not being supportive." Isabel knew she was rambling. "Anyway, I'm here to help."

"You done?" He sipped at his coffee and looked up at her.

The sun streamed white and crisp across the planks of the porch. His watery blue eyes looked into Isabel's, and she saw the sincerity she'd come to depend on. He passed her his car keys.

"Here, these are for you."

"Are you giving me the keys to your truck? I feel so special." Isabel was teasing but she was a little confused at this gesture. He had recently purchased a new SUV for her, claimed he wanted Pickle to be in the best of hands on the road. "You've been more than incredibly generous already."

"You kidding? You'd go through a clutch a month if I allowed that."

Isabel was confused. "So why your car keys – you want me to load up for the ride home? Am I a fishwife already?"

Mac laughed. "No, silly, these are the keys to this cottage. You'll get the keys to the main house when I finish building it, over there." He gestured toward the horizon. "We own this whole fifty acres of property."

Isabel was stunned. "What? I thought this was owned by the …" She was dumbfounded. "You said the ground would be broken at least three miles from here in that brush-land. Hello? Remember—our wedding reception? I thought that was the spot for breaking ground?"

"I lied. But a good one don't you think? Piper knows, in fact, I'll throw her under the bus again because she said not to tell you." He stood and reached out his two hands to her palms up. "This is all ours for as far as the eye can see."

Isabel took his hands in hers, and he pulled her to a standing position. They were face to face, lip to lip. He was waiting for an answer to a question that was not even asked.

"I don't even know what to say except where do I sign?"

She'd never dreamed she might someday live in such natural surroundings. She was married to a man who was going to build her a farmhouse after he'd already built her a romantic cottage. What world had she fallen into? Isabel knew Mac had come into a substantial amount of money from his best friend who died on 9/11, but she had no idea how much. When he first found out about Sean's will, he didn't want to inherit anything. He was angry and Isabel came to realize when he passed her the keys that the only way Mac could say thank-you to his late friend was to honor him by using the money to build this ranch. Her reaction put a broad smile on his face.

"And there's a highly ranked grade-school less than ten miles from here. Pickle will fit right in, small class sizes and individualized, old fashioned curriculums." Mac's voice rose with each word he spoke about his dreams, and Isabel saw passion in his eyes. "What do you say, Izzy? Let's build our dream home with a cool room for Pickle and a nursery for our future babies. It took a couple of years, but I finally grew the balls to commit to it and build this guest house. The farmhouse is next. We can live in this little place until I finish, I'll bring in some help and the ranch house should be completed in eighteen months, god willing. I'm sick of part-time firefighting, Iz. Morristown is great and all because you're there, but this is what makes me happy." He gestured to the endless sky, streaks of white clouds against a cerulean background that seemed to go on forever and the sun, like a mythical icon looking over the mountain ridges. "Been sneaking up here more than I've been honest about. Just finished this place a month ago. I honestly couldn't wait to show you, Izzy."

"It's awesome, Mac, really. In my wildest dreams I never imagined living like this." It was surreal and Isabel was euphoric, but she needed to ask Mac, "Are you really ready to give up fire-fighting?" Isabel knew he could financially afford to walk away from his career, but could he leave it emotionally? She wasn't sure. When she watched video footage of the days after 9/11 – Isabel saw camaraderie and brotherhood between policemen and firefighters that would rival the longest-standing Greek fraternity. Could her husband walk away from all the positive memories of his career as well? Mac had honor and bravery and had done his time as a fire fighter and first responder, but Isabel also recognized he was a bit of an adrenaline junkie.

"I figure when I'm done building the Mac Casa, this finished barn can be a cozy guest cottage for Clare and Piper when they visit. You sell your father's house like you planned and you wouldn't have to work outside of taking care of Pickle and all the future critters. We can grow our own vegetables and fruits. Have a few chickens."

"Well I wouldn't go that far, I'm not a very good farmer. I kill house plants." Isabel stopped. "But …"

She was willing to move Pickle lock, stock and barrel to wherever Mac wanted to live. Isabel knew his passions lay working with his hands, creating and designing beautiful structures, then living off the land. What she had never discussed with Mac were her own dreams, all the journals she'd kept in the hopes of someday being published. He'd always respected her privacy with her journals, but she'd never shared with him her desire to be a full-time writer.

"But what, Mrs. McAfee?"

Isabel squeezed her lips together and cleared her throat. "Well, I've always wanted to take creative writing classes. I'd love to write magazine articles or maybe even a novel someday." She felt kind of silly saying this out loud for the first time but she trusted Mac. It was her turn to find herself.

"Darling, there are several fine-arts programs we could look into." At that very moment, Isabel loved him for saying *we*. "Nowadays, you can take classes on the computer from home and still be able to be there for Pickle. I promise you will have my undivided cooperation with whatever you decide to pursue. New York City is not that far away, and isn't it considered the book and magazine capital of the world?"

Isabel couldn't believe how fortunate she was to have this man, and she took him in his entirety while he spoke.

"All I know is it was always my dream to live in the country and have a family and horses and dogs and maybe a cat or two." He sighed. "But it's also my dream to be with you and to make you happy so I have to be flexible. "What do *you* want? What makes *you* happy? That's all that matters, love."

Isabel was sure of the answer to that one. "You."

PIPER

After Isabel's nuptials, Piper found herself wanting the same thing for Clare and her. They'd been together for years and she knew she wanted to spend the rest of her life with her. Piper was well-aware this would be a union not recognized in the eyes of the law, an irony certainly not lost on the lawyer in her. Regardless, they could still have a ceremony and exchange vows.

One night while Isabel spent her honeymoon in the mountains, and Pickle was sound asleep in Piper's spare bedroom, *his* bedroom as a matter of semantics, she decided to broach the subject. Clare and she were curled up together watching *Breakfast at Tiffany's*, Clare's favorite movie.

"Would you ever consider settling down?"

"We are settled down. Look at us like two sillies here, we couldn't be more settled if we were dead."

"I mean, tie the knot, so to speak. I think I want to be married." Piper waited for her Brazilian to come out.

Clare sat up. "Are you serious? Of course I would marry you." She leaned in and kissed Piper's cheek and they resumed snuggling. "I was just thinking how I'd maybe like to have a baby in the near future. Just like Pickle but a girl, maybe call her Peaches."

Piper giggled like a silly school girl. She tried to sit up, but instead got stuck in the blanket and Clare rolled off the bed onto the floor.

They spent the next few moments laughing perhaps in an effort to avoid such serious issues. When things simmered down and they lay cozy in the center of the bed again.

"I would love to have a baby with you," Piper said. "Not sure exactly how we'd do that but yes, I'd love that."

They sat quietly then Clare spoke. "I give your sister so much credit. She gets raped and still goes ahead with having the baby. I don't know if I could've done that."

"I know, Izzy's amazing."

Isabel had never discussed the details of her rape ordeal with Piper, but she had to assume humiliation was the main reason Isabel never reported her rape. What did it do? Less than twenty percent of rapists are ever prosecuted. It was a disgusting fate to befall anyone – such a violent act that may ruin the very act held so sacred and connected to love in a woman's life. And yet, Isabel's rape yielded Pickle.

"I think us planning a family of our own would be good." Clare allowed a few tears to slip from her eyes. "I think it may help me focus on something else besides my parents returning to Brazil. I miss them so much."

Clare's parents made the decision to return to their native country shortly after 9/11 and after several attempts to coerce their daughter to come with them, heartbroken, they went back home without their only daughter. Clare was so far from her family and it had to be tough. Piper knew that –she couldn't imagine going a week without seeing Isabel. And now she couldn't imagine going a day without seeing Clare.

"Let's adopt, Piper! If Pickle is any indication of the child you and I would have then I say let's go for it!"

Piper hugged her tight. Clare was so right. Either of us could carry a child and give birth but there were so many children already in this world that needed the love of a family as much as they wanted to give that love.

"Adoption takes time, but with me as an attorney I should be able to move the process along a lot quicker. First thing Monday morning I'll get that ball rolling, meanwhile we can plan a small wedding ceremony."

"I'm so happy, Piper. We have both come so far, literally through disaster and here we are with a life worth living."

ISABEL

Mac spent his weekdays in Pennsylvania working on the ranch and came home every weekend to be with Pickle and her. She expended most of her time with Piper at Piper's local law firm in Morristown. When Pickle wasn't in school, he either came with Isabel to Piper's firm or spent time with Mac in Pennsylvania learning how to be a carpenter. They were a family.

Isabel was fortunate to have a part-time job with Piper and she did everything possible to be on time and do the work in an expedient manner. For the first time in her life she actually felt important in the business world. Isabel knew it was silly, but she was thrilled to be in the up-and-coming legal scene in Morristown. Somehow, in just a few short years, Piper had managed to pull together a few associates she had known from law school. She'd succeeded in building a lucrative practice and had enough assets to move out of their father's house and into a beautiful modern apartment in a high-rise on the Green just up the street from Piper's favorite haute: the courthouse. Clare moved in with her and they were slowly becoming more and more domesticated and settled.

Isabel was happy for them. After 9/11, Piper went through some very rough patches and Isabel was sure the only thing that got her sister from week to week was Isabel's ever growing abdomen.

In that first year, other than supporting Isabel through her pregnancy, she slept a lot and spent at least three hours a week in therapy. Isabel never knew any of the details of Piper's travail to Ground Zero that day with Mac. She'd respected their privacy and never mentioned it when they were all together. Not surprising, Mac and Piper had a permanent bond ever since.

As Piper's law firm grew, Isabel's job changed from reception duties to learning how to be her sister's legal assistant; Piper had given Isabel her own office. Isabel was also the manager of the new receptionist. Once a month, Piper allowed Isabel to select a needy client for pro-bono work, and Isabel witnessed a subtle change in her sister as a litigator and business woman. Piper involved herself in local politics for which she had a real knack and volunteered at fund raisers and bake sales at Pickle's school. Her razor-sharp edge was gone, replaced by an empathetic demeanor, which ultimately made her an even better attorney, once again in demand. Isabel was proud of Piper and how far she'd come. Before 9/11, she had dreaded the hour train ride into the city sitting next to Piper's scrutinizing eyes. In just hours afterward on that tragic day, their dynamic had drastically evolved and years later Isabel was finding it a pleasure working for her sister every day.

Isabel delved into client files and couldn't help but create storylines based on their situations. The characters that came in their office were interesting, and by the time Isabel had been with Piper's firm for a year she had started writing a legal drama. Of course, she didn't tell anyone because she was sure she wasn't very good at it, her first attempt at a novel and all, but she couldn't stop plowing through pages of dialogue and narrative.

Clare got a job at an exclusive club in the same high rise where she and Piper lived. It was the perfect set-up. Not only did Clare not have a commute they had joked, but she didn't even need a coat to walk to work. Isabel acknowledged the move had to be a challenge for the two of these high profile New York women, but it seemed to suit them.

One weekend a month, Piper and Clare would take Pickle as though it were a legal custody arrangement and Isabel didn't dare mess with that since her sister was, after all, an attorney and she often reminded Isabel of it on those rare occasions that Isabel pretended to withhold her nephew. On those weekends when Pickle was with his two aunts, Isabel spent the weekend with Mac at the farm. He was making such progress and she was excited about his plans for their home. When Mac first started the plans for the farmhouse, he wanted to show her the blueprints but Isabel told him she wanted to be surprised. She gave him a list of all her favorite color palates and house accoutrements: a bedroom fireplace, a kitchen with built in bench seating, stained glass windows in the sunroom and a plantation style porch with a swing. Mac agreed to design her dream home without her but it was up to Isabel to choose furnishings. While spending a weekend every month at the ranch, she watched as walls and rafters and roofs went up and she grew excited every time she visited knowing the final reveal was just around the corner. It was truly going to be a special moment for Pickle, too.

Meanwhile, some of the time was spent handling her father's estate. Isabel never imagined she would enjoy doing that sort of job; she'd never been a morbid person, quite to the contrary. This was a labor of love and Isabel found so many special memorabilia and was painstakingly slow in packing everything up that Piper and she wanted to keep. Most of their belongings, it was decided, would go to Goodwill and some of the remaining pieces of furniture which were custom-made, for certain rooms, would stay with the home when it was listed for sale. Piper and Isabel would split the house profits when it eventually sold. Then Pickle and Isabel would go to live in the guesthouse at the farm. She was ready for the life that awaited her and with her share of the house proceeds she'd have enough savings to go back to school and focus on her life and maybe begin her writing career.

Real estate agents in Morris County were the original ambulance chasers scouring the obituaries every day looking for estates needing to be dumped by families. Often they scored with out-of-town relatives of the deceased simply looking for a quick and painless cash payout. Isabel was grateful that this was not the case for her father's estate. Given the property acreage and the curb appeal of the house, of course Isabel was contacted by many of the top-of-the-market agents. She chose her agent wisely based on numerous referrals and Piper's approval. In a slumped housing market the For Sale sign was staked in the lawn less than one day resulting in a drive-by sale the first day at full asking price. Isabel knew it would sell, just not quickly. Whether it took a week or a year it was going to be very difficult to turn over the keys and walk away for good. The Henry family would forever be ingrained in that house and the land it rested on; it was their legacy, their past. As hard as it is to say good-bye, Isabel knew it was time to begin creating new memories.

Her new life awaited her and her future held wonderful distractions for her when she had to shut the door to her childhood home for the very last time. Life was certainly hectic but grand. The plan was to move while Pickle was on winter break. Isabel was a bit concerned for Pickle having to leave the few friends he'd made in grade school, but her son was over the moon with the ranch and his colt, Jigsaw that he seemed thrilled about the move. Isabel hoped the transition to his new school would go well.

Early one morning, in her father's sparsely equipped kitchen,

Isabel made Pickle's school lunch and felt true domestic bliss, even though she missed Mac immensely. Pickle sat on one of the two stools at the counter that served as their kitchen table and ate his bowl of cereal.

"When is Mac coming home, Mommy?"

"Well, love." Isabel licked peanut butter from her finger. "He should be home in a few days. I know he misses you, a lot! And soon we'll be joining him and Jigsaw on the ranch – how fun will that be?"

"Yay!" He was so excited and Isabel prayed this enthusiastic momentum kept going.

When the sandwich was in his lunchbox and packed into his backpack, Isabel reached for her lukewarm tea. She took a sip and was suddenly overcome with a wave of nausea. She barely made it into the bathroom off the den where she heaved whatever liquid had just landed in her stomach.

PIPER

Adoption didn't just entail a ridiculous amount of legal paperwork, it required detailed biographies of both Clare and Piper; drug screens, criminal background searches, credit checks and addresses of six personal and professional references, an extensive home visit, and both of them had to have complete physicals. It went against every grain in Piper's body to succumb to what felt like a strip search, but the idea of a baby of her very own kept her on target.

The day of her medical exam was overcast and seasonably chilly. The wind blew the weeping willows lining the roadside into swoops and fits like clusters of heaving war widows. Piper wasn't feeling very well and the weather wasn't helping her attitude. The doctor must have sensed her gloom because she drew several vials of blood that afternoon and scowled at her clipboard obviously stumped by Piper's existence.

About a week later, Piper got a call from the medical assistant that it was time to schedule an appointment for the results of the physical for adoption. Clare had to work early, so she couldn't go with Piper but Piper had never seen Clare so excited. She'd already bought a few baby items. Piper didn't have the heart to tell her the process could take years.

After meeting with the doctor, Piper didn't want to go home to her empty apartment. Clare wouldn't be home until dinnertime at which time she'd interrogate Piper about what the doctor said. She drove for about twenty minutes in a trance and when she took in her whereabouts she realized she was on Isabel's street, her old homestead just a few houses down. Isabel and Pickle would be finger painting as that was what her sister had said they were doing when Piper spoke with her earlier that day –back when Piper was happy not knowing the truth. That conversation with Isabel seemed so long ago, just a half a day away and an entire lifetime gone by in a flash.

Piper parked in the driveway and didn't see Isabel's car, but then she remembered it was with the mechanic getting snow tires put on for the harsh Pennsylvania winter around the corner. Piper couldn't help but smile over her brother-in-law. He was an expert at the unwritten, manly obligations women had come to rely on for centuries. On Isabel's behalf, Piper had somehow made the perfect choices for her sister, first convincing her to have Pickle then convincing her to have Mac. Was her purpose in life to make sure Isabel found happiness? If so, then Piper had succeeded and should get that place in heaven right up there in the front row.

They all deserved a decent life and they all may have secretly felt a tad bit entitled. September 11th was a part of them on the cellular level. It inextricably connected them forever, even after they were gone from this earth, Piper was certain. A permanent bond like a shared tattoo, never completely understood nor could it ever be taken away. It could be subtle, in the little things, the way they joked, the way they hugged good-bye, the way they respected each other for their different ways of coping. Like Isabel trying to keep the precocious Pickle busy with fun stuff because she didn't watch television since 9/11, only had one in the house so Mac could watch football. Pickle was only allowed to watch educational television, but Isabel would never have it consume his time when *he could be creating his own world,* as she put it. What she meant was she didn't want him to be exposed to *breaking news at eleven.*

Piper made her way up the steps of her old childhood home. In the past, she took the steps two or three at once but not this time. Those eight simple steps had been witness to her comings and goings. Since she had moved out to share a place in town with Clare, Piper always knocked on the front door of her father's house simply out of deference for Isabel living there. She had a key just in case, but she never used it unless she knew no one was home and only if they asked her to look in on something. Piper had nostalgia surrounding the house but it wasn't as intense as Isabel's connection. Isabel deserved to live there and call it her own.

Piper peeked through the glass sidelights and saw boxes stacked high in the two front rooms, straight ahead into the family room Isabel and Pickle were sitting on the floor with newspapers spread around them. Pickle was wearing the art smock Piper had given him for Christmas the previous year. He looked so grown-up to her all of a sudden. She'd been so focused on newborns lately that she forgot they don't stay that way. Pickle was a boy of school-age and she now more than ever, saw life ripping by at warp speed.

Her nephew was animated and although she couldn't hear what he was saying, he looked totally in the moment. Piper swallowed back tears. She'd been so lucky to share in Pickle's life and knew she was being selfish to have wanted more than what she'd been given already in this lifetime.

Isabel happened to glance up at the sidelight and saw her peering in so Piper rang the bell simultaneously announcing her nosy self. Truth be told, Piper could have watched them interact all day. Isabel popped up from the floor but not as fast as Pickle who beat her to the door, unlatched it with his fumbling little boy fingers and greeted her.

"Aunt Piper!" Pickle reached up and hugged her.

"How's my Peter Piper Pickle, huh, big man?"

"I'm not a man yet, silly."

"Okay ... *How's my big Lady?*"

Pickle giggled. Piper adored this little person. He, like her sister, was absolutely angelic looking, always had been. All blond curls and tiny nose, but they all knew there would come a day with this smart child that they'd have to explain his turquoise eyes. No one in the Henry family tree had green eyes. Piper knew this because after her father passed away she'd done a little genealogy search on the computer and was amazed at how far back she could go – not even any hazel eyes, just brown and blue.

"What are you making?" Piper inquired as though she had no idea.

"We put my hands and feet in paint then Mommy put me on the canvas. We're gonna hang it over the fireplace in our new house."

"Can I see it?"

He took his aunt's hand and led her down the hallway runner to the family room. The canvas was propped against the coffee table for anyone who came into the room to see. It was done in lovely pastel colors. On first glance it looked like an abstract oil mosaic but when really studied, the feet appeared one little toe at a time and then the shapes of the small foot pads. Fingers were intertwined and every print was in a different color.

Piper recalled when Pickle was born and how she was enamored with his little asterisk fists and pudgy feet. As a result of her obsession with his appendages, her thoughtful Isabel had his newborn hands and feet pressed into clay and then kilned to a shine to hang on Piper's wall. She said it was one-of-a-kind *just like*

Pickle's aunt. Isabel hadn't even made one for herself which rendered the gift even more precious.

The carpet at Piper's feet was strewn with papers and dry brushes. There must have been thirty different shades of paints lined up in Isabel's art caddy, which she remembered with fondness had been the same one their mother used. She lovingly recalled the smells of turpentine and oil paints when her mother was alive. Their mom had a real talent in fine arts and painted several pieces that Isabel and Piper placed in storage after their father died. The pieces were probably very valuable as their mother had made a name for herself in the New York art world for a brief stint before her illness. They'd never sell them though, they were too personal.

"Pickle, this is one of the most beautiful canvases I've ever seen!" Piper ruffled the hair on his head. She looked at Isabel who was searching Piper's face questionably.

"What's happening? It's three o'clock. Didn't you have court today, Piper?"

ISABEL

When Isabel glanced up to see Piper in the sidelight of her front door she couldn't have been more relieved. Funny how sisters know just when to show up. Before she dropped her car off at the shop and grabbed a cab home, Isabel had stopped at a drug store in town. She knew that her nausea was likely due to pregnancy, but there was still that fear she could be getting sick just like how she fretted before she knew she was pregnant with Pickle. Isabel always erred on the side of caution with her excitement because she hated setting herself up for disappointment. Imagine believing you are joyously pregnant only to find out you're ill.

Isabel decided not to wait with the test even though the label had advised it best to use the first urine of the day. If she were sick then the hormone was present in her system and it would show up at this point. Pacing the bathroom, Isabel kept glancing down at the test stick. The last time she did this she believed, at the time, it was the worst news she could have expected and then she gave birth to the best thing that ever happened to her. This time around Isabel was so excited for it to be positive, did that mean things would only go south?

When she saw the double lines like an equal sign in the tiny window her heart leapt for joy. Okay, she thought, here we go again. This time Isabel had people to share the joy with, Piper, of course, but Mac was the person she wanted to surprise with the news most of all. It was as if she had the best gift in the world to give him. He'd feel the way Isabel felt that night he proposed to her. She would plan something elaborate, and she knew Piper would be happy to help her with it. Isabel couldn't wait to tell her.

Pickle, of course, beat her to the door and when Isabel caught up to him Piper was squeezing her son in a hug. Isabel leaned into her for the obligatory cheek exchange. The way Piper was with Pickle never ceased to amaze Isabel. Here she was, a tough as nails attorney, a childless lesbian and yet she was more maternal than Isabel was with Pickle some of the time.

Isabel wasn't just expecting a son or daughter, she was expecting a niece or nephew, a brother or sister. She got a shiver of excitement with the idea of a sibling for Pickle, such was the ripple effect of a new baby in the family. It wasn't just about her, it was special news all the way around. She'd wait for Mac to come home from Pennsylvania and together they'd tell Pickle. Isabel couldn't believe her good fortune.

Piper raved about the canvas and Isabel had to admit she was proud of their accomplishments. Pickle had been quite cooperative in staying on the newspapers and tarps until she washed his feet and hands between each color. He giggled each time he hovered with painted soles over the canvas. Sometimes his attention to detail surprised Isabel for a kid his age. When they were finished bragging about art, Pickle decided he wanted to return to a Lego project he'd been working on for weeks.

Piper and Isabel went into their late father's sunny kitchen to chat. Isabel never believed she'd feel as though this was her own house without her father around, but just then with Piper sitting at the old kitchen table it felt like home. Moving to the farm in

Pennsylvania was going to be perfect timing with a new baby on the way, but this would always be Isabel's first real home. A bit of melancholy settled over her. The sensation was probably hormonal and it made her smile. Isabel was busting to share her news with Piper, but she decided to act casual, start a conversation and somehow slip it in.

"So, how are things? It's the middle of the day? I thought you had court."

"Yep, well, figured I was in the neighborhood and I'd stop by."

"Hello? Piper? You live a few miles from here. Is everything okay?" Isabel looked over at her, while she prepared them some tea.

"It's sort of a long story, but I'll make it short. Clare and I wanted to adopt a baby and so we both had to undergo complete physicals and blood work."

Isabel looked over at her sister and smiled. "Oh my god, Piper, that is so awesome! So when do you think it will happen?" The news of them wanting a child coincided with Isabel's own pregnancy, and call it weird, but she wanted to do this with Piper, together. Sure, Piper topped her news as usual, but this would be a new kind of motherhood. They had come from such a conventional family only to grow into being the strangest of family dynamics Isabel had ever witnessed. Just Pickle's existence alone was a phenomenon in many ways.

"It's not awesome, Izzy. I have the same disease Mommy had, and I have about three years left so unless I adopt an eighteen-year-old who will be a full-fledged adult when I kick, well, I just won't get approved as an appropriate match. I'm deemed an unreliable quote risk as a parent."

Piper was talking just quick enough that it took a few seconds for Isabel to comprehend what she had just said. Isabel dropped the tea saucer she was removing from one of the moving boxes and the shards of bone china that had been their mother's covered the floor at Isabel's feet. Pickle ran into the room.

"Mommy, you broke a glass!" He cocked his head at her. "What's wrong?"

Isabel knew she needed to react but she felt paralyzed. "Um, nothing is wrong, love – just sad because it was Grandma's china I dropped." She held onto the counter for support having not yet looked at Piper. "Go in the family room because I need to clean this up. You aren't wearing shoes."

At first Pickle didn't move, as if he was trying to pick up on something he couldn't see. His brow furrowed and his lips pouted for a few seconds then relaxed. "Okay." With that he was gone from the kitchen.

Isabel didn't bother to sweep up the china, but stepped around it and went to Piper. She sat beside her and grabbed her hands. "Is the doctor positive?" This was the stupidest thing she could've asked. Piper would never take an afternoon off from work to stop by and chat.

"Isabel, we knew one or both of us could get this. You're off the hook because you had to be tested when you had Pickle, remember?"

"But you said you'd been tested too? Why didn't you get tested?"

"Why? So I find out ten years earlier that I am going to die before I see forty. Not my style, you know that. I just didn't want to have you worry; back then you were already dealing with a lot of shit." Piper looked so level-headed. It wasn't her lawyer mode either. It was reality. "So I told you I was fine back then, and I was, not getting the test was just a slight lie of omission, that's all."

"Okay, counselor." Isabel felt her cheeks heat up. "What else haven't you told me? I can't believe this, Piper. We're just getting over Dad's death, and it's been almost two years since he passed."

"Chill out, Isabel. If I am okay with the news then you should be too. I haven't even told Clare yet, just trying it out on you first, you know, my delivery and all. I think it needs some work." Piper looked into her wet eyes.

"Not fucking funny, Piper. This is serious. I can't even believe I'm expected to accept this. Please don't go and leave me without any family left." Isabel started to cry.

"Oh love, this isn't something we can control. There isn't a thing we can do now or a thing we could've done back then when you thought I was tested. It is what it is."

Isabel's hands were clammy and she pulled them away and wiped them on her jeans. "You're right. I'm so sorry. It's just such crappy news, Piper. I want you to be around forever." Isabel thought about Pickle and how he loved his Aunt Piper.

"Anyway, sis-kabob." Piper stood to go and Isabel grabbed her arm.

"Don't go, have some tea." Isabel let go of Piper's arm. She sat back in the chair.

"I can't stay, honey. I have things to do – not a lot of time and all that …"

"Don't you do that, Piper! This isn't a joke." Isabel's lower lip quivered, but she refused to break down. Anger was easier.

"Okay, okay, no jokes. I really just need a bit of time to figure out how to tell Clare. She's over the moon about the prospect of us having a baby. Imagine her disappointment; she has no idea about this genetics crap."

Isabel started to say how sorry she was, but Piper cut her off.

"Don't Izzy. Let's get one thing straight – I won't joke about dying if you don't feel sorry for me. Deal?"

"Deal." Isabel took a deep breath and sighed it out. "What can I do? Anything, anything at all? You name it."

"Okay – clean my toilets." Piper chortled.

"Seriously, how 'bout I be with you when you tell Clare?"

"Oh, god no, Clare will be a mess and she won't want any hostages. Just don't be sad and morose. I can't do the whole soppy thing. I need you to be my light like you always are. Please." Piper took the straps of her purse and pulled them onto her shoulder. She winced and Isabel couldn't help but note that same grimace to the simplest of movements on an increasingly more frequent basis. "I'll call you tomorrow. Don't forget to clean up the broken china." Piper leaned down and kissed Isabel's cheek and left the room.

It wasn't until sometime later when Pickle came into the kitchen that Isabel realized she'd forgotten she was pregnant.

PIPER

After leaving Isabel's house Piper started driving and the next thing she knew, she was headed toward the Holland Tunnel. The day was damp and grey and had lost all structure, and she decided to take a little time to feel sorry for herself. Just one day, get it out of her system and then move forward and make the best of whatever time she had left. Piper made her way to Ground Zero.

The past several years Piper had avoided going anywhere near lower Manhattan. She saw news features that talked of the rebuilding of WTC and she tuned them out. There was nothing there for her anymore. She had done her level best to mourn the people she'd lost, so many people she'd loved and respected, people she came of age with in her twenties. But they were gone and Ground Zero was gone, replaced by reflection pools and oceans of reflecting.

Piper parked her car in an expensive garage and walked along the avenues not sure what she thought she would see, headed to nowhere in particular. It was like being inside a human body with its frenetic activity, the vessels and smells and secretions. She passed a church that advertised a 9/11 sanctuary and decided to go inside. The place reminded Piper of a picket-fence holocaust museum. When she slipped through the double doors, she was greeted by a woman who handed her a brochure and said if Piper had any questions she should feel free to ask her. Piper couldn't think of a single question, and she knew answers were non-existent.

She strolled along the pews, taking in the surrounding backdrops of memorabilia. The scene was equal parts sad, horrific and tragic; yet she couldn't look away. This was as close to the emotions from that day in September Piper could ever get, mere photos of the victims. A timeline of events that day caught her off-guard. She remembered where she had been at 9:30 that morning and then again an hour later. Tastefully done, it astounded her, the patience of the volunteers who put the whole shrine together. Piper must have spent an hour inside the church. She was an agnostic, but lit a candle just the same and prayed on bended knee. As if she hadn't given enough of herself to this story, she left a hundred dollar bill in the donation basket.

Back out on the street Piper passed people and it was as if she was in the past and these people were all living in the current day. These new, resilient New Yorkers probably went full days and weeks without thinking about 9/11. Not a day went by that it didn't dawn on Piper how lucky she'd been. She would never forget and it made her feel separate from this city of seventeen million.

She ended up on a bench outside the North reflecting pool which turned out to be quite lovely. She didn't focus on any one name engraved there, just sort of blurred over her eyes and stared. She'd sat on this bench a hundred times, not this exact bench but one in the same vicinity was her favorite, and this time, granted it was different but it was no less breathtaking. What used to be a view of glass and steel and crisp reflections of the sky above was replaced by the actual sky, a broad view of the other side of New York. New York City was missing its front teeth.

The signage showed pictures of what the site, which was under heavy construction, would look like in five years but Piper didn't need to know. It wasn't WTC to her anymore. It was no longer Piper Henry's Manhattan. It was time for her to go back home and back to her life with Clare. What was left of it, anyway.

ISABEL

Mac arrived home from Pennsylvania later that week to find Isabel in the kitchen preparing dinner. She hadn't mentioned anything about her sister or the pregnancy in their nightly phone chats because he sounded so upbeat and Isabel didn't want to wane his enthusiasm for the work he was doing for them on the farm.

She was making his favorite meal of grilled steak and baked potato. Isabel enjoyed taking care of Mac in that domestic way, clean home, dinner on the table, fresh flowers and crisp bed sheets. She figured that made her a bit old fashioned. She especially liked the idea of him building their home from scratch. All of it was a huge turn-on and she told him so.

"I'm a real sucker for a man in faded jeans and work boots, ya' know." Isabel winked at Mac across the table and his smile made Pickle giggle. "Then again, I said that about fireman clothes, too."

"So let me get this straight, you like men who look like they work for a living?"

"Yes, a man with a job is a good thing."

"I like fireman's clothes, too." Pickle would not be left out of any conversation.

Mac and Isabel laughed. "You're six," Mac said, "You're supposed to like fireman things."

"Six and a half and besides I want to be a fireman when I grow up. A policeman too." Pickle smiled proudly at Mac.

Isabel imagined if someone were looking through their dining room window just then, they'd see a perfect family. A mother and a father and a little boy who was just old enough to participate in his parent's conversations. It would warm their hearts to watch this family. But for as long as Isabel could remember, for every great situation there was always an underlying doomsday. Awesome childhood but no mother growing up, met a guy she actually thought might be the one and he raped her, discover she's having a baby on the worst day the world had ever seen, and she's finally in love, a baby on the way and her sister and best friend was dying.

As soon as they were done eating dinner and Pickle had fallen asleep on the couch, Mac carried him up to his bed on the second floor, Isabel's old room, and then came back down and snuggled in next to her on the couch. She knew she had to get the bad news out of the way first. She cried through the story of Piper's disease and Mac held her and listened to her anger over her sister not getting tested, how it wasn't fair that she got the disease and Isabel didn't get it. It was the short straw. The tears were for every injustice she'd ever suffered. Isabel cried until she was dehydrated, emptied out.

Mac, of course, brought her fresh water and assured her he'd be there for her when Piper was gone and Isabel couldn't help but be brought back to that day on the train to work, the day everything changed for everyone, when Piper reassured her that she'd be there when their father died. How long ago and far away that scene seemed. It wasn't about a safety-net, it was about genuinely missing her sister when Isabel couldn't be with her anymore.

The two of them sat together on the couch and flipped through the photo album on the coffee table. Pictures of Pickle as a baby, Piper dressed as a nun for Halloween, Thanksgiving when Pickle tipped the turkey off the table. They laughed at some of the memories contained in those pages. Isabel's father was prevalent even in the last few days of his life there was a photo of Piper and her in their pajamas on either side of him and he was grinning from ear to ear. There was Piper holding Pickle on her shoulders at the zoo, and then later on Mac at the farm on his horse, Matilda, and Isabel on Paisley, the Paint horse she'd come to adore.

"I'm just going to have to take a ton of pictures, it will be good to have for all of us I think." Isabel closed the album and turned to Mac. He took her face between his strong, calloused hands.

"Ya' see, that's what I love about you." His thumb traced her lips. "You figure out how to make lemonade out of shit. That's why you are so good for me." He kissed her full-on and she couldn't help but melt into his body. Mac scooped her up and she giggled. He shushed her so as to not wake Pickle, and she obediently gave into his every move while they made their way to the bed. They hadn't been together in over a week and Isabel opened herself to his touch. There was an urgency to their lovemaking and the time and space that followed left them breathless and spent. They spooned until they fell sound asleep.

Mac wasn't in the bed next to Isabel when she woke at three in the morning. She threw on her robe over her naked swollen body and realized her positive pregnancy stick was still tucked in the pocket where she hid it. Her secret felt warm and delicious. On her way downstairs, she stuck her head into Pickle's room. He was splayed out on his back, Mr. Wiggles on the floor. Isabel tiptoed in and put Mr. Wiggles back on the bed next to him and lightly kissed her son's head. She made her way down the steps looking for her husband.

Mac was in the office at the large mahogany desk that belonged to Isabel's father. He had plans laid out across the top and all the stuff that had been on the desk was now on the floor in a neat line.

"What are you doing?" Her voice came out deep and sleepy.

Mac turned in the chair and gave her his complete attention. He was naked and she flushed. "Just looking over what I still have left to do. You look beautiful, Isabel Henry."

"Oh stop, I just woke up. Now, you, you on the other hand are gorgeous." Isabel walked to him and ran her fingers through his thick, dark hair. It would've been so easy to interfere in his work and distract herself once again from the reality that was Piper. Mac had always given her space when she needed it for her journaling or time with her sister, whatever she had going on. The least she could do was give him the room he obviously deserved. Besides, she loved seeing him using her father's study and his desk, it hadn't seen any activity for many years.

"You go back to work, I'm going up to bed. Love you."

"Love you, too." He swiveled his chair back to the desk.

Isabel leaned down to kiss his cheek. They were going to have a baby, and she would tell him when the time was perfect. Before she left the room, Mac turned to the floor where the pencil holder was sitting and scanned for some strange drafting implement she supposed. He glanced up toward her and blew her a kiss. As she had done so often with her dad, she pretended to catch it.

"Oh, before you go babe, can you hand me that black marker over there on the chair. Must've slipped from my satchel." Mac gestured to the corner and then turned his attention back to his drafts, his left hand extended behind him for the marker.

Isabel went over and picked it up and placed the object in his hand and he gripped it in preparation of removing the top, he looked down and it took a few seconds for it to register what he was holding. He spun the chair around and jumped up and grabbed Isabel and pulled her in to his body.

"Please tell me this is real?"

"It's real, we're pregnant."

Mac gripped the pregnancy stick over her shoulder and stared at it for the longest time while they rocked back and forth. He gently tucked his head down next to Isabel's cheek, and she felt warm tears run down between their faces. She wasn't sure whose they were, his or her own.

ISABEL

The Sunday after Isabel told Mac, together they told Pickle they were expecting another baby. Pickle was delighted at the whole prospect of a baby sister or brother and Isabel was touched by his reaction. Later that day, Mac and Isabel let Pickle tell Aunt Piper and Clare. They were all having dinner together as they tried to do at least once a week ever since Isabel could remember. Twice she had to tell Pickle to settle down. Isabel could tell he was busting at the seams for dessert to be served so he could share his news with his Aunt. When the second bowl of ice cream hit his placemat he stood up on his chair.

"Guess what Aunt Piper, you're gonna have a sister or brother!"

Mac and Isabel had neglected to explain the baby would be Piper's niece or nephew just like he was and of course, this got a laugh out of everyone. Piper put her hands to her heart and then to Isabel's abdomen and she knew Piper was thrilled for them. Then she whispered something that would stay with Isabel forever.

"It's a girl."

Isabel knew Clare's heart had to be breaking over Piper's illness and their inability to adopt. They all focused their conversation after dinner on Pickle who talked incessantly of how he couldn't wait to have a kid smaller than him in the family. He seemed to go along with whatever was going on in life; his grandpa dying, a new baby, the upcoming move to another state, he just took it in stride. The only thing Pickle had not been told was that his aunt was dying.

Piper and Isabel stole some time alone after that Sunday dinner and discussed the best way to tell Pickle about his aunt's illness. He was going to take it very hard, no question about it. They decided to only tell him when Piper started to display the signs of illness. Otherwise, they would all put up a brave front when he was in the room. Isabel was pretty sure Pickle wasn't quite old enough to fully understand the concept of death, but it would be something he'd adjust to, in life it was something they all had to adjust to, didn't they?

Piper and Isabel made a pact with each other that no matter what the situation, they would do as much together as a family as possible, go to parks, or travel into the city, something Isabel had been reluctant to do since 9/11. She didn't even watch TV for fear of seeing another catastrophe. Though it had been several years, she still woke up in sweats at night from images of her desk falling through the floor into a blazing fireball, or trapped in the elevator with the building falling on top of her.

Every other Saturday, they let Pickle plan the day and Isabel and he would pick up Aunt Piper and take her on a surprise journey. Piper had started to lose weight and Isabel noticed she was fatiguing a lot sooner lately. Once she had seen her take a handful of pills and wash them down with expensive Chardonnay. Clare said the pills were a new form of chemo-therapy. It was helping somewhat with the symptoms of the disease, but wouldn't prolong her life.

On one of their days together, before they visited Piper, Pickle came up with the amazing idea of getting a puppy for his aunt. He said he learned about companion dogs in school. Eleven hundred dollars later they showed up at Piper's apartment with a blue bow around the neck of the cutest chocolate lab puppy Isabel had ever seen. When Piper realized the puppy was for her she fell to the floor and stayed there while the puppy licked all over her face and then peed right their next to her on the polished hardwood.

"I cannot tell you how happy this makes me."

"I know Aunt Piper, since you and Aunt Clare can't have any kids."

"Pickle!" Isabel was astonished at his candor.

"We could never have a kid that measures up to my extra special nephew so why bother trying. We will just pretend this little puppy is our son."

Isabel saw tears in Clare's eyes, but she held her composure.

"He may even be cuter than you Pickle. Uh, oh, you have some competition." Piper lifted one of the dog's front paws and examined it. "They're the size of dinner plates, he's gonna be huge." She kissed the puppy's head and then cuddled him in her lap. "I already love this little creature, I promise. And, yes, Pickle, my love, Clare will help me take care of her. So, what shall we name him?"

"Hmm? Let's think." Pickle was deep in contemplation.

Piper hugged her nephew and the puppy perked up from Piper's lap and licked at his face. He giggled. These were the moments Isabel needed to save amongst her memories forever; her sister and her son laughing together while the new puppy licked their faces. They watched the puppy run around the room and slip and slide on the shiny floor. At one point, he jumped onto the side table in the den and knocked over the lamp and proceeded to lift a bottle of pills off the table with his jaw. Calamity ensued with all of them chasing the dog around the room and then the house just to get the pill bottle from his mouth. They laughed so hard that at one point Pickle had the puppy's torso, but the child was giggling too hard to hold him only making them laugh harder. Finally, Piper had him cornered in the kitchen and was able to give him food in exchange for the amber bottle. Isabel squeezed her eyes shut and tried like a camera's shudder to take the picture into her memory bank for as long as she was alive.

They slouched in chairs around the kitchen table with grins slapped on their faces and watched the puppy crunch down gourmet croutons.

"Dog's got taste," Piper said. She shook the bottle of pills, then stared at the label and laughed. "I'm going to name him Prozac. He'll be my antidepressant with legs." Piper kissed the soft tuft of her puppy's hair and then Pickle's head and they laughed.

"What's a Prozac?" Pickle, curious as always, asked Piper.

"It means happy, kiddo – happy."

~~~~~~~~~~

Isabel lay next to Mac in bed and listened to his smooth breathing. His body rose and fell with each deep breath, the hairs on his chest looking shimmery in the moonlight coming in through the bedroom window. She snuggled in close to her husband. Isabel figured her life was about as perfect as it was going to get, a great man, a beautiful son and a new baby on the way. Nothing was ever a hundred percent and Piper's illness was a cross to bear. Once again, Isabel envied her uncanny ability to move forward, to never dwell. Piper always made the best of things and Isabel was sure her personality had influenced Pickle in so many positive ways.

Pickle somehow knew that a puppy would bring out the best in all of them. Of course, it was a perfect idea. Prozac would occupy her sister's time, distract her for a while and stay by her side till the end. When she passed away, Isabel assumed Clare would have the dog to help her through. How did her son know this was therapeutic for all of them? Isabel wasn't sure but she said a thank-you to the moon and curled in closer to Mac. Her last thought before falling into slumber was that sometimes there were those moments when she knew she wouldn't want to be anywhere else but right there in that moment.

Over the next several weeks they enjoyed the company of Piper and Prozac coming to visit. One sunny Saturday afternoon, Isabel stood in the kitchen and stared out at the backyard where her sister and Pickle played keep-away from Prozac. When the puppy got the ball they ran around laughing and rolling in the grass. Piper had an extra kick in her step since they'd gifted her Prozac and Isabel wanted so much for this to last forever, but she knew it would not. Regardless, this was her pink cloud every time she watched her sister having fun with her only nephew. Isabel prayed to god Piper would still be here to celebrate the new baby with them.

PIPER

As Isabel's abdomen grew, so did Piper's disease. There were weeks at a time when Piper felt pretty well, but then she'd end up hospitalized for tests and procedures. By the time Isabel was six months pregnant Piper found it difficult to walk Prozac for more than ten minutes without having to rest. A year ago, she had been able to spend ninety minutes in the gym and barely broke a sweat. Piper planned to stay healthy her whole life ignoring the huge white elephant always in the room. So they say, *Man plans, God laughs.* Or was it best laid plans? Whatever, she could feel her body, slow and steady, giving into death.

Piper wanted to make one more trip to lower Manhattan before she underwent the next round of experimental treatments. She had a few places she wanted to share with her nephew, and she knew Isabel would go with them even though she never travelled to the city since 9/11. Not only because of the memories attached, but because she never believed she belonged.

When the day came for them to go see a show in the city, Piper was feeling somewhat well. It had been a good few weeks of remission, and she wanted to take advantage of the extra energy never knowing how long she'd have it. She had even felt strong enough to go back to work a couple of days a week. Piper was well aware the bottom was bound to fall out, but for now she was still kicking. They took the train as Isabel and Piper had done so many years ago. Clare stayed back at the apartment with Prozac because she was scheduled to bartend at a huge private party later in the day. Clare didn't have to work. Piper had made plenty of money and made wise investments over the years and since most of her travel was business related – her firm always picked up the tab and then some. It was something Piper admired about Clare. She had an excellent work ethic even if her career was serving drinks, she did it with style. She also insisted on covering some of the bills they incurred in the apartment but unbeknownst to her, Piper put aside all the money Clare gave her and opened an account for her. Clare would learn about it from Isabel when Piper was gone.

They spent a marvelous afternoon taking in Broadway's *Lion King* and with Pickle in tow, roaming the streets of the Village and cabbing from here to there. They ended up down by Ground Zero, or what had been Ground Zero. It was a vast, dirt filled construction site, a few cement foundations appeared to be in place. Those reflecting pools were still there from the last visit Piper made to the city.

"You ever notice how every year, on the anniversary of 9/11, we endure the listing of the names of everyone who died that day?" Piper spoke as they made their way around the new and improved Financial District. Isabel didn't respond. Having Pickle running around the city with them was like being with someone on LSD and her sister had to pay attention at all times. "I understand the whole ceremonial piece of it, I get it. I often wonder, though, if all the families even want their loved ones name forever associated with this event. Maybe they don't like the reminder ever year. But the biggest issue I have is this many years later, I resent that we still give credence to those fu … umm, frigging terrorists." Piper tried to be on her best behavior when it came to cursing when her nephew was in earshot.

"What does frigging mean, Aunt Piper?"

Piper was warmed by the sing-song in his little voice until she looked at Isabel who was glaring at her.

"Yes, Aunt Piper, what does it mean?" Isabel was smirking.

"It means poopy. Hey look, Iz, there's the block the grocer's on, remember where you first met Mac." Piper pointed ahead and hoped that would change the subject.

"Poopy?" Pickle repeated. "Okay, poopy. Poopy terror men."

"Yes, my love, you are so right!" Piper tried to sound amazed. "Poopy is so much better!" She was so grateful she hadn't used the actual word. It may have carried on for hours or days.

"What we tell those 'poopy' murderers is what they did is worthy of attention every year, this many years later. I liken it to people who kill presidents and other celebrities so their name becomes associated with that particular famous name forever. It's true in cases of renowned mass murderers like Oklahoma City and Twin Towers, we always remember the names of the bad guys, but are hard pressed to recall any of the victims even though year after year we hear their names. I spent a good part of my life in those buildings and if anyone would want to honor the innocent victims from that day, it's me, but enough is enough. Rest in peace and all that. Of course none of them will ever be forgotten by those who loved them."

They crossed the street and Piper talked. "I just think the whole grieving process needs to come to a close at some point. It's a very private thing. I wouldn't want to be here every year and be reminded of how my loved ones died, no way!"

"Everyone grieves differently," Isabel cut in. "No one says you have to attend the ceremonies held every year. And for that matter, no one says you have to turn on the television that day every year."

Piper was impressed with how reasonable Isabel had become.

There were so many little nuances she began to notice, a maturity in her kid sister that was refreshing. Isabel had really grown into such a lovely young woman. Here she was, expecting her second child after raising Pickle, who was a real handful but bless his little heart, he saved all us in so many ways.

They stopped and waited as Pickle caught up with them. He had never seen such tall buildings except on television and he had the reaction that New Yorkers recognized as a visitor, a newbie to the great city just like his mom all those years ago. They were across the street from where the deli had once been.

"Wow," Isabel broke the silence between them. "Manny's gone. Just seven years and no trace of the store, how sad. I am so thankful I met my husband when I did. I hope Manny wasn't forced out."

"Look Mommy!" Pickle cut in. "There's a pet store over there. We need to get something for Prozac from our trip, a silver nail!"

"Souvenir, darling." Piper had to laugh. "The silver-nail store is in the vampire district." Another topic she regretted bringing up, as they made their way to the doors of the store. She had to explain that silver stakes had to do with vampires and got further and further into taboo country for a six-year-old. Needless to say, she was never so relieved to reach the pet shop where the puppies in the windows instantly distracted Pickle.

Inside the enormous pet store – like the Hammacher-Schlemmer of domesticated animals, Pickle easily found several hundred dollars' worth of toys and treats for Prozac within seconds of entering. Piper didn't care. It gave her such pleasure to watch her nephew run from cage to cage exclaiming to each and every creature, even the tarantulas and how he was going to come back when he saved some money and buy them.

Piper took in how dedicated the store employees behaved,

making any customer who wanted to pick up an animal use disinfectant before and after giving instructions and anecdotes about each critter. They meandered around the aisles while Pickle pretended he was in the circus. Piper told Isabel about the cruise Clare and she had planned for the following month to Clare's native Brazil. It was so far so good for her, well, she was still dying but her latest blood work was unchanged and she wanted to take advantage of her current state of wellness. Piper was looking forward to a long break from reality.

"You'll babysit Prozac, right sis?"

"Of course we will." Isabel turned to Pickle. "Honey, we're going to be taking care of Prozac next month so pick out a few extra surprises for her."

When their basket *runneth* over, Isabel held onto Pickle's hand while the three of them waited in the lengthy checkout line. These were the times they cringed and worried Pickle would blurt out something ridiculous that would, of course, completely embarrass Isabel but make Piper laugh in hysterics. This time, though, he seemed preoccupied with the people in the line behind them. Who knew what he was thinking and Piper had learned long ago never to ask until Pickle was old enough to understand the concept of discretion.

Piper found herself enamored by a gorgeous bird that was caged along the checkout area. It was an African Grey, a velvety tapered grey parrot with a brilliant red tail. He said "hello" while Piper stared at him so she said "hello" back. He then let out a loud cat-call whistle and she screeched and laughed. The sign read that the bird's name was Beaker. Beaker would eventually learn to say about 5000 words— the vocabulary of a five-year-old. Piper had always been fascinated with birds, a species that could fly, something humans could never do.

"Look Pickle. His name is Beaker."

"Make him talk again, Aunt Piper." Pickle got up close to the cage and the bird's eyes pinned down on him. "Beaker wanna cracker?" The bird cackled a laugh and all of them lost it, including other customers. "I love Beaker, don't you, Mom?"

Isabel bent down and whispered to her son, "No, look how expensive he is, he costs $1500.00! For now we have to be satisfied with Prozac."

"Okay." Pickle moaned loudly. "I do love Prozac but I can love Beaker, too."

Piper knew Isabel was tempted to turn to the line of customers and explain that her dog's name was Prozac, but then she'd hesitate because it may be offensive if someone were actually on the medication. Piper knew her sister's thought process as well as her own.

Isabel and Piper watched as Pickle leaned back in and spoke in a high, sweet voice to the bird who seemed to be listening intently to the child. When the bird responded with, "Make my day" in a perfect Clint Eastwood impression, Piper was so tempted to lay out the cash for the bird. She adored her nephew so much and wanted him to be surrounded by as much love as possible, especially when Aunt Piper left for a dirt nap. She just couldn't do that to Isabel who already had a full plate and oven.

The man standing directly behind Isabel interrupted their rare sisterly moment of silence while Pickle tried to get the bird to say something.

"African Greys can live sixty years. The kid is actually the perfect age for a bird like this, how old is he, gotta be like what six, almost seven?"

"I'm almost seven." Pickle never looked away from the cage.

Isabel and Piper turned at the same time. Piper was surprised, the man looked vaguely familiar, very nice looking, perhaps French heritage, dark wavy hair and brilliant blue-green eyes, eyes like Pickle had, actually. Before she could come back with some witty retort, she watched the color rush from Isabel's face as she slumped to the floor at Piper's feet. *Here we go again*, she thought.

Piper cleared everyone away from her sister although several of the customers and staff offered to help. She explained that Isabel was pregnant and tended to do this in the oddest of public places. The manager brought some smelling salts, explaining some people reacted badly to the snakes in the event one got loose. He had all sorts of remedies in his black bag from anti-histamine to anti-venom. Piper glanced behind Isabel and there was Pickle, the man in the suit was squatting next to him, arm slung over his shoulder, kindly comforting the boy. Piper rushed over and thanked him and pulled Pickle back toward her without appearing paranoid, after all the man was just trying to help. Didn't matter, this was New York City and there were predators around every corner. The guy looked okay, actually looked kind of cute next to Pickle, fatherly, similar to Mac's demeanor. Still, she didn't trust anyone with her favorite little boy.

Piper's cell rang. It was Mac and as soon as she answered, Isabel slowly came around. "Hey Mac, let me call you right back."

"What's wrong? Izzy's not answering her cell." Mac sounded concerned but relieved to get a live voice at the same time.

"She probably doesn't even have it with her. She's fine, Mac, just feeling a little faint."

"Where are you guys?" Mac's voice waivered. "Is she okay, can I talk to her?"

"We're still in the city in a pet store. Izzy will call you in a few minutes, promise dude."

When Piper ended the call, Isabel finally sat up and appeared fully alert when she held her head in her hands and shouted, "Where's my baby?"

ISABEL

"The baby is fine, Isabel." Piper rubbed Isabel's abdomen and tried to calm her down, but she didn't understanding what Isabel was saying.

"Where's Pickle?" Her eyes raked the store in every direction.

"I'm right here, Mommy." Pickle came from behind Beaker's cage and ran over to her. She grabbed him and hugged him tight and tried her damnedest to stop the tears but they came anyway. For years she'd ignored the possibility of this very moment, and she hadn't a clue how to process this reality. How many times in her life was she going to have to keep repeating the phrase; *this can't be happening?* She wasn't going to say it this time. It was happening.

"Ouch, you're hurting me, Mommy!"

Isabel let go before someone called the authorities.

"Can I go wait by the bird, Mommy?"

It took a second for this to register, and then Isabel gestured with her hand for him to go ahead. "Be right where I can see you, right there on this side of his cage." Isabel jerked her head toward her sister, "Where did that man go?" Spit flew from her mouth.

"What man?"

"Sorry," Isabel breathed in and out, slow. There was no hiding the panic in her voice. "There was a man standing behind us, the guy in the suit, the guy with the eyes, where did he go?"

"Well, I'd probably be more apt to remember him if he didn't have eyes – hello? What kind of …?"

"I'm not kidding, Piper!" Isabel furtively glanced back and forth from her son to the aisle by the register. "That man that was behind us in line!"

"I don't know, Izzy, why?" Piper looked around the store just as the manager came over to check on them.

The manager wore a scowl, seemingly annoyed at their continued disturbance. "Are you sure I shouldn't call an ambulance?" He held a cordless phone in one hand.

"No," was the abrupt answer from both of them.

"Okay, okay." He grabbed a chair from behind the register and propped it in front of Isabel. "At least sit in the chair. You're making the customers uncomfortable."

Isabel made her way into the chair all the while apologizing to the man. It wasn't his fault. "Why does this always happen to me at the worst possible time?" Isabel put her head in her hands. "You sure that guy is gone?"

"Yeah, pretty sure." Piper went to the main aisle and looked both ways and returned to Isabel's side. "I don't see him, why? He was just being nice when you fainted, calm down, honey."

"He's my rapist, Piper." Isabel was pretty sure she said it out loud. "He's Pickle's biological father."

~~~~~~~~~~

It was difficult for Isabel to leave the house since that day in the pet store. She never wanted to experience the terror she felt when she encountered her rapist again up close and personal. Piper stayed with Isabel the first few days after that while Mac was in Pennsylvania. Isabel refused to tell him nor was she going to allow her sister to tell him, not over the phone. She'd give him the whole story when he got home. Meanwhile, having Piper stay with her was a blessing since she was convinced in her state of hysteria that the rapist would climb in her bedroom window.

All along she had believed her rapist was dead. She never thought it odd that of all the nightmares Isabel experienced after 9/11, not one involved her rapist. For some reason Isabel dismissed him after the tragedy. He had supposedly worked in the North Tower on the 90th floor. He was a banker, looked the part, lived in a high-end apartment on the lower Westside and had died in the collapse; she had been so sure that she never thought anything else. Once again she was proved the fool, believing he must have worked in the North Tower. She had read the list of names of the deceased, but she didn't know his name so it didn't do her any good. Was he that diabolical to have trolled the elevators looking for his next victim? Of course he was. Isabel made assumptions and was wrong about every bit of it. Her rapist was very much alive and still roaming the streets of New York City. She wondered how many other women he had raped over the years.

The rapist had gone as far as to inquire about Pickle's age that day in the store. It made sense he'd figured it out based on the resemblance that he was Pickle's father. Isabel was so frightened at that point and grateful Piper was there to listen to her outlandish scenarios. She kept reassuring Isabel that he wouldn't have a legal leg to stand on if she had anything to say about it. He wouldn't get within a hundred feet of her nephew. She'd get a restraining order for all of them if she had to but no matter what action was taken – any action came with its share of repercussions. Isabel's main goal was to protect Pickle from knowing his father was a rapist, is a rapist. Pickle had a father out there, a man that was a sexual predator and Isabel would sooner die than let him get anywhere near her child.

It was tough having to wait until Mac came home so she could tell him all these terrible issues in person. He'd be upset with Isabel that she didn't tell him right away but she knew he was up to his ears in last minute details at the ranch; this week he'd run into a few glitches in the plumbing but the ranch was just about done, and through his frustration over the septic not working she could hear the absolute pride and joy underneath over building the ranch from scratch. Every time they spoke, Isabel got a sense of peace, it was like he was her mountain. He was the one area of her life that she didn't have to worry about these days. Lucky for her, she could spare Mac the specifics of the pet store and dump them on Piper for the time being. Anyway, he'd be home in a few days so no reason to share bad news over the phone. There was a part of her that feared when Mac discovered the rapist was still alive he'd move heaven and earth to hunt him down and take justice into his own hands.

"Should I cancel my cruise?" Piper casually asked Isabel one evening while they cleaned up the dinner dishes. She was still staying half-time with Isabel and half-time at home and seemed to have her illness under control for the moment. Isabel knew Piper was looking forward to getting away. No way would Isabel let her miss out on that trip.

"Listen, big sister, you have earned this trip. Sleeping on my guest bed for two weeks and putting up with all my rapist neuroses, you deserve a vacation. You've already paid for the installation of the new alarm system, we'll be fine."

"Who you calling big?" Piper's hand went to Isabel's protruding abdomen. "Don't leave the house until Mac gets home on Saturday, promise me. Clare is going out tomorrow and buying you a full house of groceries that will last until we get back. Then I know you'll only leave for your OB/GYN appointment and Mac will be home for that."

"I promise not to get in the car with anyone who offers me candy." Isabel tried to be glib in an effort to convince herself she'd be fine. She needed to believe at the very least her parents were up *there* looking out for her. Besides she had Mac, he was her husband and once she told him about the encounter she was sure he'd be over-protective to a fault. Piper had every right to get away and have a relaxing vacation. Neither of them ever mentioned it may be the last trip Piper ever took simply because they knew it was.

"I'm not kidding. At least you'll have Prozac for the ten days—sure he's just a puppy, but he can pee on a shoe quicker than an old-school gunslinger!" Piper reached out and gave Isabel a hug. Piper would have her trip and if luck was on our side, everything would be fine. As a matter of fact, it was better than fine. Her big sister taking this trip was incredible and Isabel was finally feeling decent as she entered the last trimester of her pregnancy. She'd be damned if she'd allow that horrible man to ruin her life. Again.

The day after Piper and Clare left for their trip, the doorbell rang and of course Isabel was extra careful as instructed by Piper five thousand times, but also because she wasn't expecting anyone. Pickle was up in his room with Prozac behind closed doors. She looked out the sidelight and saw her favorite delivery guy, Sal. Isabel swung open the door and saw he had a large box and a smaller box with Isabel's name across the top of both boxes. The large box had caution markings on it and perforations along the edges. The smaller box was less descriptive.

"Sign here, Ms. Henry … er, I mean McAfee, and may I say you are looking radiant today."

"Yes, you may, Sal, and if you weren't ten years younger than me I may leave my husband and have to ask you on a date."

"Aww, you sure know how to crush a guy." He pretended to be wounded in the chest as Isabel signed the receipt pad and then studied the box.

"Here, let me bring them in for you." Sal carried the package to her dining room table. "They're not that heavy, just bulky. No idea what's in these but whatever is in this big one, it needs air. It comes with instructions in this envelope." From under his signature pad he produced a thick envelope and waved good-bye as he left her home.

Isabel's curiosity was piqued when she shut and relocked her front door. The labels on the sides read "Penny Lane Pet Shop." The boxes were from the store where Isabel fainted. On the front of the envelope written in black marker was *Read this first*!

She carefully pried the envelope open and shook out the papers from inside. There was a picture of Piper smiling and waving with Clare at her side, their cruise ship in the background. They looked so relaxed and content. The typed note attached read "*For my Pickle, you deserve only the best.*" Isabel realized Aunt Piper had done something really crazy here.

She hadn't noticed Pickle come down from his room and lean over her shoulder until Isabel heard Prozac bounding down the staircase and skidding across the hardwood flooring in the hallway, frantic paw nails clicking to get their footings.

"That note says Pickle! Is the package for me, Mommy?" Pickle pulled out the chair next to her and climbed up.

It was an odd sensation standing eye to eye with a seven-year-old. Isabel smiled at her son. "It is. It looks like Aunt Piper sent you something from that pet shop in the city. Remember, where we bought all those goodies for Prozac?"

As soon as the dog heard his name, Prozac jumped at Isabel's knees and licked them until she picked the dog up and sat him on the chair next to Pickle. Together, Pickle and Isabel unwrapped the package.

"Mommy!" Pickle exclaimed.

Isabel set Prozac back down on the floor. She couldn't believe her eyes. Piper had sent them the bird Pickle fell in love with in the line at the pet store. Beaker. Isabel stood stunned. It really was a gorgeous creature, but the bird was only a year old at best and these birds lived forever. Isabel had no way of reaching Piper out on the ocean so she had to wait for her to come home to kill her sister. By then Isabel would have the perfect speech and perfect murder planned for her because Pickle would be perfectly attached to the critter by then.

"I always wanted a bird named Beaker!" This made Isabel laugh. That said, Beaker let out an ear shattering squawk that sent Prozac scampering and whimpering to a corner in the room.

"Don't be scared boy, he's a nice birdy." Pickle went to the puppy and wrapped his arms around his neck. "You two can be friends when I go back to school."

Isabel wanted to cry over Pickle's pure sensitivity to all things. It was at that moment she knew they were going to keep this creature for better or worse. It was a caged bird. How hard could this be?

"It's gonna take a while for the two animals to become familiar with each other. Meanwhile we need to protect Beaker from Prozac because eventually Prozac may try and eat him." Isabel knew this was harsh but she had to be honest. The last thing she wanted was for Pickle to deal with the heartbreak of losing a special pet. Loss of his Aunt Piper would be inevitable but maybe having Beaker to talk to would help Pickle work through his grief. Isabel knew she sounded crazy but the reality, there was a reason Beaker was sent to them. There was a method to Piper's madness. Isabel just didn't know what it was yet.

The other box contained a massive cage and it was packed with food and toys for the bird. Pickle and Isabel spent the better part of the afternoon rearranging furniture in an effort to give the bird the best view of the outside. A corner of the den by the largest window in the house seemed the best place. When Pickle went to bed that night and Prozac was curled at the bottom of his bed, Isabel got comfortable at the computer in the office and did a little Internet research. What she learned about African Greys was amazing and this was going to be an incredible learning experience for her son.

She was startled from her reading when her cell phone vibrated. It was Mac. They spoke briefly and Isabel kept it light. Once again, she didn't mention this latest development, wanting to tell him in person. Isabel realized she needed to start a list at this point. The rapist being alive was in the negative column, the bird had potential to fall under the same column in Mac's eyes. Only time would tell. Maybe she'd let Pickle tell Mac about Beaker, this way she could be an innocent bystander. Isabel was so fortunate Mac was an animal lover although she wasn't sure how he would feel about a bird that lived longer than most humans. It dawned on her that she was starting her relationship with Mac off with a bundle of *I'll tell you laters*. Whom was she protecting by doing this?

Isabel patted her swollen belly just the same and her skin warmed knowing this baby would have a real, honest to goodness father. As per the instructions, Isabel covered the birdcage with a sheet for the first time in what would likely be one more nightly routine she'd have to establish. As she retreated to her bed, she was taken aback when she could've sworn she heard Beaker say *goodnight* and make a kissing noise.

ISABEL

Mac came home after two long weeks at the farm and just in time for Isabel's' obstetric appointment. Pickle charged him before he stepped over the threshold and Prozac got so excited over all the expressed love that he peed on the foyer floor and proceeded to dance around in it.

"Shit! I mean shoot, Prozac!" Isabel, as usual, wasn't quick enough to catch the curse before it flew from her lips.

"Uh oh, Mommy said a bad word." Pickle giggled.

"Yes, yes she did but she is still the best mommy in the world, isn't she?" Mac looked at Isabel and his smile made her breath catch in her throat. His bronzed taut skin, from laboring under the sun, his glossy blue eyes and dimpled cheeks and chin stopped her in her tracks. Her husband was gorgeous and his attention was rapt to her; this man truly loved her. Isabel turned from his adoring gaze toward the kitchen to get cleanup supplies and Mac grabbed her arm, pulling her into a strong embrace. He kissed the top of her head, leaving his lips pressed there for a while. Mac inhaled deeply. Never one to be left out of a hug, Pickle wrapped his arms around their thighs. Mac whispered in her ear, "If I didn't have a doctor's appointment I'd take you upstairs and show you how much I've missed you."

Their reverie was sorely interrupted by a clear, high-pitched screech of *Who the fuck is this asshole?* It was Beaker. Isabel had not only the daunting responsibility of explaining their new pet, but also what they were going to do about his foul language of which she had no clue. Her reservations were immediately put to rest. When Mac finally finished laughing at the new addition to the family, he instantly bonded with Beaker when he gave him a pistachio nut from his well-worn barn jacket pocket. It was like love at first sight. Whatever Mac said, the bird repeated. Within two days, Mac was able to get Beaker to stop with the obscenities and take to whistling tunes like the theme song from *Andy Griffith Show* and Hi Ho Hi Ho, It's off to work we go…. it was uncanny.

When Mac was home Isabel was at her happiest but she realized while Piper was away that she missed her sister beyond words. Finally the day came for Isabel to pick them up from the airport. When Piper strode down the airport terminal, tanned and bright-eyed, she was the sexiest, healthiest sick woman Isabel had ever seen. It was apparent the trip did her wonders. Clare was by her side and was also radiant in her clingy black dress and dark sunglasses. The two were laughing and had eyes for only each other and for a split second Isabel felt like a voyeur.

The three of them stopped at a burger joint on Route 3 and ordered junk food and sodas. When they were seated with their greasy food, Piper went into details about their trip.

"There were mansions where we stayed, oh my god, Izzy, the place was palatial, amazing!" Piper was gesturing wildly with her hands. The passion in her voice was palpable. Isabel loved her ability to see the glass half-full in light of everything past and present.

"Anyway, like only two miles away are homes, I mean, sad isn't even enough to describe how some of these poor Brazilian people live. It's worse than sad, it's where sad goes to commit suicide." Piper sighed and took a sip of her drink. "It really affected me, ya' know? I mean, I'm lucky to have the life I do even if it's a shortened version. Any one of us could die tomorrow, Izzy, we all know that so well but this trip really allowed me to put my life ... or death, I guess I should say into perspective. For every day I am allowed to live in the manner that I do without a worry for food, money or family - I'm going to be grateful. Each and every day."

"She's serious." Clare's accent was heavy and as usual betrayed her polished English when she was passionate. "I, for one, never saw my own country this way until I saw it through Piper's eyes. Very real and honest, almost too raw."

"Well it sounds like you two had a life-affirming vacation. I, on the other hand, have been vacuuming feathers and trying to curtail the curse words coming from the bird."

Piper was always so great at pretending she didn't know what Isabel was talking about. "What bird?" She could've won an Emmy.

"The bird from the pet shop – c'mon Piper, you know exactly what I'm talking about."

She stared at Isabel unblinking. "I have no fucking idea what you're talking about. You actually went back and bought that bird, what was his name Butchy, Binky? He was pretty expensive if I recall correctly."

Isabel couldn't believe what she was hearing. "Beaker, Piper. His name is Beaker and you're telling me you didn't send Pickle that bird before you left for vacation?"

"Are you serious? Of course I would never do that to you. I have a feeling you'll be pumping out kids like a Pez dispenser so I would never contribute to your nightmare." She and Clare chuckled. Isabel did not. "So someone sent you a parrot? Who would do that? Mac?"

"Of course it wasn't Mac. I'm so freaked out right now if you're telling me you didn't send it, then who did?" Isabel's heart jack-hammered in her chest and she had to get out of there. "Can we go, I don't feel so well."

Piper put her hand on Isabel's shoulder. "Is it the baby?"

"No it's not the baby. I just want to get home. Can we please just go, Piper?"

"Hey, calm down, honey, we'll call the pet store tomorrow and find out who sent the bird. They must keep a record of exotic pets they've sold. I gotta run to the ladies room and then we'll jet!" With that, she stood and slung her purse strap over her shoulder and moved to the back of the burger joint. Clare jumped up to join her and arm and arm they trotted to the ladies room.

Isabel stood and walked to the counter to pay the bill in an effort to quicken their departure. The kid at the counter ran her credit card while she took note of the pre-prepared food they had just consumed; the fries stood at attention glistening with salt in their cardboard cups, red bulbs shined down on burgers as though they were paper-wrapped movie stars.

"Lady, hello, you need to sign."

"Oh, sorry." Isabel had to pay attention and yet she was apparently trying to keep her thoughts distracted so as not to focus on the issue at hand. She scribbled across the receipt and moved near the hall where the bathrooms resided to wait for Piper and Clare. The kid at the counter glanced at her a few times and then nodded in her direction as though her lurking by the bathrooms was okay with him.

The rest of the ride home Isabel listened to stories about snorkeling and the massage therapist who had a voice that reminded Clare of dolphins. Isabel was really only taking in a small percent of what they were saying. She kept coming back to the only person who could have sent her son that bird. Her mind veered back to that day in New York in the store when the rapist was standing behind them. He knew Pickle's name, he knew Isabel was pregnant, and he knew Pickle was his son, but even worse than all that, the rapist was taunting her.

PIPER

It was classic behavior for a rapist, almost predictable. Piper knew from the second Isabel told her about the bird that it was sent from the man who raped her. It was about control. He manipulated her sister into keeping a pet by pretending it was from Piper. Somehow, he knew Piper was going away on a cruise, he photographed them on the dock. He knew Mac was away, and he was sure Isabel wouldn't say no to Pickle if she thought the gift came from his aunt. The bird would grow on everyone before they learned the reality of the situation. What this meant was they were being followed by a predator and that didn't sit well with Piper at all.

Piper believed she owed it to Isabel to find out as much as possible about the rape. She was a representative of justice, she practiced law for heaven's sake and she knew law enforcement officers, judges, and prosecutors throughout Manhattan. She found it hard to believe there wasn't a damned thing she could do about this situation. The rapist was apparently alive and free and he had looked Piper in the eyes that day in the pet store. If it was the last thing she did, she would bring this monster to justice.

She knew Isabel hadn't heard the last of this guy. Piper had encouraged her to tell Mac as soon as she was able because he needed to know there was an enemy out there, someone who could harm her and Pickle in more ways than one, even come after Mac. Isabel telling Mac would be difficult because she feared Mac may do something crazy, something rash that would complicate everything. There was a part of Piper that wanted Mac to do something to hurt the monster, but Piper had attorney experience with sociopaths and there was no predicting an outcome with a person who put no value on human life, not even his own.

Had Piper been in her right mind, not so sick although that wasn't really an excuse, she'd have known what would happen next. She was not at the top of her game so when Isabel was blindsided again following the encounter in the pet store Piper had been lulled into believing it would all go away because her disease would not. Unfortunately, God wasn't working deals with her that day. Clare made her start focusing on her own survival, eating right and exercising, taking vitamins, and she was able to stop some of the drugs and had been doing really well. The doctors at the oncology unit at Morristown Hospital said she was an amazing example of "remission." That's what they called it, Piper called it life.

She had to wonder when she heard that word if it was exactly what Isabel's rapist was doing. Residing comfortably in *remission*, waiting for the perfect moment to resurface and begin killing again, one cell at a time. Not dissimilar to the disease that was killing her.

PART THREE

Before you embark on a journey of revenge, dig two graves.
~ Confucius ~

ISABEL

Mac and Isabel had a few more weeks before their big move and they were sharing a rare private moment on the couch, one of the last pieces of furniture in the Morristown house. Her head was resting in his lap, and he innocently twirled a curl of her unruly hair around and around his forefinger.

"I'm going to miss this place." Mac sounded so sincere. "It's such a gorgeous home. All the old school crown molding and the tall stained glass windows, I don't think you realize how classic all this is. All I know is you were damn lucky to have grown up here. So upper middle class, it was ridiculous."

Isabel watched the cleft in her husband's chin as he spoke, his strong Adam's apple moving up and down. She ran her finger along his throat. "I'm going to miss the place, too, Mac but I am so excited to finally see the ranch house you've built. I want us to have a new start; me and you and Pickle and our new baby."

"I know you're gonna love the place but the fact that you wanted no part in the planning other than the decorating – well, if you hate the place you can't hold it against me"

"Ohhh, the whole idea of *holding against you.*" She giggled.

He leaned down and kissed her, his tongue intertwined with her own and tasted warm and minty. She loved this man which made sharing her secret about her rapist encounter, the bird, all of it, all the more difficult. There just never seemed to be the right time. Besides, every time he came home from working on the ranch there was some sort of bad news. Isabel was tired of being the harbinger of doom. This bit of news was major and might affect the close dynamic between Mac and her. Added to it was her concern that Mac would want to settle the score with the rapist. Since there was never a good time for bad news, she figured just then was as good a time as any. He was relaxed, Pickle was out of the house and more importantly he was her husband and he had the right to know. No more secrets.

"Mac, I need to tell you something."

"Is it bad? Pickle? Not the baby is it?" His voice cracked.

She adored him for his primary concern for Pickle. "No, no, nothing like that, really it's just something that you need to know."

"Okay, I'm listening, shoot."

Before Isabel could form her words the doorbell sounded in the foyer and echoed through the room.

"Hold that thought, Izzy, I'll get the door." Mac gingerly lifted her head and stood, replacing his lap with a pillow. With heavy feet, he went to get the door.

Literally saved by the bell, Isabel thought. It gave her a minute or two to get her thoughts together. Suddenly it dawned on her she should be nervous. Pickle was playing at a school-mates house for the afternoon, what if he got hurt somehow? Her throat clenched and she sat up looking toward the expanse of the foyer and listening for voices. When she heard a woman say Isabel's name, her full name, she stood and went to the door.

"What's this in reference to?" Mac was facing a woman that looked as though she just stepped from a Sear's catalogue.

"I'm Isabel Henry." Isabel stood behind Mac, her words sounded more like a question. "Is my son okay?"

"I'm here to deliver these papers, Ms. Henry." The woman reached around Mac like a pro and handed her a blue, folded packet.

"What is this all about? Am I being sued?" Isabel turned the packet over and back again as though she'd never seen paper before.

"Not really my business, Ms. Henry. It's all in the papers there. Consider yourself served. Have a good day." The woman turned on cheap, flat shoes and walked toward a black, still-running sedan.

Isabel unfolded the papers and began to read. Before she even reached the second paragraph she realized what she was holding and dropped the papers to the floor as though they weighed a thousand pounds.

"What the hell is this? Why are you being sued?" Mac bent down and picked up the blue packet from the floor.

"I'm going to be sick." Isabel ran for the bathroom and made it just in time to lose her lunch down the drain. She looked up to see Mac in the bathroom doorway.

"What the fuck is this, Izzy?"

"It's my rapist, Mac." She stood with the support of the towel rack. "Apparently he didn't die on 9/11, and he now wants shared custody of his son."

As she'd predicted Mac went nuts over the news. "I'm going to kill the mother-fucking creep! He will get nowhere near Pickle if I have anything to say about it. Where does he live, Isabel? Tell me where he lives. You must know—you were there!"

"Stop, Mac, please stop yelling at me. He doesn't live where he took me, trust me, and that was eight years ago anyway. This is exactly why I didn't say anything. I'm freaked out, too!"

"You didn't tell me what, Isabel? What?"

"I saw him a few months ago, in the city at that pet store – it's why I fainted, remember." Isabel grimaced, waiting for Mac to explode. Isabel knew Mac would be pissed but what came next was so surprising she felt slapped.

"No, Izzy, I don't remember the part about the rapist because you didn't fucking tell me!" He grabbed his car keys off the hall table and pointed at her face. "That creep can never get anywhere near Pickle." He turned toward the door. "Damn it, Isabel! If you had reported the rape when it happened then this wouldn't be happening. Call Piper because you're going to need a good lawyer. Your fucking irresponsibility back then for not reporting the douche bag has now put your son in danger." The house rattled when the front door slammed shut.

Isabel gingerly sat down on the couch as though she might crumble. She needed to get her heartbeat under control, the rapid beating wasn't good for the baby. Mac had never even said a terse word to Isabel in the past, better yet storm out. She deserved it in a way. She'd been stupid in not trusting Mac with the truth as it unfolded. Her attempts to protect him from the truth might result in him never trusting her again.

She also knew Mac would feel terrible about raising his voice to her with such vitriol. What really got to her was his mention of her putting Pickle in danger. Ever since her decision that day on Piper's steps to keep the pregnancy, she was committed to this child and would never intentionally allow anything to happen to him. All she could think was she wanted Piper, she needed her sister more than ever.

PIPER

Normally Piper had to beat things out of Isabel so when she got the phone call at three in the afternoon and heard her crying in hiccups and gasps she locked up her office and went to her rescue. Twenty minutes later when she pulled her Porsche into Isabel's driveway she saw her sister sitting on her porch, the sheath of papers in her hand.

The runny grey day with its heaving clouds seemed apropos to Isabel's mood. From the distance of the car window Isabel looked pale, down-trodden. It occurred to Piper lately how Isabel and she had always see-sawed their personal calamities. When she was up, Isabel was down and visa-versa. It's sort of funny how they were considerate that way, a sort of sisterly volleying of disasters. This time however Piper knew based on their brief phone conversation that this situation may be the worst one of all. Isabel didn't say a word, she just handed Piper the papers as she took a seat on the stoop. She slung her arm around Isabel's shoulders and squeezed. Isabel cried and shook in her arms and she waited patiently, though deep down she wanted to tear through the papers on her lap and begin a strategy.

"This is so bad, Piper."

Piper held up a finger. She spoke with trepidation while waving the blue packet.

"Before I really study this absolute garbage, I want you to know that this bastard will not get away with this. I will do whatever I have to, use whatever legal pull I have left to make him accountable." Piper didn't know why she was saying this. She didn't need to read the papers to know that Isabel hadn't a legal leg to stand on. A woman couldn't accuse someone of rape this many years later, although Piper would damn well try. According to the US judicial system, this scumbag had a right to see his son. She wasn't going to be able to change the law, but she would do her damnedest to slow the whole process with reams of red tape.

"Mac's not back yet. But at least Pickle's having a play date at a new friend's house." Isabel blew her nose in a tissue she'd pulled from her sleeve.

"Dear god, Izzy, tissues up your sleeve, really? Who are you? Auntie Em?" Piper shoved her sister sideways and managed to get a chortle out of Isabel. "Listen, love." Piper touched her elbow. "It smells like pennies; it's gonna rain. Let's go inside." Piper knew what she had to do. What she had to ask. What she had to know in order to help her sister. She stood and reached for Isabel's hand. "Mac will be back, just give him time to blow off some steam, maybe he'll have a drink or four."

Isabel smiled up at her through puffy, red eyes, took her hand and stood to go back in.

"He's gonna win, isn't he, Piper?" She stood rooted. "I mean, can he take Pickle away from me? Please tell me ..."

Piper cut her off while holding the front door open and encouraging her inside. "Stop wasting energy on ridiculous thoughts, Izzy!"

Resignedly, Isabel slumped and walked past Piper. Piper followed her to the couch.

"We need to focus on the possible and move from there.

Reading through this is going to take a while but I already get the gist; he wants visitation with his son."

Isabel bolted from the couch and ran for the bathroom where she retched a few times. Piper held her hair. "Oh god, Piper, what am I going to do?"

"Calm down, love. You have to think about the baby." Her sister still had two months to go.

Isabel stood from the toilet and moved to the sink to wash her face. When she turned and looked Piper in the eyes a chill ran down Piper's spine.

"Piper, please don't ever refer to Pickle as that monster's son."

"Oh, Izzy, I'm so sorry, I was in lawyer mode and not thinking emotionally." Who the hell was Piper kidding? She was freaking out, tasting her stomach in her mouth kind of sick as well. "He's a monster and he deserves nothing from you, but the law will prevail whether we like it or not." Piper knew she was talking out her ass. After escorting Isabel back to the couch, she brought her a glass of flat ginger ale – a staple in Isabel's home because of her tendency to hurl undigested food at the least provocation.

They sat in silence while Piper flipped page by page through the summons and occasionally glanced at her while she was half-lying on her side, feet still on the floor, head on a throw pillow where fresh tears had stained a ring into the satin cover. A few hours ago, death was the prominent issue for Piper and this house had been a happy home. How quickly everything could change. Piper wanted to further reassure Isabel, basically lie through her teeth that everything would be okay but Isabel was so much smarter than that, she knew what would happen when they went to court next week. The monster had served her with "emergent hearing" papers. Isabel was a paralegal in Piper's firm, so she knew exactly what that meant. This guy was out for immediate blood and he obviously had the money to hire one of the best child-custody lawyers in New York City. Piper knew Gerry Stein, and the firm, well, when it was a firm in the city dreaded calls from Stein, Stein and Wiesel, the biggest predators in the business. It was immediately apparent to Piper but likely hadn't occurred to Isabel that if Stein senior was taking the monster's case then the guy had a squeaky clean record. The Gerry Stein Piper was familiar with only tried cases he knew he'd win, slam dunks so to speak. Gerry had no idea that his client, Carson Stossel was a rapist, and probably didn't care.

"What?" Isabel caught Piper staring at her. "Mac was right. I should have reported it when it happened. I had been so completely humiliated and embarrassed by the whole experience that I pretended it didn't happen."

"Honey, no one can judge you for your decisions. After all, you held onto Pickle and wasn't that the best decision you ever made. It's why Mac fell in love with you and why I'm the luckiest aunt on the planet in spite of the whole dying thing, really, you're amazing and Mac knows that. He's just very angry because he can't do a damn thing about all this right now. A man like that feeling helpless is not a good situation but he has to work that out for himself. Right now my main concern is with Pickle."

"Oh god, Piper, I hate even thinking about it, I mean sure I had images running through my mind all afternoon of having to leave Pickle with this man but that's not the worst of all. The most difficult part of this will be telling Pickle his dad is alive and is a rapist that he now has to spend one on one time with ..."

"Fuck-all no!" Piper hadn't meant to raise her voice but there was no way Isabel was going to tell Pickle his father was any such thing. "You will not tell him the rapist detail, no way, why would you do that?"

She sat up. "I don't know, I guess so he can be warned about who he is with ..."

"Fuck no squared! The kid still believes in Santa and sleeps with Mr. Wiggles and a nightlight. Telling him will only make him more frightened. He doesn't even know what sex is so don't ruin that for the kid before he even has his first wet-dream. It is going to be difficult enough having him digest that he will have to spend time with a complete stranger."

"Ugh!" Isabel collapsed back down on the couch. She had no idea that the worst was yet to come.

"We need to talk about something else, Izzy." Piper let that much sink in.

"Shit, what now?" She sounded utterly defeated but then shot back upright, startling Piper. "Are you okay? It isn't your illness is it? You look so healthy lately!"

"Relax, Izzy, no it's not my disease." Piper gently pushed her back onto the pillow. "We have needed to have this conversation for years, and I think now is a good a time as any."

Isabel turned a lazy head up toward Piper, her brows pushing into a V formation.

"You need to tell me exactly what happened that Fourth of July."

ISABEL

There were only two other people who knew about her rape and they were Piper and Mac. Neither had ever pried for details until that afternoon with Piper. It wasn't going to be easy and not because it would slay Isabel to talk about it. She didn't know if it would be painful because she tried never to even think about it better yet discuss it. Like poking at a hornet's nest.

"I don't mind telling you about it, Piper, if you think it will help with this whole law suit. I just don't see how."

"It'll certainly give me some insight into the monster's head, that's what I'm calling him by the way. I need to know who I'm dealing with here, Iz. Like for example, I don't even know the rapist's name. Or at least the name he gave himself."

"Trevor."

Piper was going to be very upset when she heard the whole truth almost as much as Isabel would have telling all the sordid details. "Okay, here goes."

For the next two hours, Piper sat quieter than Isabel had ever seen. She started with that day when she was at the picnic and how much fun she was having. Before she got to the *after the picnic* part of her story, Pickle came home from his play date and they stopped so Piper could shower him with love.

They finally exhausted the child with questions about his "big boy" day and he left the room but not before posturing and stating unequivocally, "I'm not a baby anymore, ya' know. I have a real friend." He jumped the stairs to his room two at a time on his way to confront his latest Lego project. What a dichotomy Isabel had on her hands? The best thing that ever happened to her came from the worst thing that ever happened to her.

"After the July 4th picnic he said he had a great view of the fireworks from his balcony, so I acquiesced and went home with him. How stupid was that, Piper?"

"I don't think that's so unusual, you'd been on a few casual dates with him, saw him at work, of course you believed you could trust him, I mean at what point does a woman believe she can trust someone. Shit, a month seems very conservative on your part, quite frankly. But then again I'd probably have been a whore of a heterosexual."

Isabel laughed. "I don't think it would have mattered how long I'd waited. It still would have happened. If you had seen his dark eyes. Not the eyes of the man in the pet store. His eyes when he was with me were dark and mysterious or so I told myself. Must have been contacts."

"Okay, what else?" Piper was so attentive.

"Well, at first when we got to the apartment I was in awe. The place was exquisite, all sleek and modern, quite masculine actually. In retrospect, I'm sure it wasn't his real home, more like a furnished monthly rental. He offered me a drink and we sat out on the balcony and watched the fireworks. He held my hand but that was it. Actually I was a little disappointed he didn't lean in for a kiss."

Isabel knew how strange that sounded in hindsight. How had she not picked up a bad vibe? "The last thing I recall of that part of the night was how soft and comfortable I felt in the cushy lounge chair with the New York City fireworks exploding above and the skyline on the distant horizon. I guess I fell asleep or passed out or whatever." She had to stop. Isabel sat up and leaned forward, head in her hands.

"You okay, Isabel?" Piper patted her back and she shrugged her away. "We can quit for now. I think I heard your cell phone buzzing anyway, I bet Mac called. Besides, I'm hungry – let's order pizza."

It was easy to switch gears away from her dark, looming thoughts. Isabel tried to change the subject. "Piper you shouldn't be eating pizza. Remember? The disease diet says ..."

"Screw the diet, I want some pizza and I'm having pizza with my sister and nephew and besides, I feel really good this week." Piper's face drew back. "I mean, all things considered, not that our discussion hasn't had an effect on me but ..."

"Now it's my turn to say shut the hell up, Piper! Let's get pizza. Two pies in fact, extra toppings, you know, in case Mac shows up." Isabel slung her arm around Piper's shoulders and they made their way to the kitchen all the while somehow laughing.

According to the cell phone message, Mac had called twice to say he ended up at his old fire house in the city and he'd explain when he saw Isabel later promising to be home before midnight. He apologized for being such a hothead and he reaffirmed that he loved her a few times throughout both calls. When she returned his call she tried to sound upbeat and told him they'd talk when he got home.

Piper and Isabel ate pizza with Pickle telling stories about his day and Isabel tried to listen to his every word, but too often found herself drifting back to that sordid, humiliating night. The can of worms had been opened and it would never fit back in there, it was way too large, having grown exponentially over the decade Isabel kept it hidden away. It was time for the story to be told. As though reading a first person narrative Isabel spoke the part of her story she's never told anyone.

~~~~~~~~~~

When I awoke in my date's apartment that Fourth of July night in 2001, I was no longer relaxing on the lounger. My skull felt splintered and opening my eyes was like manually raising garage doors. I was pinned. When the blur cleared, I saw myself in a ceiling mirror above, naked and tied spread eagle to a massive four -poster bed with a rag of some sort shoved in my mouth. My hands and feet were duct-taped to their respective posts on the large bed.

Once I realized my predicament I found it tough to breathe. For fear I'd hyperventilate, I maintained stillness, keeping my eyes closed and body limp figuring Trevor—if that was his real name, was probably waiting for me to come to, so he could torture me or kill me. Fear coursed through my veins like a clot, and I couldn't stop the warm tears that ran down my cheeks.

A toilet flushed in another room. Methodical footfalls sounded and I knew the monster was just outside the door. The door to the bedroom remained closed and the footsteps moved away from the door. This was a bad dream, it had to be. Whenever I had bad dreams as a child I ran to Piper's room and she let me climb in and sleep with her the rest of the night. I opened my eyes ever so slightly and realized it was not a dream, it was a living nightmare. Kitchen noises, I was sure that had been what I heard. A plate placed on a ceramic tile counter, silverware clinking, an electric can-opener. Scraping, and more scraping. Was he making food before he gutted me?

I needed to prepare myself for when he returned, needed to fake sleep, the drugged sleep I had obviously been in. A rufie or some other paralyzing sedative must have been in my drink. How could I have so grossly misjudged this man? When he asked me back to his place for fireworks it never crossed my mind he'd drug me and tie me up. I was more concerned with the two of us progressing to a point where he'd discover who I really was, a loser librarian. Turned out he was the loser, the monster. He also had the upper hand, and I was quite sure he was sociopathic.

The bedroom door was closed but the light was still on, and I took a quick glance at my immediate surroundings. The room was sparingly furnished, a black lacquered dresser on the far side of the room with a tall vase full of sunflowers arcing over its rim. I thought it seemed such a dichotomy, my favorite flower in a torture chamber.

When the door finally opened I tried to squint with one eye. I watched in disbelief as this man I trusted came through the door carrying a cat in one arm and a bowl of what smelled like cat food in the other hand. "Prince wants to watch, he gets off on it. Then he'll have his dinner." He placed the fat black cat on a chair I hadn't noticed until then. The bowl was left on the dresser next to the sunflowers. "Don't worry boy, you'll get yours." His voice was gentle but his tone suggested he knew I was awake.

His body was a specimen of perfection and his penis was erect. He kneeled on the bed between my legs and before I could protest he sunk his member into me and thrust in and out and at first it was painful without lubrication but then it just became numbing and I went somewhere else in my head. I just needed to get out of this alive, that was my main goal, and if it meant I had to lay there and bear it I would. I wanted to live no matter the cost. When he finished raping me, he pulled away and knelt between my legs again.

"Was that good for you? I do want you to cum before you go." He laughed at his own pun. He removed the rag from my mouth and dared me to scream. He was sick, I knew that from the moment I came to, and I knew I couldn't rely on him letting me go just because he said so but I had to hang my hopes on his word.

The liquid running onto my upper thighs felt like acid. My arms felt yanked from their sockets. *"Please let me go now?"* It came out as a question, but sadly I already knew the answer.

He took his finger and ran it between my legs until I quivered. *"Ohh, you like that huh, bitch?"* He rubbed his finger back and forth ever so gently and I tried to numb my body to his touch, tried to wriggle away but it was useless, there was no slack in my tethers. My arms were useless and this made him somehow proud. He mounted me again and when he penetrated me, I tasted bile and felt my bowels tense. I concentrated on not vomiting. When he finally stopped, I wept.

As though something had just dawned on him, he leapt from the bed and made his way to the dresser and opened the top draw. I watched, sure my eyes were as wide as they'd ever been. He withdrew something small and black and when he turned I knew what he was holding because he pointed it at my head. This was it, I figured – he was going to shoot me with a grin on his face. He moved closer to the bed. My eyes never moved from the hole in the gun's barrel.

"Here's what's going to happen." He sat down next to me, and I instinctively shifted my body away but I was only able to slide an inch or two. He grabbed my hair and yanked my head up so my shoulders were no longer on the bed. *"You will make love to me and you will enjoy it or you will die."* The pain in my neck was intense. When he let go of my hair, my head and neck stayed in the overextended position for a few seconds before I slowly allowed it

to cogwheel back to rest on the bed. He grinned down at me. "Do you understand?"

I nodded ever so slightly and he seemed to relish in the look of fear I saw on my face every time I glanced in the mirror above me. He forced me onto my side. My limbs were heavy as cinderblocks, but acquiesced to his demands. He lay down next to me and wrapped his arms around me. The steely cold gun rested between my breasts as he stroked my hair telling me I was a good girl. It was as if the haunting indignities were somehow my fault.

Two hours later, after he raped me two more times coaching me through the moves, he then dragged me to the bathroom and forced me to take a thirty minute shower and douche three times. All the while he spoke in a voice that was calm as though I was a child.

"I know you won't tell anyone because I video-taped you moaning in ecstasy." His way of making it consensual, I guessed. "Now tell me you loved it and you love me." I hesitated. "Say it bitch or I'll fucking slice you up!"

I was naked in a shower with a sick sadistic man and so I said it. I shuddered but somehow separated each word whereby a hope of losing its meaning. The precious three words I'd yet to say to any man. Wasted on this monster but it was either the words or me. When he deemed me clean enough, he dragged me by my wet hair back to the bed and retied my arms and legs.

"I thought you got what you want so let me go, please." My heart was punching me from inside. Was I going to die?

"Shut-up."

The monster retrieved the bowl of cat food from the dresser and dumped it between my legs and let the cat have his dinner.

He finally released me from his terror after making me kiss him as I left. Once out of this high rise apartment I ran, I stumbled a few times, but I kept running past locked down store fronts and bums asking for change. It wasn't until I was sufficiently away from the rape scene when I hailed a cab.

Slumped in the backseat of a cab and smelling like putrid cat food, I rubbed my tender wrists where the tethers had been tied. I was sure I had bruises to accompany the swollen and sore wrists and ankles along with an aching pelvis. But I had survived. I knew as soon as I left that chamber of horrors at three in the morning, I would never tell a soul. I convinced myself that if I ever told my sister, she'd go crazy and force me to get the monster arrested. Then I'd have to endure the video images of disgusting scenes. I was quite sure I couldn't handle the humiliation.

While the taxi rolled ahead chasing its own headlights to New Jersey, I brought my knees up to chest and wrapped my arms around them trying to make myself as small as possible. It was July and yet I was shivering. I tucked my head down and tried to cry but I couldn't. I ran my fingers through my damp hair and froze. My mom's charm bracelet was no longer on my wrist. My rapist had even stolen that from me, my favorite keepsake from my dead mother. A chain full of memories ripped from me.

On that long, silent ride home, my head screamed. I made two decisions that night. The first was other than my father, I would never ever trust another man again, for that I was sure. Second, I would never repeat a single word of the humiliation I had just been subjected to, not a word to anyone. How could I? Trying to comfort myself, I rationalized that this monster had taken a whole lot from me that night but I was somehow spared my life.

PIPER

Not once did Piper interrupt Isabel and only when she started crying did Piper reach in for a hug. At one point, Pickle must have heard his mom's few choked sobs and snuck into the hallway. How much of Isabel's story he'd heard, Piper couldn't say but none of it was good. Hopefully he'd only heard the crying afterward. After Piper made sure he was safely tucked in bed seemingly asleep, she encouraged Isabel to go to bed as well. Piper promised to stay until Mac got home. Prozac had probably ripped the apartment to shreds, but there was no way she would leave her sister alone. Isabel had fallen asleep in her bed, completely spent after telling Piper the rest of her story. Piper would stay until Mac got home so she got comfortable on the couch and thought of her sister.

This rapist was a sick fuck and evil as all get out, but he was also smart, rich, and clever and Piper had learned from Isabel's story, the man had a gun. She found herself at a loss for words when she reviewed the gruesome details. It was no wonder Isabel never told anyone what happened, especially the police and their typical prying shitload of questions. Piper wasn't sure if she would have reported it either. What she would have done was set out on a mission for revenge and kill the bastard.

When Mac stumbled through the front door at half past one in the morning, Piper could tell he'd been drinking way too much. Piper had never seen Mac drunk before and she felt like an angry parent while she sat on the couch in the dark waiting for him to plop down next to her.

"Please tell me you didn't drive, ass-wipe?"

"Gee, sis, nice to see you, too. And no, I didn't drive, and anyway my last drink was two hours ago." Mac fell back next to her on the couch. "What's with the dark? Oh, can you drive me to the train station tomorrow to get my car? Where's Izzy?"

"Whoa, slow down cowboy. Yes, I'll drive you to the train station. Keep it down cause Izzy's asleep, and I'm in the dark because I'm practicing for my time underground."

"Aww, stop that shit, Pipes." He leaned in and hugged her.

Piper wasn't sure why she always tested Mac's sensitivity from the moment they met. I guess it was her feminist side rearing its ugly head.

"You know you're my favorite sister-in-law, right?"

"I'm honored considering you have like seven, is it?" It was obvious he was pretty wasted but Piper needed to talk to someone and Mac was the right person, the only person really that she'd ever repeat this story to. "I'm sitting here in the dark, Mac, because I need to tell you something pretty serious and trying to think of how to do it." She quickly remedied the fright she saw in his face. "It's not Izzy or the baby or Pickle for that matter. Just something you ought to know and before you ask, it's not me either, I'm fine." Piper was relieved to see his posture relax as he leaned back on the couch and sighed heavily.

"Jeez, you really know how to ruin a guy's buzz."

"Trust me, it's not the first time."

They laughed at that and then went quiet.

"Shit, Mac, you smell like a distillery, I'm glad Izzy's asleep."

Piper shoved him in the arm and his head fell to the couch pillow Isabel had been crying on earlier. "Seriously, dude, I need to tell you a bunch of things, but first is that we're pretty much fucked when it comes to not letting the asshole near Pickle. The rapist will have rights."

"I wanna kill that son of a bitch!" Mac tried to upright himself, but ran out of steam halfway up.

"Shhh! You'll wake Izzy."

"So," he shrugged into the couch, "I want to see her, I need to tell her that I'm sorry, I love her, Piper."

"You already told her on the phone earlier. It's the only reason she was able to fall asleep. She's exhausted, she needs her rest. Let's get you some coffee and sober you up a bit." Piper tugged at his sleeve. "C'mon, I ain't no diesel dyke who's gonna carry your drunk ass to the kitchen. Let's go."

Over steaming cups of coffee, Piper told Mac the story that Isabel had shared earlier. She didn't get through it without both of them shedding a few tears. She hated retelling this story but Mac needed to understand why Isabel hadn't gone to the police, why she hadn't told anyone.

Mac stood up and paced a few times and came close to slamming his fist into the wall before catching himself. "How can I not want to kill this mother fucker? Huh, Piper? Please tell me." Mac was so red in the face that Piper feared he might have a stroke. "I'm going to Google him and find out where he lives and smoke the bastard!"

"Sit your ass down right now, dude." Piper grabbed his arm and he took a seat on a kitchen chair. "I can smell your frigging testosterone with whiskey mixed in all over the place. Cool your heels, Mac. Izzy is very fragile right now, not to mention seven months pregnant *and* has a dying sister whom she adores. Just simmer down and deal with it because Isabel has, don't go running off like some jealous tool. Get your act together and help her through the custody suit. Just be there for her." Men always needed a woman's help with matters of the heart it seemed.

"Jesus, all the more reason to rid the earth of this scum. How is Izzy going to manage when this guy gets visitation?"

"Don't do anything stupid, Mac. I'm going to handle this from a legal standpoint, and I'll try and keep this going back and forth between lawyers and buy some time for Pickle's sake. A Pickle at eight is better than a Pickle at seven, get it? So don't fuck this up for us by getting up your testosterone. I mean, we just keep buying as much time as we can."

"Still, Pipes, when Pickle actually has to go to this lunatics place, what then? I think I may become a stalker." The tendons stood out in Mac's neck and his face was ashen, he was scared for the first time she'd ever seen and she'd seen him at many a bad event.

"I don't know. We'll have to wait and see how this plays out. What I do know is that's when you'll need to be there for Izzy."

"Haven't we all been through enough?" Mac shook his head and raked his fingers through his thick hair. He stood. Piper grabbed his hand.

"You realize, Mac, that as angry as you may feel right now, if Isabel had not been raped, she would have not had morning sickness the day after 9/11 – you may have never met her in Manny's store. Everything would have been different— we may have been in work on time the day before."

"I'm going to bed now, you staying the night?"

"No, I gotta let Prozac out, otherwise I may have to move back in here because he's likely eaten his way into the neighbor's apartment." Piper stood and grabbed her handbag. "I'll let myself out."

"Like hell you will. Here," Mac held open the front door. "After you, counselor."

They walked slowly to her car. Dew had already settled on the surfaces of everything, the drops twinkled in the moonlight.

"Well now, that's not too safe." Mac gestured to the open car window. He proceeded to check the backseat and the trunk.

"What are you doing? I left it open so sue me." Piper stood back while her darling brother-in-law went through his machinations.

"Just making sure there are no monsters." He winked at her and before she got in the car he hugged her tight. "What will I ever do without you?"

"You'll do just fine." Piper was so grateful for Mac. Isabel would be able to cope with everything coming her way as long as she had this man to catch her before she fell. "I will do my best to keep this particular monster as far away from our boy and our Izzy as humanly possible, you know that right, Mac?"

"I do know that." Mac released Piper from his embrace. "But as we used to say after blazing fires took one of our own— *Sometimes you eat the monster and sometimes the monster eats you.*"

ISABEL

The next morning Isabel awoke in that blissful vague haze before she remembered the day before and the memories flooded back in and she sat upright in bed. Being served custody papers by her rapist and then finally telling the truth about her rape to Piper seemed like eons ago. Mac was not in bed next to her. Sun glared through the partially open slats of the window blinds, and she was relieved it wasn't another rainy day. Isabel was going to start anew, make the best of her life while she still could. Isabel would apologize to Mac. She needed him by her side more than ever. When things got unbearable, she'd do whatever she had to do as Pickle's mother to keep him safe, at whatever the cost.

Isabel's tongue felt thick and dry from so much crying and she became concerned for the poor little critter growing in her being subjected to all this recent negativity. She realized how the rapist had ruined the first part of her pregnancy experience with Pickle and here he was doing it to her unborn baby again. Isabel could say it was like being raped all over again, but no rape short of a fatal one could be worse than the one eight years ago. The bottom line was this man was out to ruin her and her family, but she'd be damned if she was going let that happen. The man needed to be out of their lives permanently and Isabel would risk everything but her family to make that happen.

In an effort to control what she could think and not think about the man or the memory, she donned her bathrobe and went to the kitchen to guzzle a bottle of spring water for her baby's sake. It wasn't until she moved to the living room that she saw Mac passed out on the couch, still in his shoes. He looked so peaceful so Isabel decided to cover him with a blanket and let him sleep. When she came around to his side of the couch she noticed a small wrapped box on the coffee table with a note taped to it.

Izzy, you were sleeping so soundly last night I didn't want to disturb you and besides Piper said she'd kill me and as you know she intimidates the crap out of me. Wake me up when you get this note. I love you. M

"Silly man," Isabel whispered and gently kissed his ear and he startled, limbs shooting out and eyes popping like a cartoon character. He rolled off the couch, unable to get his bearings. Isabel stepped back and laughed. As sad as her mood had been the previous night, the way she felt just then seeing her husband was the direct opposite. She was ready for what life brought down upon her. Perhaps some of it was unburdening her story to Piper, then knowing her sister would tell Mac. Like losing a set of baggage only to begin packing more baggage of a different nature. At least she could move forward with less weight on her shoulders to deal with the road ahead. The next few months would not be easy, Isabel knew that, but knowing she had a plan was what she would cling to, what she would rely on. Isabel just didn't know what the plan was yet but she couldn't ignore some of the extreme ideas she had the night before.

"Very funny." Mac extricated himself from between the couch and the thick butcher block coffee table. "I can't tell you how happy it makes me to hear you laugh, even if it is at my expense. I certainly deserve it." He straightened himself and still appeared sheepish when he cleared his throat before speaking. "If you need to talk, Izzy, I know I'm here for you. Piper told me everything, and I'm so sorry for my behavior yesterday. I was way out of line. Forgive me?" He was teary eyed with arms extended and palms up as if waiting for Isabel to slap hand-cuffs on him. She laid her hands on his hands.

"I'm so sorry, Izzy, for what happened to you all those years ago. I seriously love you and need you to know I'm not just *here* for you, I'm *part* of you." He gazed down at my budding abdomen.

"Thanks for being in my life," was all Isabel could think to say. She didn't want pity, she wanted a plan.

Mac placed both his hands on her abdomen; over their unborn baby. He didn't have to say anything; the gesture told her she needed to start focusing on the goodness in life. She had Pickle and a husband who loved her, not to mention Piper and Clare.

"So, are you ready for some good news?" Mac let go of her and picked up the box, peeled off the note but he didn't hand it to her. His demeanor lightened and he all at once was beaming.

"Am I ever?" Isabel smiled at her husband and the idea of something good.

"The castle, my queen, awaits you." He took her right hand in his and placed the box on her outstretched palm. "There's still a little bit left to finish in the basement, but we got the certificate of occupancy meaning we can move in tomorrow." He bowed his head and humbly finished his thought. "If you like; your highness."

"This is the best news I've heard in a while." Isabel hugged Mac while clutching the little box. She knew what was in the box, of course it was a house key. Mac had already given her the keys to a new car and to the renovated barn house; this was the next obvious key. It was cute – he was a key-giver. She sat down on the couch and Mac sat next to her.

"Open it, love."

"I will, Mac, and I am so happy the house is ready but what about this lawsuit thing. I know, timing and everything. I just don't want this new phase in our lives to be tainted with rape talk and custody battles." Isabel tried to stop the tears, but her hormones won out and she reached for Mac and he pulled her into him.

"Listen, Izzy, there's always going to be something – I say starting fresh is a good thing, I mean it can't hurt, right?"

She shook her head and pulled away. "You're right. I'm just so emotional."

He brushed an unruly curl of hair from her eyes. "It doesn't matter where we live, as long as we're all together as a family. In fact, Piper says it's better to go now before this guy's lawyer puts limitations; a radius on Pickle. Besides, she told me with the way the judicial system works it will be at least two months of interrogatories before you'll even need to appear in court."

"What about the request for an emergent hearing?"

"Can't happen since he has no grounds for concern for the child's well-being. Piper says she'll make that go away first thing tomorrow." Mac was so confident and it made Isabel nervous.

If Piper could make that happen then at least she'd have several weeks to perfect a plan. "Let's do it. Let's move next week! I'll call the moving company tomorrow. I'll be so happy to stop living out of the boxes." Isabel was eager to have something to focus on while she strategized and tried not to forget she was with-child. "And let's not leave a forwarding address."

"Fine by me." He kissed her full on the mouth and he tasted like stale beer and morning and Isabel knew she was home with this man. She allowed her shoulders to give in to him, so grateful her story being unleashed the night before didn't force Mac to run the other way. "Now can you please open your present?"

"I almost forgot." Isabel smiled in spite of knowing what the box would reveal. She peeled back the paper covering and lifted the lid. Her breath caught in her throat at what she saw before her. Isabel gently lifted the charmed bracelet from the velvet pad and just stared at the shiny icons already adorning so many of the loops. They were tiny charms dangling and nearly identical to the ones her mom had collected, a new and exact replica of her bracelet full of memories lost so many years ago. It was the same bracelet, just brand new.

PIPER

It didn't take much persuading to get the judge to dismiss the emergent hearing. Piper was willing to take full responsibility for the child until a proper hearing could be scheduled down the road; she believed it was a small victory for Isabel. Although the attorney for the plaintiff argued, the judge ruled in Piper's favor. She had known Judge Clemont for many years, grew up with his daughter and when Piper claimed her client was having pregnancy issues and produced a note stating Isabel was to be on bed rest for the next few weeks, he was more than happy to grant the motion. A white lie, Piper figured.

Isabel's rapist was of course present in the courtroom, but Piper tried never to look in his direction. Pretending he didn't exist was about the best way to deal with him at that moment in time. There was no way Isabel would be exposed to him if Piper could help it. Piper couldn't protect her all those years ago, but she was damn-well going to try and keep her sister safe this time.

Although Piper was the victor that day in court, the monster did pass the paternity test with flying colors and the judge refused to further run his DNA through a crime database. *This isn't a criminal trial, Ms. Henry. Denied.*

It was only the first round, but Stossel the monster didn't look defeated. He knew full-well he'd eventually win out and at least get partial custody of the boy he referred to over and over as *his son*. Piper knew why Isabel was so angered at her when she used that reference.

He sauntered from court, head held high, his demeanor jovial only betrayed by his clenched fists and a smile cold as a zipper. Piper followed closely behind him and his attorney until they stepped into the men's room. When Carson emerged alone she took the opportunity to sidle up to him.

"I understand you have a heart condition."

He stopped and peered down at her with curious eyes, lips thin as worms against his white strained smile. "What the hell are you saying?"

"You don't have one." Piper moved past him and turned. "You better watch your back now dirt-bag cause I'm coming for you, and I have not a god-damned thing to lose."

Before he could respond Gerry Stein was by his side.

"Now, now, Ms. Henry, no fraternizing with my client. I realize he's quite an attractive man, but I heard you prefer to swim with the other beavers." He snickered. "One small step for your client today." He made quotation marks around the word client with his two chubby index fingers. "One giant step for my client come trial, you and I both know that, don't we?"

"Your client is a perverted sexual predator and rapist and I would sooner have my tits cut off than see him get anything but jail time. Ask him about his penchant for duct-tape and cat food. Good day."

Piper needed to get away from them so she pushed through the ladies room door with a false nonchalance and once inside she leaned on the stained sink for support. Lucky for her the bathroom was empty. Piper had promised herself earlier that she would not lose her cool. It was her Izzy for crying out loud, but she was a lawyer first and a sister second in this case. If she was a sister first, she'd lose the case for sure because she'd have killed the fucker weeks ago.

Piper stopped by Isabel's house on the way back from court to fill her in on the details and wasn't too surprised to see a moving truck in her driveway. Isabel was outside in a pair of coveralls seemingly directing the process while Pickle rode his bicycle up and down the sidewalk. When her nephew saw her pull in, he dropped his bike on the spot and ran to the car. The responses she received from him and her dog washed over her like a sunbeam. It filled her with such purpose that she finally felt significant for the first time in this world of six billion people.

Isabel came over to the spectacle; both Pickle and his aunt in a hug fest and tickle time balled in one. Pickle was just seven and still so very innocent. Piper would risk her life to keep him in that protective bubble.

"Hey Piper, guess what?" Isabel hugged Piper around the neck since her son was around the rest of Piper. They pecked cheeks, a habit they somehow picked up after 9/11. Piper noticed people did hug more these days.

"Oh gee, I don't know, you're doing what you told me at least six times." She mouthed *I'm dying not becoming dumb.* "Let me guess. You're moving to the farm and taking Pickle to live at the zoo with the monkeys?" Piper really needed to keep it light which she hoped conveyed to her sister.

"Aunt Piper! I am not going to live with the monkeys, besides I like chimps better. Beaker's moving with us too and he gets to come in the car next to me."

"I figured you were going to make him fly there. He'll be such great conversation in a closed in space like that." Piper winked. Her last encounter with Beaker was the previous weekend when she refused to share her apple with him and he called her a pig and kept making oinking sounds until she left the room. "Pickle, why don't you show me some cool moves on your bicycle to keep me awake while your mom talks boring to me."

Isabel shoved Piper. "He loves to ride that bike." Isabel grinned but Piper saw a twitch in her lip and Piper knew that Isabel knew what was coming by way of conversation.

They watched Pickle pedal standing up as he made his way to the upper part of the long driveway.

"Be careful, Pickle, no skinned knees!" Isabel looked at Piper. "What happened in court? I'm dying here."

They sat on the front steps of their childhood home while Piper told Isabel the details of the hearing. Isabel listened without comment. Every so often they'd yell whoops to Pickle's "Watch this Aunt Piper!"

"I'll remember his amazing talent when I'm dead." Piper meant it. She'd take these everyday moments with her: these were moments with energy and that never went away. For that she was sure. Her nephew had unconditional love for her just like his mother. She stared into the bright light of reality that she was loved. Funny how one only recognizes truly being in the moment when their moments are limited. Isabel broke her quiet stare.

"I can't even respond to you not being here. Let's just change the subject." Isabel turned to Piper. "I really mean it when I say I could not do any of this without you or Mac." Isabel held out her arm and Piper took her delicate wrist in her hand. "Oh, I almost forgot." Isabel raised the wrist Piper was holding a little closer to her. "Look what Mac gave me the other day, Piper. A new charm bracelet to replace the one I lost. And look, he added a charm of a pickle and a horse and a dog and a few others." Isabel extended her arm in front of her sister and twisted her wrist, admiring her new bracelet. "I love him, Piper, and I have you to thank for bringing him into my life."

"Oh bullocks, you two would have found each other regardless. And I knew about the bracelet –I didn't know how you'd lost it, only that you'd lost it. Mac's timing is impeccable as usual. Besides, curly girlie, how do you think he knew what Mommy's bracelet actually looked like?" Piper examined the charms resting on her sister's delicate wrist. She stopped at the one that read *sister* inside a heart. Her lungs filled with beautiful fresh air. "I love Mac too, Isabel, and you have given me so much more than I could have ever had on my own, and we both know that." Piper let go of her sister's wrist. One of the charms represented her and that said everything. "You know what makes this bracelet so special don't you, sis? Not the silver dolphin or the ones representing Pickle and Beaker and Prozac. Not even the ones that stand for Mom. The best charm of all is not even on the charm bracelet. It's the guy who gave it to you."

ISABEL

While Piper stayed behind to fight Isabel's battles in court, Mac and Isabel, along with Pickle and Beaker got settled into their new digs. The place was perfection for a country ranch. The entrance had an exquisite, frosted oval beveled glass inset in the arched doorway welcoming friends and neighbors. A traditional wrap-around porch replete with a swing, led the way inside Isabel's dream house.

Isabel told Mac the picture perfect scene needed to be photographed before they allowed Pickle, and his soon-to-be sibling, to wreak havoc on the place. This pristine look would diminish after a year of living there. There was a piece of mail, a manila envelope taped to the door so Isabel pulled it off and then took a few photos of the warm and welcoming entrance to their new home. It was truly magazine material.

Mac and Isabel stood holding hands on the porch before they went inside. Isabel silently said her thanks for everything she had been blessed with. Without warning, Mac lifted her up into his arms, pregnant belly and all, unlocked the front door and carried her over the threshold of their home sweet home. While Pickle giggled at their silly behavior, Isabel walked around in her new life in awe. Despite the stacks of boxes the movers unloaded the day before, everything was exactly as she'd hoped and better. Mac had truly outdone himself. She couldn't wait to see the place when the large furniture arrived later that day.

"You, my love, are a genius." When he put her down Isabel kept her arms wrapped around his neck, her belly standing in the way of a tighter hug.

"Can I go see Jigsaw? I know how to open the horse pen and I'll be super careful." Pickle had run from room to room and then rejoiced over his own area of the house on the third floor loft. Isabel knew Pickle had some energy to burn from the trip from New Jersey, so she sent him outside to say hello to his horse.

"First go get Beaker from the car and put him over there by the window for now until the movers unpack his big cage. Then you can go say 'hello' to Jigsaw but that's all until we come out." Isabel hadn't seen him this excited since their wedding.

Mac and Isabel stood on the landing outside Pickle's room and watched as *their* son tore down the curved stairwell and out into the massive farm yard. It was breathtaking and a boy's dream world all balled into one place. Mac's smile made her realize how all of them living together there in that home was as close to his dream come true for this property as he could get since he'd purchased it so long ago with Sean.

"I know you want to be out there with Pickle so go ahead, I'm going to start unpacking before I weigh 600 pounds and can't get out of bed." Isabel rested a hand on her belly.

"You don't have to tell me twice to go outside. I'm going to take Pickle for a ride on the trails. We'll see you in an hour or so." He took Isabel's chin in his hand and kissed her full on the mouth and headed down the stairs. "Don't lift anything, okay? Got it?"

"Yes, sir, I promise I'll save all the heavy stuff for you."

Mac seemed relieved not to be asked to put anything away and made his way down the staircase as Pickle had just done, two steps at a time. He was halfway down when he turned back to her.

"Take as long as you need to move in and really, Izzy, please don't lift anything heavy. Remember, you're the best thing that's ever happened to me."

Isabel watched out the picture window from the landing at the vast stretch of yard and the fields off in the distance. What a wonderful place to raise children. She rubbed her belly as her unborn baby stirred. Happiness squeezed its way around the pit she'd been carrying in her stomach since she was served. She found herself grinning in spite of herself. Isabel made a mental note to add a tiny farm house to her charm bracelet. Thoughts of her sister back in New Jersey, ill and having to fight Isabel's battles came seeping in and tried to ruin her special moment but she blocked them. She wanted their first day in their new home to be a lovely memory and not tarnished by the evil that loomed at a distance like an impending storm.

Isabel distracted herself with the daunting task of unpacking. Organizing everything would take weeks but she had to start somewhere so she began with Pickle's room, so he'd have a comfy place to sleep for the night. The things they'd accumulated over a lifetime and then carted around with them until they died amazed Isabel when she saw it all in stacked boxes. Granted she had gotten rid of so much stuff, but it was astounding how much one accumulates in the smallest of spaces, worlds unto themselves lived under kitchen sinks or behind bathroom mirrors. She glanced around the vast space of house. There had to be a hundred boxes full of stuff. No one really *owned* anything, but it was more like one rented the things they considered their belongings. What a joke. When they passed into the next world all they'd have would be the clothes on their backs – some not even that much. Yet the things that were most important to Isabel were not in boxes, but were outside horseback riding.

After about an hour of arranging Pickle's belongings, she needed to get a drink of water or juice. Isabel was sure Mac had something in the fridge. She took the oak curved staircase carefully because she was not familiar with the steps and had nightmares of falling belly first. At the base of the stairs lay her purse. Isabel smiled at the thought of her dropping it there when Mac carried her over the threshold. She leaned over with a groan to lift it and saw the manila-envelope under it. She lifted Mac's mail as well as the bag and went to the kitchen to check things out at her own pace. The fridge was stocked with all sorts of goodies and, of course, bottles of cold water.

The room was expansive and Isabel was almost embarrassed with a kitchen of this magnitude when the most extravagant recipe she'd ever cooked was chicken parmesan. She took a stool at the amber granite island and after a long swallow of water for both her and the little-one; Isabel looked around and took it all in. Her eyes eventually settled on the manila envelope next to her purse. It wasn't mail for Mac at all, but rather it was addressed to Isabel.

"What the ...?"

No return address made her curious so she reached for it and tore it across the top. There were three pieces of paper inside, she lifted them out and that was the last thing she remembered.

ISABEL

"Izzy, it's me honey, wake up."

It was Mac, his voice was soft and firm all at once and Isabel found that peculiar. Two opposites occurring simultaneously like sun and rain. She thought of her rapist and how they were so completely different and yet they were the same in Pickle.

"Izzy, open your eyes, you're scaring me. I've already called 911."

In her entire life, Isabel had never called 911. The irony that 9/11 was the ultimate 911 didn't escape her. Isabel's brain felt spongy and dull and her eyes were so heavy it was like they were magnetized shut. She finally was able to flutter the lids to allow a little light to penetrate. She thought of eyes and how people take them for granted when they have good vision. Given the choice, it's the last sense she'd give up. Yet there were times that her eyes were a window to a world she'd give anything not to see. When she opened her eyes fully, Isabel registered Mac hovering over her.

"You're going to be okay, the ambulance is on its way."

"Where's Pickle?" Isabel didn't want him to see the contents of the envelope.

"It's okay, Iz, I hid the envelope in the cabinet before he saw them and now he's out front waiting for the ambulance. I reassured him you were okay and gave him the job of ambulance announcer when it arrives. Are you okay?"

"I'm fine." It came out gravelly so Isabel cleared her throat. "He sent me those pictures Mac. Oh my god they are so humiliating." Tears hung on her lower lashes and began to drop.

"Here babe, sit up and I'll get you some water." He grabbed her bottle from the counter and gave her a long sip.

"Thanks. I'm okay, I don't need an ambulance. This is just me, you know I faint. The baby's moving too, I feel it kicking."

"We are going to err on the side of caution, Izzy, I'm not taking any chances with you or the baby. It can't hurt to …"

"Ambulance is here, it's here, Mac!" Pickle dashed into the room. "You okay Mommy? You were subconscious." He sat down on the floor next to her, his head leaning on Isabel's shoulder.

She couldn't help but smile. "Everything's fine, baby, just had a little fall."

Before Isabel was allowed to enjoy the first night in her new life she had to spend six hours in an emergency room. They all went home aggravated and hungry but feeling very blessed that all was healthy and safe. Mac carried Pickle up to his awaiting bed since he'd fallen asleep on the ride home. Isabel went to the kitchen and retrieved the photos from the cabinet. She stared long and hard at them before holding them over a stovetop flame. She cringed at her naked body on its hands and knees, her head between a rapist's legs, each photo the same and by the third enlarged photo it was clear that she was aggressively sucking on a man's penis. The photos curled as they melted then Isabel doused them in water and shoved the charred distorted images down the garbage disposal. It felt good in spite of the fact that it was evidence and Piper was going to kill her.

It took some time for Isabel to lose the intense anxiety over the idea that her rapist knew where she was and was continuing to taunt her. She dove into getting the house in order and over the course of the next several days the ranch took shape. Mac commented how great the place looked with all her personal touches, but she was most proud of what she'd accomplished when Piper showed up with Clare and they raved at her interior design abilities. During their first visit to the ranch, Prozac urinated on the foyer floor followed by Beaker cackling in laughter when Piper yelled at the overly excited dog. Isabel believed just then that their house became a real home.

Piper and Clare spent the weekend in the renovated barn and Mac treated them as if they were staying in a five-star hotel. He brought them warm muffins and fresh coffee in the morning and saddled up the horses for them to take a mid-morning ride around the property. Prozac had the time of his life running haplessly for what seemed like hours and then fell dead asleep on the porch in the shade for the rest of the day. Pickle was beside himself having his aunts visiting. Isabel did everything she could to keep him from constantly bothering them without hurting her son's sensitive feelings.

Sunday morning, while Clare and Pickle watched a movie together in the den, Piper found Isabel in the kitchen straightening up after breakfast. Isabel turned and Piper was there staring at her.

"What? I'm fat, right?" Isabel wiped her hands on a dish towel.

"No, you look gorgeous." Piper handed her a thick sweater. "Come sit outside with me for a bit, just for a little chat."

"What's wrong?" Anxiety nicked Isabel's cozy demeanor.

"I just want to catch you up on what's happening in the case, that's all." She gestured to the den where Clare and Pickle were slumped on the couch. Piper wanted to talk in private and that scared Isabel. They had gone three days without a word of business.

"Okay, I'll make us some tea and be right out." Of course Piper needed to talk to her. Isabel was in denial. All weekend she had avoided any conversations about the legal proceedings, figuring if something was pressing from the judge, Piper would have told her when she arrived; Piper wouldn't just spring bad news on her, would she? The pit in Isabel's stomach suggested otherwise.

PIPER

When Isabel invited Piper and Clare to stay for the weekend Piper was somewhat reluctant. She knew the news she had to share with Isabel was not going to be well-received, and if they were going to be stuck on a farm all weekend clearly it wouldn't be a grand time, to say the least. She'd refrained from ruining everyone's weekend and waited until the last possible minute to tell Isabel.

When Isabel had called Piper a few weeks back and told her about the photos she'd received and that she'd burned them, only saving the envelope in case Piper needed it for fingerprints, Piper had to laugh. Isabel was quite possibly an attorney's worst nightmare as a client. Piper would have been angry with her sister, but often those sisterly lines blurred. This time Piper understood that Mac seeing those photos was horrific enough, no one else should have to witness her rape.

Piper desperately wanted to see Isabel and was looking forward to getting away to be with family – what could be better. She missed them all so much since the move and before Isabel knew it, she'd be back in the hospital spitting out *Thing Two*. Piper decided she'd take her sister up on the offer to come and stay for the long Thanksgiving weekend even though Piper was feeling weaker and weaker by the day.

As it turned out, the weekend was one of the best, most relaxing times Clare and she had spent together since the cruise. The new medications were kicking Piper hard, but she had no choice but to take them unless she wanted to spend the rest of her short life in bed. The day before they left for Pennsylvania, Piper had gone in for blood tests but it was a waste of time, she already could tell the disease had progressed to the next inevitable stage. Her skin was blotchy, she was barely urinating and she experienced daily migraine headaches. Piper's sole concern was over Isabel's reaction when she saw how much weight Piper had lost in just a few weeks. Truth was Piper had been living on coffee, oranges, steroids and top of the spectrum pain killers. And it made life tolerable.

Mac had shown them a real dude ranch experience that weekend. At home, Piper had spent a lot of time sleeping but Mac would have none of that on the ranch. After a fitful but comfortable night sleep, on Saturday morning she and Clare rode horseback, which lasted until afternoon. Isabel and Pickle dog-sat back at the ranch, while Mac, their escort, brought them to an open grassy glade with daisies and wild lavender lace swaying their greetings. Mac tied up their horses and produced a straw basket and spread a red and white checkered tablecloth on a low patch of grass for Clare and her to have a picnic. He galloped off on his steed for a long ride while the women snuggled together sharing champagne with strawberries and slices of sour dough bread with chunks of rich cinnamon butter.

"What a sexy man he is." Clare made a low catcall whistle in Mac's direction.

"He's simply amazing." Piper lay back and smiled. "It's important to me, Clare, that Izzy has someone to take care of her when I leave for Never-Never Land."

"Oh Piper, don't say that," her Portuguese coming through.

"I know it's old fashioned, but I'm proud of the woman my sister's become. This lifestyle," Piper swept her arm across the vast expanse of the glade with its flitting butterflies and the buzzing and chirping of hidden insects, "is perfect for Izzy. Mac makes her feel like *princess on the prairie* and it suits her. I can't tell you how happy that makes me."

"That makes you a neo-feminist, my love."

Piper laughed. "There were two things I was sure of before this weekend. I was a feminist and an arachnophobe, but after sleeping amongst spiders and wearing an apron to do the dishes, I'm questioning my long-held sensibility. Truth be told, I could get used to this sort of peace and serenity. Home-cooked meals and pick-up trucks, the smell of linens fresh from a clothesline, and fireflies in a jar." Piper didn't want to ruin the moment by mentioning her impending trip to heaven or wherever she may be headed.

Back at the ranch that night they all enjoyed grilled steaks, redskin potatoes and buttered corn on the cob by a blazing fire. Prozac went from person to person begging for morsels and they didn't need music because Beaker whistled and sang all sorts of songs throughout the night in his outdoor cage. Pickle entertained Piper with stories of his latest adventures on the big frontier. His new school seemed to be a great fit. Moving at any age could be traumatic, but he seemed to have adjusted beautifully to the change.

"Last weekend I caught a big fish, Aunt Piper." Pickle was too excited to stay seated at the picnic table, having his favorite people surrounding him. "It was a puppy fish so I threw him back in the water and he swam away back to his mommy."

"You mean a guppy, with a 'G,' Pickle." Mac cut in laughing. "It was certainly a nice healthy catch." Behind Pickle's back Mac took his thumb and forefinger and displayed the inch sign. They all laughed at that, even Pickle joined in without a clue what was so funny.

It warmed Piper's heart to have everyone around each other having a great time and making memories. When Beaker chimed in with a screeching version of Madonna's "Like a Virgin" they all looked at Isabel's protruding belly and laughed. When Beaker stopped singing and yelled in a woman's voice, *"Shut that crap off!"* they all lost it, all of them except Pickle who proceeded to scold Beaker for saying a bad word.

These were not just Piper's very specials moments. These were her loved ones' cherished memories as well. She knew it would go a long way for Isabel to see her sister having fun on her way out the door, so to speak. It sickened Piper to think about the monster who was trying to ruin all this and there wasn't a damn thing she could do about it unless she had him killed. All Piper knew for certain was she had to take care of herself, had to keep taking the medication and stay strong because her work in this world wasn't finished.

Sunday morning was a bit overcast, lending to a chill in the air and not unexpected for early fall in the mountains. Piper sat in a bright orange Adirondack chair, her feet propped on a matching ottoman. Prozac lay at her side on the cool ground, only perking up when she lit a joint. Ironically, Prozac had had the best time of all here at the ranch because he was capable of strictly living in the moment. Piper was envious of that trait ever since her diagnosis. And her dog was the best medicine of all besides her nephew.

When Isabel emerged from the house, Piper's face froze. From a distance she was astonished to see how much Isabel looked like their mother, pregnant with Isabel at the same age Isabel was at that moment. Granted, her sister's abdomen was practically hanging to her knees under the weight of Piper's niece or nephew, but still,

Isabel was so beautiful. In each hand her sister carried a cup of what Piper assumed was tea. Isabel crossed the gravel path leading from the front porch and made her way over to Piper. The song, "Two for Tea" ran through Piper's thoughts, *me for you and you for me, forever.* Piper prayed that what she was about to tell Isabel wouldn't cause her sister to hate her.

ISABEL

"Are you smoking marijuana?" Isabel couldn't believe what she was smelling. Piper was holding in a puff of smoke and when Isabel sat down next to her she blew it out with a ratcheted cough and laughed at the same time. The sweet condensation sat in the still chilled air like a low-lying cloud.

"Is this the new medicine the doctor put you on? What you need to discuss with me out here today?" Isabel air-quoted the word *medicine.*

"Yep. It's an antiemetic to combat the nausea and vomiting, a side effect from the high doses of dexamethasone and synthetic opiates." Piper grinned in Isabel's direction. "Sorry, I'd love to share a drag with you but you're pregnant, besides it would be illegal. For you, that is."

She seemed content and Isabel was in no position to judge. If anything, it frightened Isabel to see her Wall Street sister smoking pot because for her to resort to anything mind-altering like opiates and marijuana meant this disease had to be really taking hold of her.

"I'd kill for a bit of a buzz right about now. I have at least a few weeks before I can chemically induce euphoria but forget about fat ole me; I'm more worried about you." Isabel was afraid of where this was going. "What did the doctor say on Friday?"

"He did more blood work, but I can tell him the results before they come back. I'm dying." She took another long pull from the joint. "I'd say we're all dying, but I refuse to give in to maudlin clichés."

"I am so sorry." Isabel reached over and touched Piper's knee. No crying for her, she needed to be supportive. This was Piper's moment and Isabel refused to fall apart. "I'll come by whenever you need me other than when I'm in labor, I swear to you. Mac can stay with the kids and I'll be by your side. I promise, Piper, I will be there for you always. You need bone marrow, you got it, a kidney, it's yours, no problem – just say the word. What do you want?"

"I want to die with dignity. How am I doing so far?" She blew out a stream of smoke and turned and winked at Isabel, then stubbed out the joint in the grass where it made a hissing noise. She cleared her throat and took a sip of her tea, cradling the cup in two hands as if it were an injured sparrow. "That's one of the things I wanted to discuss with you, Izzy, actually there are two things. Do you want the good news first or the bad news?"

"Shit, I hate this." Isabel never liked that choice, and who did? With Piper doing the asking, Isabel knew she'd hear it all anyway, the good the bad and the ugly. This was just Piper's expert way of softening the blow of the bad news. "Alright," Isabel sighed. "Give me the good first, I may not make it through the bad news."

"I want to die here."

"What?"

"You heard me." Piper said each word as though she were listing them. "I, Want, To, Die, Here. Will that be okay with you?"

"Are you serious? Of course you can di ..." Isabel paused, not willing to say *die*. "Well you know, of course you can live here as long as you want." Isabel couldn't believe what she was hearing.

Piper wanted to spend the last days of her life with her family; Isabel's family. "I'd be most honored if you'd stay here, how's that for an answer?"

Piper methodically placed her cup back on the saucer resting on the grass. "I want to be around my family, isn't that weird?" She leaned over for a lopsided hug. "I really love it here, Izzy."

Isabel knew her sister was a little stoned and that was fine. Piper released her squeeze and sat back against the chair.

"When I told Clare, at first she looked worried but then she said she'd take a leave of absence from work to come here and help care for me. When the time comes that is, but let's face it Izzy, I'm starting to see the light at the end of the joint if you know what I mean."

"Shit, Piper, quit it." Isabel hated when Piper joked about dying. "I am happy that Clare will be here too. She's an angel. I'm thrilled you are both coming –it'll be like a big slumber party."

"Calm down, let's not turn this into The Sisters of the Travelling Pants, it's not going to be pretty, Izzy."

"I know but I don't care. I'm committed to you through this whole illness. Mac and Pickle are going to be thrilled!" Isabel recognized her stupidity as soon as the words were out. "I'm sorry, not thrilled, it's just that they'll be relieved is probably a better way to put it. Do you want to tell them?"

"Mac already knows, in fact it was his idea. He suggested we come for the weekend and see how comfortable it is here. After this weekend, Clare and I are sure it's the right thing."

"Are you serious?" Isabel feigned surprised anger but she was not surprised or angry. "Let me get this straight. Mac and you once again went behind my back with a scheme that directly affects me? To use your eloquent vernacular, Piper, what the fuck?"

"Yeah, yeah, yeah, but c'mon, sis, you must admit, it's brilliant.

After we talked he told you that you should invite us and voila, the sinister plan was hatched."

"It is brilliant. I just deplore the whole reason behind the scheme." Isabel held back her emotions as best she could but a few traitorous tears slipped by. Deep down Isabel was so touched by Piper's affection for Mac and vise-versa, they had a closeness and love all their own. "It'll be a double-edged sword," was all Isabel could think to say.

"Oh sweetie, don't cry yet. There'll be plenty of time for that." Piper put her hand on Isabel's leg. "I won't come here until I'm ready, promise and I'll know when it's right." Piper may have had a few glistening tears in her eyes too, but she looked the other way and Isabel didn't comment. Piper wouldn't want to hear it anyway. If her sister had something to share, she'd share it without reservation. "I'd like to see another summer."

Isabel jerked away. "Piper! That's only nine months away, of course you'll be here next summer." Isabel couldn't tell if she was serious. "You're not being serious, right?"

"Isabel, let's change the subject before this moves over to the bad news column with the other news I haven't told you yet. That's a whole other hill of beans."

"Okay, okay." This was all such heavy duty information to process and even though Isabel was more than okay with Piper coming to the ranch to die, emotionally she was never going to be prepared for losing her sister. Isabel shook her head like an athlete following a blow to the skull. "I'm ready for the bad news." Isabel lied. She was petrified of Piper's news but Isabel didn't want to get crazy for the baby's sake and her own. "Just tell me so we can be done with it, like ripping off a Band-Aid." Isabel wasn't sure why she said that; she hated when a Band-Aid got ripped off. She usually waited until she took a bath and soaked it off. "I just don't understand why you didn't share the bad news when you got here so I could at least process it before you left." Isabel was sure there was a method to her sister's madness, there always was as Piper never did anything on a whim. "I'm braced. Hit me."

"I wasn't here this weekend, Izzy, to deliver news. I was here to check out heaven's waiting room, as Mac so poetically put it." She reached across to the arm of Isabel's chair and took Isabel's hand in hers. "The monster is going to get visitation."

Isabel sat up straight in her chair. "Oh dear god, Piper! What am I going to do? I have to fight this! I hope I didn't make a huge mistake by burning those pictures, did I?"

"Izzy, his face wasn't in the pictures so they wouldn't have served any other purpose but to try and disgrace you. This has nothing to do with photos. Unfortunately, it's about the law. We can spend thousands of dollars fighting it, but we'd be flushing the money down the toilet."

Isabel was too terrified to speak. Her mind went to the plans she had conjured up for this very news. She'd take her son out of the country. She hadn't bought plane tickets nor did Pickle have a passport, but she would begin to arrange things first thing in the morning. Her thoughts were spinning with what to do. She had to do something and quick.

"I know it sucks, Isabel, but there isn't anything that can be done. We will have to be in court a week from Wednesday and the arrangements will be finalized. I can get you out of court with a note from your OB/GYN because you're like a hundred months pregnant at this point."

"I'm running away with Pickle."

"Don't be ridiculous, Izzy. I have put my practice on the line with the judge – I'm supposed to know Pickle's whereabouts at all times, remember? I'd hate to be disbarred at this juncture, Sis. Besides, you're about to give birth and no airline in the free world will allow you on board without a doctor's note. Look at you." She poked my belly. "You could be smuggling a kilo in there."

"I am not joking, Piper – okay, so it would take a while to get a passport for Pickle anyway, but what would prevent me from just taking all my money from the sale of Dad's estate and start driving. I'll disappear and set up a new identity for me and Pickle. I wouldn't involve you, won't tell you where we're headed, at least not in the beginning."

"Forget about me, little sister. You'd leave Mac?" An edge of anger surrounded Piper's tone.

"He can come with us." Isabel looked around at the ranch and realized she was kidding herself. No way could she ask Mac to leave the ranch, their dream home. He'd have to understand that it was about saving her little boy.

"Okay, so now there will be two people you'll leave behind to deal with and lie to the authorities."

"You can plead the fifth."

"Holy shit, Isabel! You're talking like an armchair legal lunatic right now!" She bolted up in the chair and her feet hit the ground and nearly spilled her tea propped in the grass. She knitted her brows at Isabel as if examining a strange insect. "For starters, you need to always put Pickle first. If you do that every time you'll make the best decisions. A little boy cannot be on the run. It's not fair to him to take all this away from him when he has just gotten settled in a new school and a new life. Secondly, you'd have to leave the new baby with Mac or that would be a kidnapping count. And that's just the start of your legal woes."

Isabel knew Piper was setting up the argument of her life and that meant she believed Isabel was being serious. She'd run but she knew she'd still be miserable. Isabel couldn't stop the tears from rolling down her cheeks.

"Oh god, Piper, what am I going to do? I feel like running is my only option."

"I'll humor you here. Let's say you take off for some small town in Podunk, USA. Kidnapping charges aside, along with violating the court order not to leave the tri-state area, you'd still be evading the law. By the way, I had to fight hell and high water to get you permission to move out of New Jersey after you were served papers. That's unheard of in custody court mind you." Piper leaned back and propped her feet back up, seeming to relax. Isabel knew better. Piper wasn't done, far from it.

"Not to mention you'd never see any of us again. It wouldn't be safe for Pickle and you'd be a fugitive always looking over your shoulder. And not just in fear of the police might I add. No, you'd be waiting every day for that monster to catch up with you and trust me Isabel, he will."

"How much time will he be awarded?" Isabel's mind was all over the board. "Not overnights?"

"No overnights at first. He's granted day visitation for the first few weeks. That has to start right after court next week."

"One week!" Isabel was shaking her head. "Then just a few weeks of day visits until he has to go overnight! No way, Piper! The guy has a gun! A gun, Piper! I can't stand by and allow my son to go with this sexual predator and spend the night. I'll sooner die."

"Not sooner than me. With you dead and me dying, Pickle would live with the scumbag permanently. Now there's a good solution. You need to be strong, Izzy, if it ends up being overnights we'll deal with it then. Let's just get used to the idea of a few hours at a time of visitation. It's the same scenario when you explain all this to Pickle, you're not going to pile on the entire story, just a little at a time."

"Okay, okay, I need to get a grip." Isabel had her work cut out for her. "I still have to tell Pickle his father is alive."

Mac was the only father-figure Pickle had ever known and Isabel was going to rip that security rug right out from underneath the poor kid. For a long time she'd been able to keep the two parts of her life separate. There was an uncomfortable tautness to Isabel's world, temporary buoyancy that wouldn't withstand any more pressure before sinking. She needed to be proactive with Pickle, tell him about the man in the pet store and allow that bit of information to sink in. Pickle would dictate how much Isabel revealed and she prayed she still had the skills to read him. Her maternal instinct suddenly felt precarious and fragile.

Every so often the opportunity presented itself when Isabel could have explained to Pickle about his father, but she didn't do it. Just the other day they'd been talking about dinosaurs and somehow got on the subject of DNA and resemblances in the family. They decided Isabel looked most like Grandma even though Pickle had never met her but he'd seen photos. Pickle said he looked most like Mac. Isabel wanted to correct him, to explain it was impossible for him to look like Mac. Truth was Pickle looked a lot like Piper. Then there were those turquoise eyes, the color like no other person in the family. The man who raped Isabel had dark eyes, but when they saw him in the pet store she realized he had masked his unique eye color with dark contacts. It wasn't just the eyes, but it was the voice that day in the store that Isabel recognized and the hair on her neck stood on end before she even turned around.

Isabel had to admit if it was just Pickle and her she'd already have been gone, next flight out of the country. When she considered Mac and their new baby she knew she was kidding herself. And lately she couldn't even leave her driveway without getting stuck between the seat and the steering wheel. As horrific as this was, and it was pretty traumatic, Isabel needed to focus on a back-up plan. Piper was right. She had to be strong and do something to fight back.

Eight years ago Isabel had not fought back. She made a decision not to report the rape and then for so many years after 9/11, it became a convenience to believe he'd died in the collapse of the North tower. It was time for her to do something, but what? Her mind floated to all sorts of scenarios, ways to handle the situation in which her son would never have to be alone with the monster. Unfortunately, most of her ideas were highly illegal. Murder and kidnapping were at the top. If she ended up in jail, her son would lose his mother and the fate of her unborn baby would be out of her hands.

Piper sat forward again in the chair. "Don't do anything stupid, Isabel."

"Call me odd but allowing that monster anywhere near my son feels *stupid*. Wait until Mac finds out. Or have you already told him?" Isabel stood from the chair and it took some effort because she felt like Humpty Dumpty.

"Isabel, you need to settle down. And yes, Mac knows. I told him this morning before breakfast while you were still sleeping. He's worried about the gun too, but unfortunately it isn't illegal to have a registered gun in New York."

"Of course Mac knows. Well, that would explain his incessant chopping of fire wood all morning." Isabel knew she sounded sarcastic and had to remind herself again why she loved the relationship Piper had with her husband. "What did he say?"

"His exact words were: 'If that asshole even thinks about messing with Pickle's head I'll mess with his head before I chop the fucker's waste of grey matter clean off his shoulders!' quote unquote."

"Wow, okay, that went well." Isabel let out a nervous sort of titter. She extended her hand to help Piper from her chair.

They headed back to the house, arm in arm, tea cups in the other, not sure who was really relying on whom as they strolled up the path. They paused at the expansive front porch steps.

"So when will the first visit be, do you think?" Isabel winced as though expecting to be slapped.

"Starting next Sunday at noon, we will have to meet on the Green in Morristown."

Isabel's heart quickened in her chest and she concentrated on quelling it, but it was no use. "I can't do this alone, Piper, you'll come with me, right?" Isabel knew there was no way Mac could go with her without exacting some sort of retribution.

"I'll do my best to intervene on your behalf. In fact, on Sunday I'll bring Pickle and you can wait with Clare at the apartment in Morristown if that makes you feel better."

"Nothing short of the death of this man will make me feel better." Isabel was shocked at her own disregard for human life, even in this situation. This was not behavior she ever wanted her children to see or hear. "I appreciate the offer to stay back with Clare, but I can't keep letting you do my dirty work for me. This is my son we're talking about and I can't show Pickle that I'm afraid even if I'll be freaking out inside. As long as the baby isn't too affected by my stress levels, I can do this with you."

~~~~~~~~~~~~

It was a few evenings later and Isabel had the perfect opportunity to explain to her son how it came to be that his father was still alive. The visitation conversation needed to be had with Sunday just four days away — there was no way around it. It was a conversation Isabel hadn't looked forward to and she wished Mac could do this with her, but this was private between mother and son.

There were no details. Just lies. Isabel told her son that she did not know his father had survived 9/11. Pickle didn't have a whole bunch of questions. Just one.

"Is that the man that has a gun?" He started to cry.

PIPER

On the morning of her nephew's first visitation, Isabel was ashen and sullen and Piper feared for her unborn baby. Piper certainly understood her sister's defeated demeanor. Pickle must have overheard Isabel when she told Piper the story about the rape. He'd gotten up in the middle of the night for water and when he glanced through the landing spindles and saw his mom crying in the family room with his Aunt Piper, he huddled on the top steps and listened. There was no way for them to know how much he had heard, but it was obviously enough for him to know this man he would be spending time with had done something very bad to his mother. She explained to Piper that she tried to get him to talk to her about it; he just clammed up or cried.

Hours of worry had obviously put Isabel into a catatonic state in which she said the bare minimum of only the necessary monosyllabic words during the car ride. Piper sat in the backseat and tried to distract her nephew. It was a brief visit and Mac still didn't trust himself anywhere near the guy so he opted to hang back and allow Isabel some time with her sister and son.

"Almost there." Piper glanced out the window and tried to sound cheerful but deep down she was contemplating ways she could legally stop this encounter but aside from Isabel going into labor or Piper dropping dead, there didn't seem to be a way out. Piper was supposed to be protecting Isabel so her sister could protect her son and Piper couldn't help but feel she was falling down on the job. There would not be a last minute stay of execution; this would be seen through until the bitter end and Piper had no idea what the "after" would look like. From the backseat, she could almost hear the sound of Isabel's heart shattering bit by bit.

"I have a little something for you, Pickle Eater." Piper reached into her purse and removed the cell phone she had purchased for him.

"Is that my own cell phone?" He was elated at this, and Piper wondered if she had made a big mistake. "Mom and Mac said I couldn't have one until I hit the two digit birthday?"

Piper saw the shoulder belt holding Isabel in the driver's seat strain a bit, but her sister didn't comment and never turned back to give Piper some sort of disapproving look. Pickle meanwhile, was seemingly stretching himself to appear bigger, probably a good attitude for him to take. *Isn't that what they tell you to do when confronted by a wild animal, make yourself look bigger?* Piper thought.

"Yes." Piper held it out of his reach. "Cool out, kid. Now, listen to me, this is what you need to push to call us and we'll come running."

Piper demonstrated a call and then he demonstrated it back a few times. It never ceased to amaze her how kids these days could navigate technology as if they were born with chips already implanted in their heads. The phone slid neatly into the backpack he insisted on taking on this trip. Piper noticed a tuft of green matted hair pinched in the larger zipper, and she knew Mr. Wiggles was in there. Big boy or not, Pickle never went anywhere without Mr.

Wiggles. Piper patted it as if to reassure herself the stuffed animal would be with her nephew with the cell phone tucked away right next to it.

"You are officially a mini-man." Piper leaned down and kissed the top of his head, his wild curly hair smelled of cookie dough and No More Tears. Her nephew smiled up at her and she swelled with pride and something else entirely. Was it fear? Piper reviewed again in her head how this whole visitation would roll out. It seemed the only way she could keep her control over the situation in check. The Serenity Prayer had come to mind often throughout this mess. Control the things she can and let go of that which she cannot but most importantly, recognize the difference.

They would park by the library on the square and wait for the two-hour visit to be over. Piper knew Isabel would never leave the drop-off spot, like a mother whose child is abducted and she keeps returning to the spot where she last saw her baby. When the overnights started in weeks to come, Piper imagined Isabel camped-out in front of the monster's apartment. She'd try but it was Piper's responsibility to remind her there was something called a restraining order. Piper realized her sister didn't want to actually be in the same breathing space as the monster so for the time being, while Isabel was *with child*, Piper was able to convince the judge that it was in her client's best interest to stay close to home in case of labor. The lawyer for the monster would send a social worker to take the child from Piper's possession and deliver him to his client for at least the first few weeks. This was costly, most of which Piper's firm incurred but she didn't care. She'd somehow managed to get the judge off to the side at one of the custody hearings, as lower Manhattan courthouses had been her home for so many years, and for the first and hopefully the last time in her meager life, she pulled the *dying of a fatal disease* card. The judge was quite generous with her but Piper knew there would come a time when Isabel would have to do the drop-off without a middle man and her big sister would no longer be around to do it.

It was such an unfortunate time to be dying. Piper just needed a bit more time to see this whole thing through to its bitter end. Even if it took until her nephew was fourteen, when he would legally be allowed to decline visitation, Piper needed that closure but she knew she'd never get it. She'd be lucky to attend his birthday party in six months.

A slim non-descript woman in a poorly fitted suit and sensible shoes met them at the Famished Frog and they all shared a cup of something so Pickle could get comfortable with the social worker before he trusted the stranger enough to walk away from his mother. Piper assured Pickle that the social worker (Sally was her name) would be there in the background in case he needed anything. Piper didn't need to remind Isabel that within the next few day visits they'd have to meet the sperm donor face to face, on their own.

It wasn't long before Sally took Pickle by the hand and they walked off together to meet Pickle's biological father. Pickle was quiet and contemplative, but didn't appear frightened. It was the look he had on his first day of kindergarten. When Pickle and the woman walked past the front window of the restaurant and he peered in to give the two of them a sheepish wave, Isabel fell apart. She was sobbing so hard that the manager came over to see if they wanted a more private booth. Isabel refused to move and eventually she settled down enough that the patrons stopped staring.

"I have never felt this much pain in my entire life, not the rape, not 9/11, not the papers being served or Daddy dying. This is the worst feeling in the world. My little boy is out there somewhere with a monster, Piper! A fucking monster!"

"Shhh, Izzy, honey, calm down. They'll throw us out." Piper glanced around the room at a few skeptical eyes and knitted her brows at them in a look of *back off*. She focused back on her sister. "Listen, honey, our boy is capable of holding his own. Give yourself a little credit, woman." Piper reached across the table and took Isabel's hands in hers.

"You have raised an incredible human being and nothing bad is going to happen to him no matter where he goes. Look at how cooperative he is with this whole mess. There are kids I've met who would have a shit-fit and go kicking and screaming. Not our Pickle. He's a trooper."

"I know but that's what scares me. He's so trusting."

"I know he's just seven but he's smart, little sister." Piper squeezed her hand.

"He'll be okay, right?" Her eyes begged for Piper to say *yes*.

"He'll be right as rain." What the fuck was she saying? Piper had never used that expression before, but she recalled it just then as one her mother used even when she was unable to walk anymore. *I'm right as rain, big girl.* "I don't even know why I said that – is rain right?"

Isabel laughed at that and Piper was able to relax a bit. For two hours they sat there and Piper drank seven cups of coffee so the employees wouldn't give them dirty looks. Isabel sipped water at Piper's insistence and because Piper reminded her she was drinking for two and needed to keep hydrated. After phoning Mac and Clare as to the status of the situation, they, or rather Piper talked about all sorts of things. How she met Mac, Beaker's foul mouth, how everyone in the restaurant saw them holding hands and assumed they were both lesbians. Isabel cracked a smile a few times and Piper even got a couple of chuckles from her.

When the social worker called exactly two hours after she

escorted Pickle to the rendezvous site, Isabel cried but this time with happiness. The social worker and Pickle were on their way back to the restaurant. Everything had gone just fine. On the car ride home, Piper drove. She'd had so much caffeine she was capable of running alongside the car while steering with her arm through the driver's side window. Pickle spent the first half of the three hour trip back home telling them about *the man from the pet store* as he referred to him. Piper kept thinking of Curious George and his man in the yellow hat every time he said it and she wished Pickle's *man* was as innocuous as George's man but she knew better.

Pickle was excited to share with them a blow-by-blow description of the two hours he'd spent with the monster. It all sounded so normal. A visit to a park with swings and a three-decker slide and then a stop in an ice cream shop where Pickle was allowed to order any toppings he desired. Isabel gasped and the hair on the back of Piper's neck stood up when Pickle said he was going to meet the man's cat next visit. Cats didn't go out on leashes like dogs did, so did that mean they'd be going to the monster's apartment?

Even though Isabel was in the backseat with Pickle and they had long since fallen asleep, Piper sensed her sister's fear. Piper felt worse for Isabel than she did for Pickle. As they made their way back to Pennsylvania according to the plan, Piper glanced every so often in the rear view mirror at the two of them, heads side by side, seemingly at peace for the time being. Mac came out to the car when she pulled onto the ranch. It was as if he was waiting outside the whole time they were gone. He carried Pickle into the house and up to his room and by then Isabel and Piper were inside slumped together on the couch.

Mac returned to the room looking silly carrying Pickle's plastic

Spiderman backpack. He tossed it on the coffee table in front of them and Piper jumped.

"Whoa, cowboy!" It took some effort for Piper to reach the backpack from where she was on the couch, and she momentarily wished she *was* Spiderman. "Your son's cell phone is in there, that is, if you didn't just crack it in half." She reached into the zipped side pocket and pulled it out and examined it. Still intact.

"Pump the breaks, sister. When did this happen?" Mac sounded like he wasn't sure how he felt about this decision. "Okay, sure I get it but he is still just a kid."

"Listen, dude, get used to it." Piper threw the backpack sans cell phone back onto the table with as little exertion as humanly possible. "It was this or a gun."

Mac laughed but Piper could tell by the resigned tone that he wasn't going to object to it any further. He knew she respected him as Isabel's husband and as Pickle's dad and as far as she was concerned, he gave her plenty of leeway when decisions had to be made as of late.

"I'm going to bed. I promised Clare I'd be home before she leaves for work in the morning. Barn house open?"

"All ready for you. I guess we'll hit the hay as well." Mac stood from his seat and pulled Isabel from the couch with both hands. She fell into his arms and they hugged.

Instinctively, Isabel plucked the backpack from the table and together they walked to the foyer. She unzipped the bag and halted in the arched foyer just as she reached to give Piper a good night embrace. Something with the bag was awry.

Isabel turned, a look of horror on her face, backpack in one hand and in the other hand, a slightly mangled sunflower.

ISABEL

After a couple weeks of visitation, Piper forced Isabel to stop stalking around the drop-off site. The baby was due any day and the doctor wanted her close to home. Isabel was able to stay at the farm, but never relaxed enough to stop pacing, anticipating how the overnights would play out. She was so grateful to Piper for all she was doing for their family. Isabel knew Piper wasn't feeling well on those Sundays as her sister was forced to stop taking her opiates for those Sundays while she drove between Pennsylvania and New Jersey, but she never once complained. The judge had no issue designating her as the drop-off agent until after the baby was born – after all, Piper was Isabel's lawyer and Pickle's aunt.

One of the only things that gave Isabel joy was the amount of time Pickle was spending with his aunt. She knew it would be invaluable down the road. Her sister needed to be close to Pickle and Isabel got that; Piper believed her nephew had saved her life on 9/11. Piper was undoubtedly sharing bits of family wisdom with her nephew, and he seemed to really look forward to the times he visited her the night before he saw the monster. One evening after Pickle came back from New Jersey, his last day visit before the overnights started, he and Mac took a walk in the woods for a little man to man. Piper was napping in the barn house and Isabel began to feel a tightening around her abdomen, which she knew was a little more than Braxton-Hicks. She paced for a bit around the house and then watched out the kitchen window as the November sky darkened with thunder clouds and rain began pelting the skylights overhead. By the time Mac blew through the front door, soaking wet with a drenched and laughing Pickle up on his shoulders, Isabel's contractions were coming every three minutes.

Two hours later with Pickle and husband and sister in tow, Isabel gave blessed birth to Penelope Piper McAfee, and she was perfect in every way. Everyone that mattered in her life was there, and she believed Pickle was the most enthused about the whole scene. He had a little sister. Mac was more concerned about Isabel's well-being, but as soon as he knew she was fine, his focus was on his baby girl.

Pickle didn't appear to show any outward signs of sibling rivalry and if anything it was the opposite. He insisted on giving his baby sister every toy he didn't play with anymore. Isabel walked into the nursery on different occasions to find Mr. Wiggles or Buzz Lightyear guarding her crib. On Penelope's shelf Isabel discovered stacks of books Pickle deemed babyish.

In those first several days post-partum, Isabel made every effort to spend all her time with Pickle while Penelope slept; even if Pickle had somehow seemingly right before her eyes, had become a much larger boy. While Isabel spent that first week healing from the delivery, she tried to be as upbeat as possible all-the-while crowding-out fears of Pickle's impending first overnight that was set for the following Sunday.

Time seemed to fly by and before they knew it, it was Saturday and Piper was on her way to pick up Pickle. While they sat outside on the porch swing in the crisp November air waiting with a small packed bag for his aunt to pull up the drive, Isabel's son surprised her.

"The man from the pet store wants me to call him 'father', but I don't want to because he won't call me Pickle."

Isabel swallowed past a lump rising in her throat. "What does he call you?"

"*Son* or sometimes *Junior*." Pickle sounded so matter-of-fact. Isabel envied his strength.

"Well of course you don't have to call him *father* if you don't want to— I get that." Isabel brushed his soft, blond locks of hair from his forehead. "What *do* you call him?"

"Mister."

His answer made Isabel smile. This man would never be her son's father, that much was certain. After Piper left with Pickle, Isabel wept. She had believed she was mentally prepared to handle the overnights, but it didn't take long for her to realize she had been kidding herself. That night after Mac fell asleep and after Isabel breastfed Penelope and put her in the basinet, she found herself in Pickle's bed. Half the night she spent trying not to have a complete meltdown and the rest of the night Isabel stared at all the simple items around Pickle's room that defined him. His snow globe collection, his Lego creations he refused to take apart once they were erected, an entire wall covered in pictures taken at all sorts of fun places including Isabel's favorite and most recent one of Pickle riding Jigsaw. She was amazed at how old he appeared in that shot taken a few weeks back. He was nearing eight and yet her heart ached at how much he was still her little boy and always would be.

She finally fell asleep around four. Mac must have come in and found her in Pickle's room sometime after that because when she woke up with the sun streaming through the sheer blue curtains, she noticed Mac sound asleep on Piper's camouflage-print beanbag chair.

"Morning, babe." Isabel whispered in his ear and he roused.

"Baby okay? Pickle?" He startled then grabbed her by the shoulders. "Sorry, love." He gently released his grip.

Isabel hated how paranoid Mac had become. It took years for him to get past the tragic loss of his best friend and his many co-workers, but the pain seemed to morph into the need to overprotect. Mac was on guard every moment of the day, even when he was asleep.

"Penelope's still asleep, I fed her at two and then came and crashed in here because I didn't want to wake you, but I guess I did anyway. Sorry."

"You're worried about Pickle aren't you?" He smacked himself in the forehead with this palm. "Duh! Of course you're worried. Jesus, what's wrong with me? Half asleep still, I guess. I'm worried too."

"Stop taking all this on, Mac. I know you love Pickle and I know you wish he never met his father but we have to deal with this together. I am holding up as best as I can because you're here to support me. Piper is being such an amazing help by taking Pickle to all his visitations, but it won't be forever. I know that."

"It's a great thing she's doing for us, sick and all but at some point she won't be able to drive." He hit his forehead again when he saw Isabel's melancholic expression fade. "I'm sorry, babe, it's just that I am not sure I can ever come face to face with the guy. I've got two kids to worry about and would be honored to eliminate this asshole from the world's population." Mac stood and stretched his back.

"I know we've all thought of killing him but the truth remains; we have to think about the long run – this will be over in a few years when the law says Pickle will be old enough to emancipate himself from the man. Until then, I just pray to God or whoever will listen not to let the man break my son's spirit. Not mess with Pickle's head, is that too much to ask?"

Mac groaned as he walked out of Pickle's room, a sound one might make just before plunging into ice water. He turned at the door and rubbed the stubble on his chin and spoke in an eerily calm tone. "Pickle and I have an agreement. If the man steps out of line one inch I'm going to get involved and the prick will wish he died on 9/11."

PIPER

It was Piper's third trip in the past six weeks into the city to drop Pickle off for his overnight. They talked. Often they talked. She was well aware that she was trying to make him into a man before his time but she didn't give a shit. Her nephew was going to be able to defend himself.

Every other weekend Piper and her nephew had a little routine. She picked him up from the farm on Friday night, and he stayed with Clare and Piper until Saturday at noon at which time Piper dropped him off in Tribeca across the street from the monster's apartment. Of course, when they made the first trip there Piper made note of where it was located but Isabel said it was nowhere near the apartment where she was raped. Piper had to wonder if the bastard still went around renting torture chambers throughout the city.

Clare also spent time with Pickle while Piper rested – the weekend without pain medication exhausted her, but Piper didn't want to risk having brain fog when she was with her nephew, especially driving in the city. Isabel was still breastfeeding Penelope and Piper knew her sister didn't have the fortitude or strength to make the trip. How much longer Piper would even be driving was anyone's guess, but her bouts of pain and fatigue were coming so frequently that she prepared Clare for the reality she may have to drive Pickle soon. Piper would do this for Isabel and Pickle until the day she died even if she had to hire an ambulance. She couldn't help but smile. If she hired an ambulance she knew one little boy who would get a huge kick out of the sirens and lights.

As usual, when they headed into the city, Pickle had his backpack which Piper knew held Mr. Wiggles and the cell phone. He had recently lost his front teeth and, when she glanced back at him in the rearview mirror at the gap, Piper grimaced because she knew she'd probably be gone when those Chiclet-size teeth filled his smile for good. About ten minutes outside the Holland Tunnel, Piper noticed her nephew had been a bit quiet this trip.

"Hey mini-man, what ya' thinking about?"

"Nothing." He sounded so distant.

Piper knew he didn't want to have to go on these overnights. Why would he want to leave the ranch and Jigsaw and Beaker and everything that was familiar? And he was acting like such a trooper, but something was wrong and he wasn't able to hide it.

"What do you mean you're not thinking anything? Of course you are; your brain doesn't stop thinking even when you're asleep. You can talk to me Pickle. What's up?" Piper turned in her seat at the next stop light and saw his eyes were teary. They neared the tunnel and Piper needed to pull over. Doing this in Jersey City was never a good idea but Piper didn't care. She veered into a seedy vacant lot. Assuming it wasn't a good idea to get out here even in broad daylight, Piper climbed over the front seat and settled in next to her nephew.

"Aunt Piper, what are you doing?" He giggled when Piper rolled over the seat to sit next to him, but when his eyes squeezed together the tears welling in his eyes streamed down his face and he quickly swiped them away. "I'm not crying. I have a cold."

Piper took him in her arms. "Listen kiddo, you can't kid a

kidder." She handed him a tissue. "You can talk to me. What's wrong?" Somehow she knew this was not going to go well and she was grateful for only one thing; that Isabel was at the ranch with Mac and wasn't here to witness whatever was upsetting her beautiful innocent little boy.

"What is Lebanese?" He looked at her wide-eyed, uncertain.

"What? Well, people from Lebanon are called Lebanese. Lebanon is in Asia. Why, Pickle?"

"Because the man from the pet store said you were Lebanese, and you shouldn't be allowed to come near me. What's wrong about being Lebanese?"

"Oh, sweetie." Piper pulled him closer. "There's nothing wrong with being Lebanese. I am sure he is just upset because I was one of the people who fought him in court, that's all." She had no idea how to respond to her nephew. She was sure her sister had never explained her relationship with Clare to her son. He wasn't even eight at this point and she was waiting until he was old enough to ask questions about sex. He'd learn that there were many different kinds of love between two people.

"I don't want to go to the man in the pet store's house anymore, Aunt Piper."

"I know, I know, honey, it's not a great situation right now but soon enough, like just a few years from now you'll be old enough to decide if and when you go to visit with the man."

"I'm old enough now. I'm allowed to have a cell phone." He reached for his backpack as if that would prove he was grown up. Then he stopped short of unzipping the bag and looked at her. "I don't like him, he's mean."

"I know this is not great but until we can figure something else out you have to just be a strong man and deal with this. It's just two nights a month – easy-peasy." Piper took his two hands in hers.

"You can call me any time you need to, day or night, got it? Anytime." She kissed him on his damp cheek and started to climb back over the seat, not easy in a sports car while dying.

"Do I still have to drink the pink stuff?"

"What pink stuff?" Piper rolled back to the spot next to him and took his chin in her hand. "What pink stuff, Pickle?" A wave of nausea pushed up in her throat.

"The man from the pet store makes me drink this gross juice and it makes me really sleepy."

"He does what?" Piper realized her voice was escalating. Her heart was racing and breaking all at once. "Okay, okay, sweetie, tell me when he has you drink this stuff."

"At night when it is time for my sleepover." He sighed and she heard his breath catch. "I don't remember going to bed, but then I wake up in the morning in a bed. He says it's vitamins and if I don't drink it, I will stop growing."

"He's wrong, Pickle!" Piper reminded herself again to calm down. "Do not drink the stuff again do you hear me?" She felt the heat rise up her neck and into her cheeks.

"He'll get mad at me, Aunt Piper."

"I don't give a sh …" She stopped herself. "Oops, I almost said a bad word, didn't I? Okay, how about this? Instead of drinking this pink stuff, just pour it out and pretend you drank it. Then fake sleeping, you know how to do that don't you?"

His head flopped to the side and he closed his eyes. Then he perked up seemingly content with this performance. "Like that?"

"That's exactly what I mean." She squeezed his knee and climbed with much effort back into the front seat. "You'll be fine and I will be back tomorrow with Mommy to pick you up. We can talk about this then, too. Mommy will want to know."

When Piper started to drive again, she had tears rolling down her cheeks. Isabel was going to lose her shit and Piper needed a plan. Think, she demanded of herself! That son of a bitch was up to something and she knew whatever it was, it was not in her nephew's best interest. Piper was so tempted to turn the car around, to say Pickle wasn't feeling well and cancel. She knew if he didn't go she'd have to contact the social worker and explain her actions. At the next gas station, Piper pulled into the lot and parked leaving the motor running. She called the social worker, prepared to leave a detailed message but the woman answered on the third ring. It didn't surprise Piper that this woman didn't have a life on weekends.

Piper told her what her nephew had just shared and gave her only the details he used so she didn't scare him with the sense of panic she was experiencing just then. She put extra emphasis in her voice when she urged the woman to please intervene before she dropped Pickle off.

"I understand your concerns, but it is not a good idea to violate this court order. Even if he is sick, his father can take care of him – he still has to go. Otherwise, you'll land in deep trouble with the judge." She cleared her throat. "Ms. Henry, are you speaking in front of the child? Because, if so, you are putting negative ideas in his head about his father and that is a very bad idea on many levels."

"The guy is drugging my nephew so don't give me that good idea bad idea bullshit! I need to intervene." Piper couldn't believe what she was hearing. "It's your frigging job to protect the child, isn't it?"

"You need to calm down, Ms. Henry. I am sure it's just Pepto-Bismol, perhaps he had a stomach ache."

"It's not a stomach ache! What, every time he visits this man he has a stomach ache? That, in and of itself if it were true, is reason enough he shouldn't have to do overnights. But it's not the case, the bastard is drugging the kid. The drink makes him fall asleep. We both know Pepto-Bismol doesn't do that."

Piper turned to the back seat. "Pickle, did you have a stomach ache and then the man gave you the pink stuff?"

"No."

She could tell he was scared.

"If I have a tummy ache then I don't have to go? I can pretend I have a stomach ache just like I can pretend to drink the medicine like you said, Aunt Piper."

"Shit." Piper knew her nephew would point out the curse words. They could survive a plane crash and her nephew would remember every bad word his aunt said. "Hold on sweetie, let me finish my conversation with the nice lady."

"Ms. Henry, this is all very unethical. You are well aware of Mr. Stossel's rights and by coaching your nephew to lie to his father is grounds for the man to get a court order against you. If Isabel Henry wants to reopen the case because she believes her son is being mistreated she has every right to do that, but meanwhile if Peter does not show up at seven tonight for his overnight you will be in deep trouble not to mention in violation of the law."

"Blah, blah, blah, don't you dare quote the fucking law to me." Piper wanted to stay professional but it was impossible. "He'll have his visitation tonight but mark my words you worthless, uptight bitch, my client and I will be returning to court Monday morning and filing an emergent hearing because I can guarantee you I have grounds to prove negligence and child endangerment. If anything happens to my nephew in the meantime, you will be out looking for a fucking job by Tuesday afternoon. Good day." Piper snapped her cell phone shut nearly forgetting Pickle was still in the car. She glanced in the rearview mirror and he looked at her, his green eyes wide.

"Aunt Piper, you said bad words." He whispered.

"I did, didn't I?"

"Do I still have to go?" It was not a question. The poor child was resigned to the inevitable fate of his evening.

ISABEL

It was torture waiting to hear from Piper every time she handled the drop-off for Isabel. Isabel feared she'd fall to pieces with the overnights. It was visceral, her reaction to the overnights. Sure, her obstetrician was very concerned about the stress even after Penelope was born and had advised Isabel to let Piper take care of those visitation issues until she was at least six weeks post-partum. It was past six weeks after giving birth but the truth was Isabel had palpitations when she thought about her little boy with the monster. When she tried to mentally prepare herself for what the future was going to look like she felt gut-punched. The idea that she may not have her sister was tough enough, but the thought of not having Pickle with them on a Christmas morning or at a Thanksgiving dinner was devastating.

It was Pickle's fourth overnight and up until that evening nothing had been amiss. The past two months, every time Piper did the hand-off, she called Isabel. When the clock rolled around to six that night and she still hadn't heard from Piper, she went into a slight panic. Mac was out with the horses and Isabel didn't want to get him upset as well so she waited another fifteen minutes and tried her cell phone again.

"Hello." Piper finally answered and Isabel was relieved.

"How'd it go?"

"It was fine, just like before." Piper's voice was low and without energy.

"What's wrong?"

"Nothing, just really tired and not feeling so great but don't get all bent out of shape. Okay?"

Isabel could tell Piper wasn't being completely honest with her, but her sister was such a strong-willed woman that Isabel figured if things got to be too much for Piper she'd let Isabel know. Or at least Isabel hoped she would.

"Why don't you rest tomorrow and Mac and I will drive into the city and pick up Pickle." Isabel surprised herself by considering this – she being a frightened mess and Mac all hot-headed about the situation. But Isabel knew her sister needed a break. She could hear it in Piper's voice – she was fading. Piper constantly reassured Isabel that she loved the one-on-one time she was spending with Pickle before Piper was too sick to enjoy it anymore. Isabel got that but it had to be taking its toll on her.

"I may take you guys up on that. Why don't you come a little early and have lunch with Clare and me before you head into the city. Break the day up a bit so you're not so anxious."

"Sounds like a plan. Pickle will be so excited that Penelope is there with Mac and me to pick him up."

After hanging up from the call Isabel made herself a cup of chamomile tea in the hopes it would help her sleep better. It was as if a little bit of her slipped away each time she was separated from her son. Isabel had never been fazed when he had overnights with Piper and Clare. They loved him nearly as much as Isabel did. When he spent time with the monster Isabel knew he was with someone who couldn't possibly love him. The man wasn't capable of love and was only taking possession of something he believed was rightfully his, like a piece of real estate.

"Who was on the phone?" Mac came into the kitchen and took one look at Isabel's face and went to her side. "No, don't tell me – of course, it was Piper. Everything go smooth with the drop off?"

"Everything went okay." Isabel turned toward Mac and they hugged. He released her to arms-length and gazed down at her with concern. "Mac, I'm so sick of feeling sorry for myself. I need to grow a set of ovaries and take charge of my own life. If not for anything else, for my son."

Mac nodded and gestured to the stools so they'd sit. "I'm here for you no matter what."

"I know, but here's the thing, Mac, all along you've been here for me and Piper's been here for me but I have not been here for me. I need to take responsibility for what is happening here and make the best of it." Isabel couldn't help but look away from his warm blue eyes. "I have been behaving like a coward. It's two sleepovers a month, I should be strong enough to handle that if Pickle can handle it. I mean, Mac, think about it, there are thousands of moms out there who must bear the pain of losing their children and here I am running the other way as soon as my son faces independence."

Isabel needed to stop running and embrace the situation at hand. It wasn't ideal but Pickle was her son and she knew deep down that not taking him for the visits had to make her son wonder. Isabel was showing him that she was afraid and therefore he too should be scared. This was wrong on so many levels.

"You're not a coward, Izzy, you're the bravest woman I know."

"No, Mac, you're wrong. I've been letting my dying sister handle my affairs and that's just down-right cruel. I'm probably killing her faster with all this stress. See, I worry about Pickle, and Piper has to worry about both of us."

"That's true – she even worries about me." Mac smiled at

Isabel. "She's that damn good, our Pipes, isn't she?" He took Isabel's hands in his. "But don't you ever underestimate the amazing woman you are – a person could open a thousand oysters and never find a pearl – I found my pearl."

"Awww, you are so sweet." Isabel squeezed his hands before standing. "I mean it when I say that I will be taking Pickle to his drop-offs from now on. Penelope is almost two months so I am out of that post-partum period, heck, I'm even allowed to have sex again!" Isabel clamped her hand over her mouth feigning embarrassment. Mac reached for her.

"Speaking of sex." He stood and lifted her into his arms and carried her up to their bedroom. After they peaked in and admired their beautiful sleeping baby girl, they fell into their bed and made love for the first time since Isabel had given birth. Afterwards, they lay in bed wrapped in each other's arms and talked until they fell asleep a few hours later.

When they had lunch with Piper the following day Isabel would tell her that from then on she would do the driving and the drop-off. Piper would understand and Isabel knew she'd also want to make the trip with her into the city for as long as she was well enough to do so. The truth was she needed to do this with Isabel because Pickle was a part of her as well. When the social worker was sure it was in Pickle's best interest to eliminate the lawyer as middle man and have a direct drop-off and pick-up with the monster, Isabel would be very grateful to have Piper with her. Mac, on the other hand would be a challenge to keep calm. As difficult as all of this was, Isabel had never felt so loved by her family in all her life.

~~~~~~~~~~~~~

Isabel was startled awake by a noise and at first she thought

Penelope had awoken. But it was her cell phone vibrating on the dresser where it was charging. The clock read 3:15 a.m. and Isabel couldn't imagine who would be calling at this hour. Isabel jumped from the bed to answer it and panicked when she saw Clare's number on the caller ID. Was Clare calling because Piper's illness had taken a turn for the worse? Isabel prayed with every ounce of faith she had in her that Piper was okay.

PIPER

After getting back to Morristown, Piper didn't waste any time starting on the emergent briefing for court. No way could she tell her sister over the phone what Pickle had shared with her. Piper was still trying to process it and not succeeding. She swiveled methodically in her father's old leather chair at the mahogany desk – the only items she wanted when the homestead sold. Piper wished she could go back to a day when she'd sat in Dad's chair and her feet didn't reach the ground, when he'd take the back of the chair and spin her until she got delightfully giddy and dizzy.

Her dad had been so proud when Piper passed the bar exam so he willed his oldest daughter his chair and desk right then and there. Piper was grateful her father wasn't around to see her demise. Slowly giving up most of her connection with the legal system had not come easy. She did a few consultations with friends but only for advice, not representation and at no charge. Isabel no longer worked in the law office, so Piper had farmed out most of her clients to other lawyers in the area. Piper's only real case boiled down to her sister versus the rapist.

Right after she dropped Pickle off, Piper called Clare. She explained the whole story to her and it surprised Piper how upset Clare got. She'd never heard Clare so adamant. If Piper hadn't understood and come to love Clare's passionate, hot-headed Brazilian moments, Piper would've been stung by her reaction.

"Are you out of your mind? Something is better than nothing!" She had shouted at Piper and Piper wasn't sure what Clare even meant by that.

As far as Piper was concerned, even if Clare didn't have a clue that most people didn't understand what she was going on about when she was passionate but Clare's reaction to Isabel's rapist being a part of their lives was certainly justified. They spent much of the time Pickle spent with the man, hashing and rehashing the implications of the poor child spending a single minute with the scum who raped Isabel. They were also well-aware of their lack of power in this visitation situation, there was nothing they could have done to stop what was happening without an emergent court order. If at any point Isabel withheld visitation without court consent, she'd lose more ground and maybe more time with Pickle. The best thing Mac and Isabel had done was teach Pickle, over the course of the past few months, how to behave and how to protect himself. Unfortunately, the drugging of her nephew went beyond any form of protection.

"We should have just run off with him, kept him from that animal! Now what Piper? You lawyers with your bright legal ideas, what do you have up your sleeve now? Let me deal with him. I'll take care of things before they go to court. Save everyone much time and dollars. Just say the word and I'll put the bastard out of his misery and leave the country. What will they do? Better yet, I'll just take Pickle far away, okay maybe Brazil with no forwarding address."

"For starters, they'd find you, silly. You're way too beautiful not to stand out to every man who's within a mile of you. Hello? Look at you, you're a walking orgasm." Piper paused and narrowed her gaze at Clare. "And don't you dare get any crazy ideas about running off to South America with my nephew, woman, I mean it! That's not to say the kid wouldn't love it, but just don't do anything extreme. If you do you better take me with you."

After Clare went to bed, Piper began to wonder if *she* should've run off with Pickle. Done something to save him? She could have just started driving and not looked back. Somehow, she would cryptically contact Isabel and when the dust settled Pickle could return under a different name. Piper knew she wasn't in her right mind so she decided to put her energy into working on Isabel's case. For the next few hours she scoured through stacks of used legal pads with every person involved in the law that may owe her a favor. The Internet made it easy to find people and if it wasn't midnight, she'd have made some calls. Lost in thought, she failed to hear the patter of bare-feet on the hardwood and was startled when Clare ever-so-gently tapped on the wall of the office.

"Sorry, I didn't mean to frighten you." Her sleepy accent was heavy. "What're you doing?"

"Sorry, I hope I didn't wake you. I couldn't sleep so I decided to get this work done while it was still fresh in my mind, not that I'd ever forget the look on his little face when I dropped him off. It was a combination of bravery and fear. I need to have this ready in less than thirty-six hours. I know, I'm whining."

"Can I make you some tea?"

Clare was so good to Piper. "No, I'm fine. I have water. I love you though." Piper smiled at her and felt her cheeks flush.

"Awww, love you too."

Piper could tell Clare was still a bit upset about everything. Like her, she wasn't sleeping well.

"Come up soon, okay?" Clare waved from the door.

"Just a bit more. Promise."

When the clock struck three in the morning Piper called it a night. Her brain hurt, not as much a headache as a pulled muscle if that was even possible. At this point she was doing more harm than good to her editing of the documents. It was best for her to abandon this for the night and wrap it up when she woke up. Piper reached in the side pouch of her leather satchel and took out the pill bottle that held her pain medication and swallowed down two Oxycontin. She wasn't sure if her sister's plight was keeping her energy level up but she had felt fairly normal over the past few weeks. The stress should have rendered her incapacitated but quite the contrary, she got a second wind. Her hope beyond hope was that she didn't have a set-back before she was able to see this mess through until its ending. Just as she shut down the computer and headed down the hall, off to bed, her cell phone vibrated.

"This can't be good," Piper said aloud to no one as she looked at the screen to see who was calling but already somehow knew. She answered, aware of her heart rate revving and the sheen of sweat bleeding on her skin. "What's wrong honey?" She did her best to keep calm.

"Come for me, you said you would. I'm scared, Aunt Piper. What should I do?" His voice quavered and Piper did everything she could not to force herself like sausage through the tiny holes in his phone's receiver.

"Okay, Pickle, calm down and talk to me. Take a deep breath. Did you pretend like we said?" Piper needed to get herself in check. She heard a long sigh.

"I took a big breath but I don't feel better, Aunt Piper. How long does that take? And how long till you get here?" She pressed the record button on her cell phone.

Piper gripped the hall table and the legs let out an eerie screech as it shifted a few inches. She saw her car keys in the decorative ceramic bowl that nearly slid to the floor before she caught it.

"You're doing great. Keep taking nice calm breaths and tell me what's going on." Piper felt lightheaded and retreated to the nearest chair in the dining room. "Start at the beginning. Where is the man from the pet store?" She hated that nickname. He didn't deserve a label suitable for a Disney character.

"I pretended just like you said. It was so easy even though I was a little scared he would figure out that I poured the pink stuff down the chair cushion. Then the man from the pet store went somewhere. I'm scared for him to come back." He was whimpering. He was just a little boy barely out of footie pajamas and bedtime stories.

"You are so brave little man. I'm coming for you, dude, don't you worry. I'm on my way. You just sit tight and keep the phone with you at all times. When I get there you have to let me in, okay. Can you do that, let me in and give me a major-league hug?"

"Yes, Aunt Piper, please stay on the phone with me, please don't hang up. Can I call my mommy? I didn't call her because you said to call you because you're nearer. I didn't want to wake up Penelope. Please hurry. Are you hurrying?"

Piper's heart broke with each *please*. "I'll call Mommy but you'll need to wait while I do that. Don't hang up and don't be frightened because I'm not going anywhere but driving to you for the next hour. I'm just putting the phone on my lap."

"No, wait Aunt Piper, don't put the phone down yet. An hour you said? That's too long! You have to come faster! You have to!" Pickle was full-out crying and she could hear hiccups, he had slipped into panic mode and she had to bring him back if they were going to be successful.

"Really it's less than an hour, love – see, the time is going fast. But remember I explained about the phone battery? We may not be able to stay on the phone the whole time, we don't want to run out of bars, remember? Check your bars, how many?" Piper waited knowing his phone was charged.

"Three bars. That's great right?"

"Yes, perfect." Now, just stay put, do you understand – I need you to be super cool. I'm going to put the phone in my pocket but if you yell I can hear you. I need to get Aunt Clare, she'll come with me." Three bars wasn't great but she didn't want him to be frightened further. Clare would have to drive her; her meds had just started to kick in. "And Mommy too, I'm going to call Mommy as soon as we get in the car."

Piper wanted nothing more at that moment than to hug her nephew, rescue her sister's son. She slid the phone gingerly into her jacket pocket and woke Clare who was out of bed, record time. They threw on clothes, grabbed their handbags and headed out to the parking garage. On the way out of the apartment Clare finally spoke.

"Did you call the police?"

Piper didn't have much time to prep for the scene that would play out in the next hour. While she was preparing the emergent briefing a few hours earlier she ran through her reaction if Pickle did indeed call her at some point. She dreaded a call where he might want to come home for no good reason other than he didn't want to be there; excuses like he was uncomfortable or was made to eat his vegetables. Piper planned a response in the event he tried this but nothing could have prepared her for this phone call, the quavering little voice cowering in a dark corner somewhere in a city of seventeen million strangers.

"I didn't call the police yet. I want to be there before they come. Besides, what if the monster comes home before the police get there and we blow this opportunity to actually bust the guy. I need this to nail the fucker! The case worker already thinks I am influencing Pickle against his father. I think I may have called her *an incompetent bitch* on the phone before I dropped Pickle off last night so she's not on Team Piper at the moment."

"Tsk, tsk … I know Piper, you don't want to do anything that could make things worse."

Piper sucked in breath for a defensive spiel but she cut her off.

"I'm frightened for him, Piper."

"He'll be okay. Remember, Clare, the social workers have no idea about the rape or the mind games Stossel plays – how could they? I have to get in there and get the evidence I need to slam the door shut on this sexual predator. I need to prove neglect and abandonment and I need to do it behind the scenes without the monster knowing. If the police are called in before I get there I won't be able to get proof and from what I already know of Stossel he somehow has the uncanny ability to get away with things. He's rich and savvy, so I have to be one step ahead of him. I'm calling the shots on this one, Clare. I haven't even called Izzy yet." Piper waited for Clare to acknowledge her rationale but all she said was that she had to trust her – that if anyone understood the judicial system it was Piper.

"I mean think about it Clare, if I could go back and bust her rapist without involving the police who didn't seem to make a difference anyway, would I do it?"

"I would have gotten my Uncle Pablo and his brothers to come and fit the man for a pair of cement shoes after they cut his dick off."

It was something that would never go away nor would it ever be resolved for Isabel, but that didn't mean Piper couldn't at least do something to keep the man from permanently traumatizing Pickle even if it meant putting her own life on the line.

Piper brought along her digital camera and some evidence bags she nicked from a crime scene class she'd participated in years ago. She knew any evidence she collected wouldn't hold up in court, but she at least needed to know what Stossel was putting in that pink drink and she would keep the specimen as clean as possible. Piper was also going to take a look around the apartment and try and collect any information that she could squirrel away for her emergent case. She wasn't sure what she was looking for but she would know it if she saw it.

Right now the goal was to catch the rapist out of the house and prove that her nephew was left alone. Pickle was barely eight and the monster may believe that was old enough to be left alone for a little while and sure, some experts might agree. Then why drug the kid? Piper needed to get to the bottom of this guy's psyche and the best way to that was a sneak preemptive attack. She also had the case worker's phone number and as soon as she got Pickle to safety, she'd contact her and of course Piper would gloat. If Piper called before they got there, the social worker would likely accuse her of trying to cause issues just like she did when Piper spoke with her the previous night. Piper didn't want to leave Social Worker Sally or the police alone with Pickle where they could twist his story. *Oh it was just a stomach ache medicine* or *His dad just ran out to the all night drug store because of his stomach ache.* No way would the monster get to explain these behaviors away, not on Piper's watch.

Driving along Route 80 Piper took the phone from her pocket.

"You still there, Captain Underpants?" Please still be there Piper begged to no one in particular and everyone all at once.

"I'm here Aunt Piper, and don't call me Captain Underpants, silly."

She sensed there may have been a smile in his tone, but then it was gone as quickly as it came.

"I like being able to hear you and Clare talking so don't hang up, okay? Are you going to be here soon? I'm kind of scared." Panic seeped back into his tone.

"We'll be there in like forty-five minutes and I don't care if he's there or not, you're coming home with us. Listen to me, stinker -boy, I'm sure we'll get there before him because we're the good guys, remember? Besides, Aunt Clare's driving like she's in Grand Theft Auto." A game he was too young to play but seemed to know all about it from the kids on his school bus. This time Piper heard a giggle, a sweet little sound of joy. She had to admit she was flying by the seat of her pants and she'd never wished time away so fervently in her life. There was hope.

Only after she made the executive decision to go pick up Pickle had it dawned on her what was happening. The man had tried to drug her nephew so he could go clubbing or some much more sinister activity. Rape women then use Pickle as an alibi, how convenient. Piper realized the legal chunk of her brain was at full-throttle, but anything was possible with this man sick with insanity. She was still trying to come to terms with his leaving Pickle all alone in the craziest city in the world. The monster had the audacity to attempt to sedate *his own son*, though she hated that reference as much as Isabel at that point. This man put thousands of dollars on the line so he could spend time with *his son*. Meanwhile, he goes out and does who knows what. It made no difference that Pickle was alone in a New York City high-rise with a sociopath. "Pickle, I'm going to put the phone back in my pocket, but I'm not hanging up. I can hear you if you yell."

"I'll wait but please hurry."

"You're doing awesome, kiddo!" Piper's brow ached from trying to hold back tears, but she could still feel them prickling her eyes. Piper looked over at Clare who stared straight ahead out the windshield with both hands planted firmly at ten and two. She was on a mission.

"I am so grateful you're driving me to do this," Piper said. Clare had been there with Piper since she first started her law career in New York City, back in the mid-nineties. They'd been employed in the city during the first World's Trade Center attack and they'd been spared in the second, a far more devastating attack. They'd shared so much and it didn't hurt that Clare was a natural with the kids. Pickle adored her and Penelope fell asleep without fuss when she was in Aunt Clare's arms. Even newborn babies saw how beautiful and warm Clare was. When Piper and Clare walked through the city together, people smiled and stepped aside as though Clare were royalty, admired from afar in the same way one would a brilliant sunset or a sleek panther.

"Are you kidding," Clare whispered. "I want to help you in whatever way I can, I don't necessarily agree with not calling the police, but I am sure there is a method to your madness and besides, you're the lawyer assigned to the custody case. I can't say my thoughts have been all that pure tonight, Piper. I want all of us to runaway, go to Brazil and never look back. If Mac doesn't want to go we'll kidnap him. I have another uncle who can get us new identities." Clare turned for a second and smiled at Piper then resumed her attention to the driving.

In spite of everything that had happened, and was still happening, Piper had to laugh. Clare was serious and Piper loved her so much for that. Piper was scared, too, no question about it. She was embarking on a new journey and with no clear idea of the outcome.

"My plan is to go into the apartment and get Pickle out of there and safe with you here in the car. I need you to take him back to Morristown, basically hang with him like you always do until Izzy gets there. In fact, I probably should call her now." Piper reached across the seat and touched Clare's thigh. "I couldn't do this without you, ya' know. Meanwhile, I'll go straight to the nearest police station and file a child endangerment charge, not to mention several other major violations of the custody agreement." A stray strand of hair danced about Clare's face and Piper tucked it behind her delicate ear. "I hate to have to call Izzy."

Clare performed the sign of the cross and as if reading Piper's mind, she handed Piper her cell phone and Piper dialed Isabel.

ISABEL

When Isabel answered the phone and heard her sister's voice a relief washed over her. It took a second for her to register that if it wasn't Piper having a middle of the night emergency then it had to be either Clare or Pickle. Piper didn't waste time with the details – she was whispering and went straight to the point.

"Just listen, Izzy, I'm whispering because Pickle is live on my cell phone in my pocket waiting for me to pick him up. I guess the monster left him alone.

"Oh god, Piper, our boy's going to be okay isn't he?"

"Of course he will be fine because I will be picking him up in the next fifteen minutes but you need to relax."

"When did this happen? I'm so glad he called you. I owe you my life."

"Cool out, Izzy, he'll be fine but hold off on the Medal of Honor until I have him out of that house of horrors and back to his mom." Piper's voice seemed to escalate. "We're almost there, gotta jet, Izzy."

"Okay, okay. Call me the minute he's out of the building. We're going to your apartment. Thank you, Piper, I love you. Please text me when everyone is safe."

"I will and then I am planning to involve the police so I may

265

need to come into the city at some point in the morning. I'll keep you posted. Love you too, Izzy."

Seconds became minutes and minutes seemed like hours of sheer terror. The trauma of being helpless was worse than anything Isabel had ever experienced before.

Mac drove at warp speed to Piper's apartment, disregarding the traffic signals. He had his flashers from his days as a fireman, but luckily there were few people on the road at that hour. Isabel sat next to Penelope in the backseat as the baby slept in her car-seat. It allowed Isabel to put all her focus on the cell phone, gripping it in her palm and willing it to ring. Piper had said they were fifteen minutes away from rescuing her son and after twenty-five minutes passed Isabel began to panic.

"Ring damn it!"

"I'm sure they're okay."

"Oh god, Mac, you can't know that! If Piper was okay she'd call." Isabel needed to settle down or she'd wake Penelope. The baby didn't stir and Isabel was grateful for this one small blessing; a child should never have to witness her mother falling apart at the seams.

"Sweetie – I promise you; your son will be fine. You need to calm down or you'll be no good to anyone. There will be some issues to deal with after Pickle comes home and that is what you need to focus on." Mac was a rock.

"My brain can't even go there yet." Isabel tried to stop the tears but they betrayed her. "This is all my fault, Mac. I should have been the one to pick Pickle up, sure I know my sister's closer and could get to him faster than me but c'mon. If I hadn't been such a baby about the drop-off my sister would have never been involved in this mess. She's sick, Mac, or more to the point, she's dying and I am so selfish." Isabel tried stifling her sobs so as to not wake the baby, but it was like she was being suffocated. She realized then that the not-knowing was the worst thing to ever get through. Even if the news was grave at least she would know. The waiting game was torture.

PIPER

After what seemed like hours of checking back in with Pickle, *so far so good*, Piper thought. The impossibility at hand was finding a parking space, especially in the wee hours of a Sunday morning in New York City. Clare double-parked and Piper turned and touched her cheek.

"It's that time." Piper leaned in and kissed her then got serious. "You'll never find a spot so take a trip around the block, I'm gonna send him out and then gather some evidence."

"No, why? Just get out of there." Clare was shaking her head. "You come out with him, no?"

"I told you what I need to do. It'll take me just a few minutes, trust me, it's the only way to get this guy out of Pickle's life."

Piper spoke into her phone. "I'm here, love."

For the first time since they left Morristown, Pickle didn't answer. Piper had no clue what she was walking into. Her only choice was to ring the buzzer and hope Pickle knew how to answer the intercom. They had one in his grandpa's house, and he should be waiting by the door anyway. That is if he was still alone. If she didn't get an answer, she'd call the police. Had she been out of her league? Should she have called the police?

Piper rationalized that once Pickle got out of there, she really didn't care if the monster came back and found her in his apartment and killed her. Her ultimate mission would be over and he'd go to jail for murder. Piper gave Clare a peck on the cheek and without another word from either of them, Piper exited the car.

She stood outside the brownstone at the buzzer board and waited for an answer for what seemed like eons before trying the cell phone again.

Before she could tap send, a tiny voice asked, "Is that you, Aunt Piper?"

"Yes it is, love, now push the button by the front door." *Thank god*, Piper thought. She breathed deep. A second later the obnoxious sound of a security buzzer crackled into the night. "I'm in. Open the front door."

Piper took steps three at a time and had to stop at each landing to catch her breath. At the massive double doors she waited for Pickle to figure out the locks. Several clicks later the door opened and there was Pickle, eyes rimmed in red and looking so pale and small she did everything she could do not to fall to her knees and breakdown in sobs. A panel next to the door beeped and she recognized the error message. If someone didn't contact the security company in five minutes, the police would come. Piper didn't care at that point. Her boy was almost home-free. With whatever last reserves of energy she had left, she swooped him up in her arms and they embraced like that for a minute or so. She heard his soft whimpers and felt the dampness from his tears on her neck. She knew it'd be tough to extricate herself from him after all this, but they had to get out of there.

"It's okay, baby." Piper rubbed his back. "Let's go home." She put him down and reluctantly he parted from her. She lifted his chin up to look at her. "You are the bravest boy I know. Don't you ever forget that Pickle."

Piper quickly took in her surroundings. The room was all white walls and a navy carpet with all navy blue couches and window treatments. There were no pictures on the walls and the only photo was framed over the fireplace of Carson Stossel himself. The surfaces were all black lacquer and sleek lines. Artwork adorned a few walls and were nothing less than pornographic. Piper wanted to say: *What the fuck?* But she didn't.

"Okay love, go get your backpack and let's blow this joint."

"We can't go yet, Aunt Piper." He pointed toward the lighted kitchen doorway and whispered his next word. "Look."

ISABEL

Mac and Isabel had gotten to Piper's place in Morristown in record time and Penelope slept while they paced until the phone buzzed. Her hands shook so much she fumbled with the simple task of pressing a button. "Hello, Piper?"

"It's me, Mommy ..."

"Oh baby." Isabel had no words that would suffice. *I love you* sounded cliché and trite. She said it anyway. "I love you Pickle." She had to sit because relying on her knees to keep her upright was out of the question.

"I love you too, Mommy."

Her breath caught. Mac was leaning in to her in an effort to hear the conversation and she saw tears welling in his eyes. She kissed his cheek and he helped her to her feet. They just hugged and rocked back and forth.

"He's okay, baby, he's okay." Isabel wasn't sure what was going to happen at that point and she didn't want to think about down the road. All she wanted to do at that point was lock her family in a room somewhere and never let anyone in or out. "He's safe for now, oh god Mac he's safe. But where's Aunt Piper?" The phone fell from Isabel's fingers and clattered to the floor. Mac reached down to get it and put it up to her ear.

"Isabel? Izzy? It's me." It was Clare on the other end.

"Oh Clare, I can't even tell you how relieved we are that Pickle is okay. What about Piper? Is she with you too?" There was an agonizing pause that seemed to go on forever while Isabel gripped the cell phone with both hands.

"Just relax, Izzy. Pickle and I are on our way back to Morristown. Piper is headed to the police station to file a report, she's fine too."

Isabel let out a breath and fell back onto Piper's plush couch. "Clare, I don't even know what to say. I've been going insane here waiting and you are my angel. I will never forget what you are doing for us. If I can't be with my son, the only other people I trust with him are you and my sister."

"Well, your sister is on a mission she'll pursue until the end. You know that about her, Izzy. I just worry because she is so sick, you'll have to help me to get her to focus on herself more. Maybe she can help you get another lawyer to handle all this from now on."

"Yes, yes, of course, you're right, she needs to not be so stressed over my shit all the time. We will all have to sit down and figure out what the best plan of attack will be."

"Well good luck getting Piper to take a second seat is all I'm thinking. She's like a dog with a bone." She took what sounded like a swig of water. "You and Mac make yourselves some strong drinks and relax, we'll be there soon, darlin'."

"Hurry home … but be safe." She wanted to see her son, to hold him in her arms and never let him go but Isabel had to be realistic, they were escaping one horrific experience and she didn't want them to be derailed after all that by a car wreck.

Isabel would spend the rest of her life keeping her family safe, even if that meant kidnapping her own children. Considering Pickle had been left alone in the monster's apartment someone would have to answer for that, but Isabel would expect the worst case scenario as an outcome because it didn't seem that the courts had her son's best interest at heart no matter what angle Piper pursued as her attorney. Isabel would relieve her sister of the huge burden of trying to protect Pickle. At this point Isabel knew Piper wasn't coming home until she was granted an emergent hearing for the following morning. Didn't matter though. Isabel would get a top-notch lawyer based on Piper's recommendation, and she'd be sure there was no way this man would get anywhere near Pickle again. She'd allow Piper to bring up the rape in all of its gory details.

Isabel needed to bask in the glory of the moment. Everyone was safe for the time. When Clare opened the door of the apartment, Isabel embraced her and kissed her cheek and then she drank in her little boy. She lifted him in her arms, no words were exchanged, all she could think about was what a beautiful sight the child was. His out-of-control curls, his luminous green eyes, his fair smooth skin. Somehow he looked like he'd grown a few inches through the whole ordeal.

"I'm good, Mommy, really, I'm okay, but I never want to go back there again. I don't have to, right?"

Mac took Pickle from Isabel's arms. "No champ, you're never going to see that man again even if we all have to disappear." Mac kissed his head and handed him back over to Isabel who gently put him down to the floor.

"Izzy, why don't you get him in his PJs and I'll make us some hot chocolate. You both must be sleepy." Clare winked at Isabel.

"I'm not sleepy, I've stayed up all night before Mom, 'member."

"I know, you're all grown up now, but even big boys need sleep. Let's go do the pajamas and see how you feel." She patted his back and he yawned. "Okay honey, let's go."

He skipped from the room and she followed her precious son to the guest room leaving Clare in the kitchen with Prozac at her heels hoping a morsel of food may fall to the floor. Mac was on the couch while Penelope slept in her carrier next to him.

After washing up, Pickle had barely finished his chocolate milk when Isabel saw his eyelids droop and flutter. They were seated, all of them except Piper and Baby Penelope, at the kitchen table making small talk, but Isabel couldn't take her eyes off her son and it seemed Mac couldn't take his eyes off of her.

"The world has suddenly become a much bigger place, don't you think?" Mac sipped on a bottle of beer.

"What do you mean?"

"I knew I loved you from the moment I saw you. I've loved Pickle when I first saw him in the nursery on the day he was born and of course I loved Penelope when she was just a swell in your belly. But I had always viewed each of you as separate entities unto yourselves. Yet, we're not. It goes way beyond that. When Pickle was in jeopardy it wasn't just about him, it was about you and Piper and Penelope and Clare and if anything happened to him that ripple effect would be so strong it could threaten everything I hold so dear, so secure."

"Oh Mac." Isabel reached across the kitchen table and took his hand in hers. She'd always heard that you never know true love until you have a child, but you never know real pain until you lose one. She often contemplated what she'd brought on herself by loving something so wholly that if she were to lose it, a huge piece of herself would be lost as well." Isabel smiled at her husband. "It's mind boggling and enough to paralyze me if I think on it too much, ya' know?"

Before Pickle's head rested on the table, Mac lifted him into his arms and brought him to the guest room where he laid him down next to his sister who still slept soundly. Then Mac and Isabel sat together on the couch. At any moment, Piper's car service would drop her off at the apartment and then they'd all be together again under one roof. For that brief shard of time Isabel would be happy. Then Isabel knew that reality would set in and the old expression that the only constant in life was change, things would begin again. The world would continue to spin out of control and life would haphazardly march on only to a new and different drummer. She didn't know what the future held, no one did but she prayed that the events of the previous night would not be in vain, that the change would be in the best interest of the family. And then there was her sister's fatal disease. She rested her head on Mac's shoulder and watched the clock. It was noon and they hadn't heard a word from Piper, nor was she answering her cell phone.

Just as Isabel began to pace, a call came in on her cell phone and she assumed it was Piper. Without checking the caller ID Isabel gave the caller out a breathy, "Hello?"

"Ms. McAfee?"

"Yes, this is she." Isabel had no idea who this man was other than it wasn't her rapist, she'd recognize that voice and its glib inflections for the rest of her life.

"This is Sergeant Jenkins from NYPD. Your sister, Piper Henry, became unresponsive during questioning. We found your number in her emergency contact list. She's been transported to New York Downtown Hospital off Gold Street. Are you familiar?"

Isabel's brain went fuzzy after the word *unresponsive*.

"Ms. McAfee, is there someone who can drive you? It's the medical center on Gold."

"Sorry, yes, I know where it is. Is she going to be okay, what do you mean unresponsive?"

Mac was hovering over her trying to hear.

"I have no further information, madam, just that she was alive but unconscious. Here is the number for the medical center, they may be able to tell you more." He rattled off the number but Isabel didn't bother to write it down.

"Thank-you." Isabel hung up.

"Now what?" Mac sounded annoyed.

"Piper is in the hospital. Something happened while she was at the police department. I guess she passed out while she was filing papers—although the cop had said *during questioning*. If anything happened to my sister because of the monster after all this I will personally murder him. "I have to wake up Clare, she's going to want to go. You need to stay here with the kids, Mac and besides, you've had two beers so driving is out of the question."

"Shit, I'm fine to drive, Izzy. I had those beers at noon, it's two o'clock." He slammed his fist on the table. "What the fuck is happening here? Can't we just get a break once in a while?"

"I don't have time to feel sorry for us, Mac. My sister rescued my son from a horrible predicament tonight, and she is now lying unconscious in the hospital and the doctors there have no idea about her disease. They won't have a clue how to treat her. I have to go!"

He then reached for her and hugged her. "Sorry babe, just hate to see you and Piper go through all this, alone. I'll stay here with the kids but you have to call me as soon as you have news."

Isabel strode to the bedroom where Clare was lying on top of her duvet staring up at the ceiling. "Clare, honey, I'm sorry to be the bearer of bad ..."

"I heard, Izzy." When she said Isabel's name it sounded like *easy*. "We'll go together. I'll drive."

Isabel wasn't going to protest or argue. She had already taken enough advantage of her sister and she'd let Clare call the shots.

The trip into lower Manhattan was silent for the most part as if even small chatter would slow them down. Clare pulled up to the emergency entrance.

"You go and find her and text me, Izzy. I have to park the car and gather my feelings."

It was tough sometimes for Isabel to know her place when it came to Piper and Clare. Neither of their relationships with her sister were any more important than the other. Isabel guessed that was the way Piper felt when it came to Mac and her. Isabel took Clare's hand. "Are you sure? I can park the car while you find her."

"No, Izzy, go, go. I'll be right in."

Isabel didn't argue with her. Piper had teased Clare about her stubbornness over the years. Without wasting any more time Isabel jumped from the vehicle and headed through the double doors of the facility.

The elevator doors opened and she registered a cheesy tang of unwashed bodies and illness. She found Piper's room at the very end of a long hallway. It was a good sign Isabel figured because she was so removed from the nurse's station – those closer beds were reserved for the gravely ill, *weren't they*? And it wasn't intensive care, at least. Outside Piper's door was an armed guard and he stood when Isabel stopped at the entrance, double checking that she had the right room number.

"Can I help you, Miss?"

Before Isabel could speak she heard, "It's okay, Fred, let her in." It was Piper, apparently awake and from the sound of her voice she was no worse for the wear.

"Sure thing, doll."

The guard stepped aside and Isabel wondered what warranted her sister having someone screening her visitors like she was a rock star. Then again, it was Piper, a lesbian with men eating out of her hand. Once inside the room, Isabel stopped and took a step back when she saw Piper grinning widely. She waved Isabel over and it was then that Isabel noticed her wrists were shackled to the bed.

PIPER

"What the hell is going on? Why are you hand-cuffed?" Isabel sounded indignant.

"See, I knew you'd focus on the negative side of this situation." It was a given that Isabel would show up and Piper would need to explain and she was as ready as one could be. It was her turn to play the tragic heroine. "The simple explanation was I woke up chained to a hospital bed with a cop next to me." Piper had thought she was in the worst possible nightmare – she was in both prison and a hospital – the two places no one ever wanted to be and certainly not at the same time.

"What happened? The police called and said you were unresponsive."

"It really is a long story and I am on some wonderful narcotics, so I don't know if what I say is going to be credible."

"Cut the shit, Piper, what did you do? Why are you in hand-cuffs. I realize your extreme dedication to protecting Pickle, but if you punched some random cop or threatened a judge, it won't help our case against the monster. You do realize that don't you?"

"Oh no, I am still very much respected by the NYPD, I have learned. What I did is not only going to help your case against the guy, it's eliminated the guy. I killed him Izzy, I killed the motherfucker. It has nothing to do with you – and now Pickle never has to spend another minute with him again. Truth is, I faked the unresponsiveness, shhh – don't tell anyone."

"Shhh? Jesus, Piper, you have a cop less than ten feet from you. What are you saying? Clare said you were reporting the child endangerment, she didn't say the police were there or that you were arrested." Isabel could not believe what she was hearing. She wished Clare would hurry up. Clare needed to hear this too. "Clare didn't say anything about my rapist being shot." Isabel sat back on the radiator, no chair in case Piper decided to become a fugitive and hurl it through the window or at a nurse and escape.

"Izzy, I shot him and that's all you need to know. Shot the bastard with his own gun. He's dead and can never hurt my nephew again." Piper looked her in the eyes. "In fact, the less you know, the better. Suffice it to say, Izzy, I'm dying and can get away with anything; shit my pants, sleep till noon, even shoot a sick, violent bastard who was trying to ruin your life. I did the world a favor. You'll get used to the idea. By the time it goes to trial, I'll be doing the dirt dance."

PIPER

After Piper's recovery and release on bail which Mac forked over without hesitation, she spent the next three months living, or rather dying in Isabel's cozy guest house. So much had happened and she was starting to have difficulty recalling some of the finer details. What she did know was Clare had moved back to Brazil, unable to handle the fact that Piper was so ill. After the monster's murder, Clare fell apart. She said she'd return after a visit with her family, but Piper knew she was never going to see her again. And that was understandable.

Everyday Piper was surrounded by her family. She missed Clare, but there were rare alone moments. At first she felt a little invasive in their lives until one day Mac walked her outside and showed her a sign he'd made. It was a beautiful wood sign that read in carved script letters; Piper's Place.

Piper had long talks with Isabel and on one of Piper's more lucid afternoons, she couldn't avoid Isabel's questions about what happened that day. She shared some of what happened and the rest she'd take to her grave. A mother didn't need to know all the details of how frightened her child had been.

"Pickle was so brave. He ran to Aunt Clare just like I told him. I found the gun on the bed in the master bedroom. The monster had no regard for leaving his son alone with a loaded gun, so I took it, amongst other things. Then the bastard came home and discovered me snooping around collecting evidence. I had DNA and the pink stuff. I planned to get someone to run the monster's profile through a database, and I'd get a lab to analyze the stuff he made Pickle drink."

"My god Piper, anything could have happened to either of you. I know you can handle things as they come and always do but Pickle, I mean hell, what will this do to him? I'm so scared for him."

"Calm down, little sister." Piper knew her nephew would be fine. "He's safe and that's all that matters." Piper believed the end here did justify the means.

"When the monster happened to walk in on me when he got back home and realized I was there and Pickle was gone, he went out of control. Meanwhile the gun was tucked in my bag. Then the monster made the mistake of locking the door and told me he was going to do to me what he did to you. When he lunged at me, I shot him. Twice. With his own gun."

"Whoa, you are so brave, Piper. And then coming forward and telling the truth. I'd probably have nightmares for the rest of my life."

"No way, and don't even go there, Izzy. The guy nearly killed you and nearly killed my nephew, my best boy! I have zero regrets." Piper was sure none of anything that went down was ever premeditated, just convenient. "It's an interesting quandary — I have no remorse and yet I feel sad about the fact that I have no remorse. Go figure."

She worried about how she'd handle the witness stand – she couldn't fake repentance. She had no idea if she'd still be above ground for the event. Isabel and she were driving to her oncologist when Piper voiced her concerns that if she lived long enough to make it to court the following month, she was afraid she wouldn't be able to pull it together. Piper's food source was in the form of a tube in her nose. She was thirty pounds lighter, no hair and she had bruises all over her body.

Isabel reassured her she'd be with her every step of the way. They were in the medical building's parking lot when Piper's cell phone rang. A rarity, she hadn't even heard from Clare since she jetted back to Brazil. It was a call from the prosecutor's office. Thus far, Piper had only been in court once, it would be a while before her case went to trial. That was thanks to a friend whose legal expertise was mainly postponements and he played the *chemo card* whenever possible. Piper assumed the phone call was in reference to meeting dates. Instead what she learned in that conversation would become the closest she'd come to self-forgiveness. Saving her nephew from the monster was sweet enough but discovering that she had uncovered a serial rapist the city had been hunting for fifteen years, a man suspected of being responsible for eighteen *reported* rapes over that time. That tally didn't include Isabel.

Piper's case was dismissed.

"Self-defense, Piper, you're free to go and do as you please."

Die as I please, Piper thought.

ISABEL

Piper had moved into the guest house and seemed to be as content as possible considering she was dying. Clare had gone back to Brazil and Isabel tried to talk to her sister about it, but Piper refused to entertain the idea of rehashing the past. All Piper would admit was, "Clare isn't good with death."

Once in a while Isabel could see her sister had been crying. She always attributed it to the pain and Isabel had to let go. Maybe some things didn't need to be discussed. Her sister was narrating her own death and Isabel had no choice but to be on-board. She tried to soak up every word of their discussions and began journaling after each encounter. Isabel's writing had never been so prolific as in those last few months of her sister's life. She took it all in and even if it never saw print or even another human's eyes, Isabel had this story to tell; a story that was so unique to just them, a story of loss and life and love built on the rubbles of tragedies, in a world reformed and redesigned, always growing and changing, a story thriving like weeds that will live long after they were all gone.

Piper was in and out of lucidity. Isabel spent all day while Pickle was in school with her sister. They enjoyed the company of Penelope when she wasn't napping. Piper had a Russian nurse who came to the ranch twice a week and did an assessment. She was reliable and efficient and as Piper put it— she had the personality and hair-coloring of Borscht. Piper's favorite part of the nurse visit was the delivery of "angel salad" or medicinal marijuana. Somehow even though Pennsylvania was not legalized for use yet, Piper had some sort of UN connections from days gone by and was given a carte blanche universal permit to toke. Isabel tried her best to keep Pickle from being exposed to his aunt's partaking – but he called them "special" cigarettes. One thing that came from this experience for Pickle was his sudden desire to hurry up and grow up so he could be a doctor. If Pickle decided to use his life to help others because he didn't believe he could save his aunt, then it became a small miracle. Lately Pickle spent hours, bless his heart, investigating cures for the disease his aunt was stricken with on the Internet. He copied articles and menus, vitamin recommendations and even hospitals specializing in blood disorders. He nagged her about the dangers of not listening to her doctors.

"Oh doctors schmoctors!" Piper had laughed. "Listen to me kiddo, if the doctors had their way I'd be in the rainforest eating tree bark."

Pickle had laughed at that but clammed up when Piper said, "Shouldn't you be putting the books down and getting yourself a girlfriend?"

"Aunt Piper, I'm only eight." This made him blush and make a hasty exit. He turned in the doorway.

"You should be on your third wife by now."

"Maybe I have a girlfriend already but don't want to bring her around to meet my crazy aunt." He cocked his head and smiled.

"Oooh you little freak, if I could get out of this bed I'd tickle you to death."

Whenever Isabel overheard these interactions between her sister and Pickle she was warmed by the fact that this was her sister's way of gently saying good-bye to her nephew. Piper and

Pickle had a very unique relationship and it had never been within Isabel's control. From day one Piper had nurtured this bond on her own and on her own terms. She'd nicknamed him before he was born and continued to shape him into a beautiful young man. In her eyes he'd gone from the baby Piper had always wanted, to the little brother she'd never had. Watching them interact was both mesmerizing and melancholy all at once.

When Pickle wasn't with them they still talked often about him. Isabel worried about her son. Sure, he was smart and gorgeous and didn't really have to worry about anything but then he had the heaviness of losing his aunt day by day. Isabel wasn't sure what that was doing to him inside and she worried about Aunt Piper no longer being in the picture someday.

In mid-January after a fresh snowfall, the two sisters were taking a horse-driven sleigh ride, just the two of them, huddled under blankets and sipping hot chocolate. Later that night, he would take Isabel back up to the top of the ridge where they'd make a fire and roast marshmallows but for now, as the sun set on another day, it was just Piper and her little sister.

The sway of the carriage over fresh driven snow was hypnotizing and Isabel never felt so in the moment with Piper. They held each other's gloved hands, while leaning back on the burgundy leather coach seat and stared up at the big snowflakes lighting on their faces. There was no other place Isabel wanted to be at that moment. Up at the ridge they took in the vast views from all angles. Mac had set up a bonfire and a chilled bottle of champagne. Isabel laughed when her sister sipped champagne somehow around her nasal tube.

"Fuck all!" Piper said through a loud giggle.

Isabel clinked glasses with her. "Here, here, and I hope Pickle treats women like Mac has treated me. He thinks of everything."

Isabel turned toward her sister. "Reality is, Piper, I worry so much because of the violent crazed father he has. Had … had. I still am not used to that. At some point, all of the ugly pieces of this family secret will slip into place for him and he'll realize his roots. It's going to be tough."

"Don't think about that now, take it as it comes. It's all a big tragedy. There's no avoiding Pickle being affected by it. He knows the man from the pet store is dead. Eventually he will figure it all out but let it alone. The kid is growing up. He knows a lot more than you think he does."

"All I know is he has hair on his legs and still sleeps with Mr. Wiggles. What will I do when Pickle gets a girlfriend?"

"Oh lord, well don't blame me when puberty hits him in the head like a shovel."

Isabel would give anything to experience those trials and tribulations with Piper. They'd spent more time than Isabel ever imagined them spending together when Piper first mentioned the idea of living with Mac and her in the end. Isabel cherished every second with Piper and then got to spend her nights wrapped in a beautiful, kind man's arms, sharing all her inner-most thoughts. Sometimes they were joyous, revelatory stories and other times they were sad and tearful.

One night Mac and Isabel were headed over to Piper's Place to extricate Pickle from her bedside. She'd lost her eyesight and saw only blurs, so her nephew sat with her and told her stories about school and things that happened in the main house. Pickle often brought Beaker in the portable cage to visit with his aunt and of course Prozac had sat vigil ever since Piper had moved in with them. Isabel knew even in death all of their connections were unbreakable. It would still be there when Piper was no longer with them, it was in their souls.

That night Mac and Isabel stopped at the door as they usually did and surreptitiously listened. Isabel's beautiful sister had her arm slung around her son while he sat next to her on her bed.

"This is corny but it's true. When I'm gone and you miss me, and I know you're going to totally miss me, maybe even cry a little. I mean c'mon I deserve a few tears."

"Aunt Piper, get on with it, what's going to happen when I miss you?"

Piper pretended to shove him from the bed and he grabbed onto the blanket and laughed. "Whenever you miss me, I want you to look up at the stars because even though you can see those stars, they burnt out millions of years ago. In twenty years, you'll still see them even though they're no longer there. Get it?" She tightened her arm around him. "If you see the stars then you see me, your kids will see me, even your grandkids!"

"Brilliant." Isabel whispered to Mac before they barged into the room and climbed on the bed with them.

"When is Pickle going to have children? He's not even married." Mac tickled Pickle's feet.

"Ewww, I'm not going to get married. I'll have dogs and cats and birds but no kids."

"You have to have children, Pickle." Piper was laughing and Isabel couldn't help but smile when her sister went on to say, "Who's going to carry on my legacy, my amazing stories, my secrets."

ISABEL

For months following *the mess* as they came to refer to it, Piper and Isabel covered a lot of ground. The two things she wanted Piper to open up about, she never did. There was never any more talk about the murder nor did she address her sudden break-up with Clare. They talked about Isabel's return to writing and the schools she was looking to attend when Penelope was a little older. Piper gave Isabel tons of advice about raising Penelope, after all she had always claimed Isabel's raising.

Piper lectured Isabel that if her dreams didn't scare her, then they weren't big enough. She believed loss was not the end but an opportunity to change. Her sister always came through so Isabel found it easy for the first time in their adult lives to really open up to Piper, to tell her about her feelings, how there were light days and then there were times when the darkness descended; audible like a door being shut.

Piper responded by abusing clichés saying things like, "Trade places with me" and "When you're in the dark working to get out — that's when you're at your best." Piper consoled Isabel over her own death.

Piper Ann Henry passed away at midnight on a starry night in late February. In the end she had slipped into a coma and was surrounded by all of them when she left this realm. She had a grin on her face throughout her final days as she controlled her death till the very end. Piper died in Isabel's arms as they spooned on the bed.

~~~~~~~~~~~~~~

Pickle was wrapping up the third grade and Isabel was in her second semester of college. She was doing an online English degree and Isabel loved every second of being a student. It was the difference between being made to go to school and wanting to go to school. Piper had been right. She's been gone a full year and Isabel suspected she'd continue to appear to her in the, *I told you so* way for the rest of her life.

During the day, while Pickle was in school Isabel took Penelope on play dates. Her daughter, she quickly learned, had the perfect middle name. She was only fifteen months old, yet quite bossy and stubborn to everyone in her vicinity including her brother who feigned annoyance. On this unseasonably warm fall afternoon Isabel pushed Penelope's stroller down to the end of their expansive driveway. In the distance Isabel heard the sound of the tractor and knew Mac was getting ready for fall harvest. Penelope was sound asleep, at least for the moment. Her little girl had a tiny dust bunny clinging to her cheek, but Isabel didn't dare pluck it off for fear she'd wake up and Isabel would have to forgo her life until the next reprieve. Yet, when this gorgeous little creature reached from her crib every morning for Mommy to pick her up, she looked more and more like her Aunt Piper. They all saw it. At times it was both uncanny and unnerving all at once.

Isabel thought about Piper all the time, and she never wanted that to change. She made a conscious effort not to feel sorry for herself when Piper popped into her mind, but she often couldn't help shedding a few tears. For the most part, Isabel wanted to be grateful. Piper had singlehandedly saved Pickle's life and as a result she had saved Isabel's life.

Penelope slept on under the shade of the stroller hood while Isabel grabbed the mail from their battered rural mailbox and sat on her designated tree stump, the *bus-stump* as Pickle referred to it, and waited for her son. As much as she relished the break it gave her when he bounded up the steps of the bus each morning, Isabel loved to see him bounce down the steps of the bus every afternoon much more. A mother could tell the mood of a kid based on the after-school body language. The kid who ran from the bus was a child who wanted to be home as soon as possible. The kid who sauntered, stopped to pick grass and throw rocks, showed a kid who was in no hurry to get home.

The sun warmed Isabel's skin while she leafed through the mail, most of it catalogs and "junk" letters, and of course, a couple of bills. She came across something that had several stamps on it and plucked it from the ridiculous stack of waste. The return heading said it was from Brazil.

Isabel's stomach clenched; her heart was blocking her throat. The mail fell to the grass. She tore open the letter knowing it had to be from Clare. There was a handwritten letter along with another sealed envelope inside. Isabel read the handwritten note first.

Dear Isabel,

Thank you for informing me when my beloved Piper passed. Please know you and your amazing family have been in my thoughts and prayers every day since I left. I needed to go back home to Brazil for personal reasons, but adored your sister. Please accept my sincere apologies for not delivering this to you in person. I miss you all so very much it hurts but most of all I miss my best friend and life's love. Give my Pickle an extra special hug from his Aunt Clare. I know you understand my grief and my reasons for needing to return to my family. Perhaps someday we can meet again. Meanwhile, be well.

Love, Clare

PS. Enclosed please find a letter from Piper.

Isabel had unwittingly held her breath and let it out in a long stream. This was big, the envelope she was holding in this other hand was light yet weighty. It was almost as if the envelope was pulsing. She recognized the writing on the sealed envelope as Pipers.

With fingers trembling, Isabel carefully peeled open the envelope flap. It would slay her to read this, but it was a gift at the same time. It would ultimately be their closure, the final puzzle piece and of course, Isabel chuckled aloud; Piper getting the last word. Nothing else would be coming from her sister after this, no more packages or envelopes, no more ghost dreams, just the memories they already savored.

Isabel hadn't realized she was crying until she tasted salt on her smiling lips. This letter had to be nearly a year and a half old. This was well orchestrated by Piper— she'd given what she deemed was an appropriate amount of time for the boo-hooing so her letter would not be tarnished by the maelstrom of misery over losing one's incredible sister. Isabel had yet to read the letter and yet she could hear her sister's voice as if they were standing shoulder to shoulder waiting together for Pickle to get off the school bus.

Isabel gingerly removed the letter and her heart quickened when she saw it was two pages in her sister's handwriting shaky as it had become in the end. Isabel unfolded it, pressed it to her chest and with a deep breath, she laid it on her knees and with just an ounce of trepidation she began to read.

Dear Isabel,

If you're reading this then I'm in Never-Never Land and I can tell you it's not the same without you, siskabob. I don't have to waste time writing how much I love you, suffice it to say, you taught me the meaning of the word Love. When you get here, look for me so I can buy you a drink, although you and I may have entirely different destinations.

I worried that when it came down to it, I was going to be judged in the hereafter for all the shitty things I did before 9/11, before I came back home, humbled myself enough to meet the real me. That was the hardest part, you know. The law played in my favor on that one since the monster was found guilty of at least eighteen reported rapes not to mention ones like yours that went unreported. And if I never told you how brave I believed you were through the whole rape thing I'm telling you now. I was never so proud of you as when you decided to keep Pickle.

I don't have any regrets about the murder of your rapist I'm sorry to say. I can only associate him with evil and even if I wasn't dying I would have still shot him just the same. All I knew was he needed to be off the street before my Penelope hit the ground running. The rapist is dead, I'm dead and Pickle is free and clear.

When the towers collapsed I made a decision to be there for my family. We had been through and conquered so much over the past decade and when I knew there was no way to win the custody case I was afraid I had failed you again. I had assured you that everything would be alright with overnights with the monster and I had lied. I lied so often throughout my life I lost a grip on who I really was. I lied about my sexuality, I lied about my passion for the law, lied to myself about Mom's disease. Granted, it didn't matter, genetically predisposed was a given in my case. I was dying but I could do something that would save your life and the life of my nephew. Writing this, knowing that someday soon you will read this and hopefully find some solace in its words – that's all I need to rest in peace. And still so many untruths I take to my grave ...

I don't want you to miss me, Isabel. I want you to remember me. I'm not talking about my birthday or Christmas or most of all, the anniversary of my death. Please don't celebrate that. I wish for you to think of me when you're doing some random thing, braiding Penelope's hair or playing chess with Pickle, walking Prozac or riding your gorgeous horse through the woods, singing Christmas carols around the piano with Beaker screeching obscenities— that's when I want you to think of me. What I wish most of all is for you to believe I was a decent person.

Even when you stand alone, I am standing right next to you. Like those towers that are no longer there, we will always stand together ... forever. And smile, please smile. And dance – I hope you dance. In the end was when my life began. It helped me learn what was important just in the nick of time and for someone who saved my life a long, long time ago by simply making me late for work, I thank you from the bottom of my soul for giving me a legacy. We've created quite a story together haven't we? And it's all yours for the telling. Write your novel, Isabel. The material is at your fingertips.

I love you for all eternity, Izzy.

Piper

Isabel was shaking. This was her sister's last words and she couldn't help but smile. Maybe someday Isabel *would* finish the story of them. She gently folded the letter back into the envelope and it was then that Isabel noticed there was something small and hard in the envelope as well. She tapped the end of the envelope and out rolled a tiny object that glinted in the afternoon sunlight. The shiny item had settled into her palm like a magic bean. It was a charm, a mini replica of the Twin Towers. On one tower was the letter "P" and on the other was the letter "I". Isabel picked it up and turned it over. The tears that had welled for months over love and loss only sisters could understand streamed down her cheeks and they felt warm and comforting. On the back of the charm two words were engraved across the towers — together they read:

Never Forget.

EPILOGUE

PICKLE

I'll use the name Peter or at least that's the name I used on my college applications. A nickname like Pickle would never fly in the Ivy League world. I was fortunate to be accepted to Columbia University to study pre-med. When I explained to my mom that I wanted to be able to help people who had diseases like Aunt Piper's, she cried. My aunt died ten years ago, and she left me enough money to attend all four years of college. Ironically, I got a scholarship to Columbia University, which is not far from the place where my life began seventeen years earlier according to family lore.

So here I was on my way from Mac Casa, Pennsylvania to the Big Apple. It was tough to say good-bye to Mac and Mom, not to mention Penelope and the twins. But most of all I'd miss Beaker, Prozac and ole Jigsaw. The three of them came into my life when I was just seven when I needed the sort of unconditional love only a pet can provide, they were there.

Mac finally had the horse ranch he'd always dreamed of having. And Mom, well following the birth of my twin sisters, she eventually found the time to pursue her writing. After a few years of failed attempts at getting published she found her niche in the children's literature market with her first middle-grade book coming out next year. It's titled *A Fine Pickle* — no surprise there and her agent was able to get her a three book deal with a major publisher. I have to admit it's a sweet story, but I also know my real story was anything but sweet. A cautionary tale that would never be told as long as I kept the secret. I recall that fateful night when I made a promise to Aunt Piper that the truth of what went down in my father's apartment would remain a secret forever.

After I called Aunt Piper and told her my father tried to drug me again and then left me alone, she came to my rescue and I loved her for that all my life. Unfortunately, before Aunt Piper got there, the man that was my real father came home. I came out of my hiding place near the front door and ran down the hall before he could spot me. But then the man came into my room and lifted me from the bed and put me in his larger bed in the master bedroom. I didn't know why he did that, but I watched through squinted eyes while he threw his jacket onto the bed right next to me and partially sticking from the pocket I saw the glinting handle of a gun. I watched without moving while the man went into the bathroom and shut the door behind him. This was my chance to escape. Before I was able to get off the bed, the bathroom door flung open and the man stood there staring at me.

"Where the fuck do you think you're going kid?" He came toward me and when he climbed up on the bed with me I grabbed for the gun and pointed it at him.

"C'mon kid," he laughed. "Give your daddy the gun or risk me kicking the shit out of you instead of just us playing around for a little bit. Now give me the fucking gun."

Over the years, Aunt Piper's version became my reality and it wasn't until she was long gone that I puzzled the truth back together. I had shot and killed my own father.

When Piper asked me to keep this special secret, that it would be the most important secret I would ever keep for her, I made a promise to do just that because she saved my life that day. I loved her so fiercely and I knew I would never tell anyone, not even my own mother because the truth would hurt my mom more than my keeping the secret. When I ran from the apartment that night, I left Aunt Piper with the gun in the bedroom. Aunt Piper shot the gun again but only so she could get the gun powder residue on her hands. When my aunt went to the police she took the full blame for what I'd done.

I was so fortunate to spend time with my aunt while she was dying. Before she passed nearly a year after that horrible night in some of her more lucid moments when we were alone, she'd explained to me how I had saved her life during 9/11, and she owed me something for that and we were *almost* even. Almost, except it was my responsibility to make the most of my life and grow to become a gentleman: a decent human being.

In the years that followed I tried to be a loving son and brother and I eventually graduated as my high school's valedictorian and got into Columbia. I will continue to do the right thing and prove myself to the world but mostly to my Aunt Piper. The last conversation we had, she explained that I may not see it as a kid but that our secret would save my life in the long run. In the end, she was right.

Made in United States
North Haven, CT
24 April 2022

18524883R00163